Praise for Secret in Whitetail Lake

"It was Winston Churchill who made the famous comment: 'It is a riddle, wrapped in a mystery, inside an enigma.' Although he was speaking about Russia, he might well have been describing author Christine Husom's *Secret in Whitetail Lake*, the latest in her popular Winnebago County Mystery Series. Multiple layers of secrets and carefully laid clues danced just on the edge of revealing the truth throughout the story. Stunning revelations concluded both storylines and, although I love to solve a mystery, I didn't want this one to end."
~Timya Owen, author of The Fernbridge Mysteries

"Gripping suspense, captivating story line, and a cast of characters so well written you will be mesmerized from the start. This fast-paced, action-filled book will keep you reading through the night, eager to find out what will happen next."
~Shelley Giusti, reviewer, Shelley's Book Case

"Christine Husom hits it out of the ballpark with *Secret in Whitetail Lake*. It is a captivating mystery filled with twists and turns that will make your head spin and keep you reading late into the night and leave you wanting more." ~Julie Seedorf, author of the Fuchsia, Minnesota Mysteries

"A local mystery from the past surfaces through technology brought to the small town, and stirs up memories. This series will not be forgotten." ~Rhonda Gilliland, Twin Cities Sisters in Crime President, 2012-2015

"Two kids are found dead—at the bottom of a lake—in a Dodge Charger—33 years after they disappeared, and that's just a few of the surprising ingredients in this twisty concoction. *The Secret in Whitetail Lake* is a delectable mixture of suspense, rich characters and cultural observations that simmers happily until the final scene." ~David Housewright, Edgar Award winning author of *Unidentified Woman #15*

"Christine Husom has once again captured the essence of a rural Minnesota mystery as she draws readers into the *Secret in Whitetail Lake*. When the Winnebago County Sheriff's Department stumbles upon a car at the bottom of Whitetail Lake, what appears to be a probable accident from three decades earlier, turns into something far more sinister that makes this story a page turner." ~Sheila Knop, journalist

"*The Secret in Whitetail Lake* is a must read for any mystery sleuth craving a good read...a *really* good read. Christine Husom has a way of weaving intricate twists and turns into her stories that, while very natural, will keep you guessing until the very end. Each and every one of her characters is so natural that you may just assume they are living, breathing human beings *in* Winnebago County, so much so that you might just want to take a drive to visit your friends in Winnebago County... Now if you could just find it on the map." ~Julie Bergh, author, *The Restored Woman*

Also by Christine Husom

SECRET IN WHITETAIL LAKE

Sixth in the Winnebago County Mystery Series

Christine Husom

The wRight Press

The wRight Press edition published 2018.

Cover design by Richard Haskin, Minneapolis, Minnesota
Cover layout by Precision Prints, Buffalo, Minnesota

The wRight Press
804 Circle Drive
Buffalo, Minnesota, 55313

Printed in the United States of America

ISBN 978-1-948068-07-9

This story is dedicated to each of you who lost a loved one in a way that left you wondering what happened, and why.

Acknowledgements

It's amazing what a team effort it is to take an idea for a story and build it into a book. I have many people to thank and give credit to. I asked about the disintegration of clothing and leather in water on the crimescenewriter message board and appreciate the responses I got from Wally Lind, Hilary Catron, and Dr. Judy Melinek, forensic pathologist with Pathology Expert, Inc. Dr. Melinek shared her expertise and provided me with valuable information and corrected my mistakes. She also consulted with Lindsey C. Thomas, MD, Assistant Medical Examiner, Hennepin County Medical Examiner's Office, on my behalf. Many thanks to both of you. Dr. Tia Larson offered enlightening medical advice and explained it so I understood it. Jake Hermansen with the Wright County Sheriff's Office gave me important details of what is involved in a water recovery, from the divers and their gear, to the towing operation itself. And my faithful team of proofreaders gave me their time, careful reading, and sound advice: Judy Bergquist, Rhonda Gilliland, Elizabeth Husom, Judy Lewis, Chad Mead, and Edie Peterson. I truly appreciate all of you and your willingness to lend a helping hand.

1

My English setter, Queenie, nudged me with her nose, so I bent over and took her head in my hands. "You want to go outside, girl?" She jumped up and down, telling me that's what she wanted all right.

When I opened the front door, the smells of spring tickled my nostrils open wider to savor them. Queenie loved the acres and acres of open space surrounding our country home, and ran around for her vigorous morning exercise.

I surveyed the grass on my lawn, still packed down from months of resting under a heavy blanket of snow. The blades were coming out of their hibernation and would be standing on end before long to bask in the warming sun.

A Winnebago County Sheriff's squad car crunching the gravel on the township road I lived on caught my attention. It slowed down, pulled in my driveway, and stopped. Deputy Todd Mason climbed out, leaving his car door wide open. The morning sun settled on his face like it was a spotlight drawn to his eye-catching features. He smiled and Queenie bounded to him, begging for attention.

"Enjoying your day off, Sergeant Corky?" He bent over and ruffled Queenie's coat.

"With the weather being about perfect, it's hard not to." I stretched my arms.

"You know it. Goodbye winter and hello spring."

I nodded and smiled. "What are you up to?"

"Just cruising by when I happened to see you." Mason's pager went off. He unclipped it from his belt, glanced at the display and said, "It's Captain Randolph." He replaced the pager, pulled his cell phone out of its holder, and dialed. "Captain, it's Mason. . . . Out on Whitetail, really? . . . Okay, I'm about five minutes from the office so I'll go change, grab my gear, and be out there in twenty or so minutes."

Mason pushed the end button on his phone and frowned. "Warner decided to try the new-fangled sonar equipment that his water division just got out on Whitetail Lake. Seems he got an indication something is down there that needs to be checked out. They're assembling the dive team." Sergeant Tim Warner was head of the recreational vehicle and underwater recovery division for the county.

"Randolph didn't say what it was?"

"Nope, just that it was a large object."

"Really? Whitetail is one of the deeper lakes in the county, and it's a long way down to the bottom."

"Yeah, seventy feet, give or take. We did a dive out there what, two, three years ago now. It's cold and clear, but once we stirred up the silt on the bottom we could see next to nothing, so we called it quits," he said.

"It's curious what's down there, anyway. Maybe a boat that sunk and just got left there," I said.

"Most likely, and we'll find out soon enough." Todd climbed into his car and backed out onto Brandt Avenue.

Queenie and I watched him drive away. "Well, girl, I best get that last report turned in and then we'll figure out what to do with the rest of our day."

The Winnebago Sheriff's Office was a beehive of activity. I met Detective Elton "Smoke" Dawes in the hallway on my way to the squad room. "You heard about the find in Whitetail?" he said.

"No details, just that the divers were called out. What's going on?"

"You know how Warner has been itching to test the new side-scan sonar. Now that the winter ice is off most of the lakes, he couldn't wait any longer. Long story short, he went out on Whitetail and found what looks like a vehicle at the bottom. On the south side."

I drew my eyebrows together. "A vehicle, on the south side? There's no road, or even a shore over there to speak of. That steep hill starts at the water and goes up fifty or sixty feet to where those houses sit at the top."

"Doesn't make sense, that's for sure. You probably don't remember this, but there used to be an old farmhouse on that site. In fact, I may have gone to a beer party there myself back in the Stone Age. I'm thinking it's some old piece of farm equipment that slipped out of gear and plunged in. From back when it was pasture land."

"Pasture land for goats?"

The corners of Smoke's lips lifted, and he raised and lowered his eyebrows. "Or maybe it's a hay wagon they couldn't get out. It would have been a big challenge without the right equipment back then."

"When you'd have to use a team of work horses to do the job?" I teased. Smoke was twenty years my senior but far from old.

"You are on a roll this morning, Corinne."

I held up my memo pad. "I have one last report I didn't finish yesterday. Then I think I'll head out to Whitetail and watch the action."

"Nothing better to do on your day off?" I lifted my shoulders, and he added, "I may do the same after I wrap up a few things here. In any case, I'll check in with Warner for the particulars."

After I'd filed my report, I left the office and drove west on County Road 35, past the road I lived on for another half mile. Whitetail Lake was mid-point between Smoke's house and mine. A number of personal vehicles and squad cars were sitting on the shoulder of the county road where a hopeful fisherman or two parked when the fish were reportedly biting. There wasn't a public access by the lake, to speak of. The launching area was tricky to maneuver, and I was a little surprised Warner had chosen Whitetail to test his new equipment. Maybe the fact that it was deep and scarcely explored added to the appeal.

Deputies Vince Weber, Brian Carlson, and Todd Mason were outfitted in their scuba gear, prepared to climb into Warner's boat, a twenty-one foot whaler with a square bow. It was tied to a sturdy post on the shore. I swung my classic 1967 Pontiac GTO around in a U-turn and parked on the same side of the road as the lake.

Warner waved at me when I got out of my car. "Hey Sergeant, wanna ride along?"

"Sure, why not?" I jogged over to the boat and climbed on behind the three divers. Warner loosened the knot on the tie rope, jumped on board, then moved to the steering wheel. He turned the key and the 125 horsepower motor purred to life.

"So there's some sort of vehicle down there?" Carlson said.

"Yeah, it's crazy, but it looks like an automobile. And that's just not logical," Warner said.

Weber pointed. "Nah. On the south side there? There's no road access. Nothin'."

"I know," Warner said and focused on the lake.

Whitetail was small and deep and almost perfectly round. The depth of the lake was proportionate to the height of the overlooking hill. And like Mason said, it had a silt-covered bottom that clouded visibility when it was stirred up. The divers had three hundred lakes in the county to practice on, and Whitetail was not their first, or even their one hundredth choice.

I sat down on a bench in the boat and studied the side-scan sonar screen and spotted a few objects on the floor of the lake. At that spot on the north side, it was around fifteen feet deep. "Tim, how does this system work exactly?" I said.

Warner pointed at the screen. "It sends out a sonar beam that does a sweep of the bottom and reflects off any object down there. Then it sends that image to the tow fish, the instrument in the water. That in turn sends it up the tow cable to the display here. You can see that we get a fairly decent view. It even works in more mucky bottoms like Whitetail here, which is why I wanted to check it out on this lake, to see how good it works."

That explained that. I watched the screen, waiting for an identifiable item to show up. "It's pretty amazing. I think I could get hooked on this technology, checking out the lake bottoms for buried treasures," I said.

"You can always join the dive team," Mason said and I lifted my eyebrows. Maybe some time.

"It'll take more than one summer to scan all the lakes we got here in Winnebago County," Carlson said.

Warner reached the site in question and the object came into view. It wasn't immediately recognizable, but as I studied it, I made out the windshield, roof, and hood. "It's not a hay wagon," I said.

"Huh?" Weber said as he, Carlson, and Mason crowded in beside me.

"Detective Dawes offered that as a possibility."

Warner split the screen, revealing a red area where the vehicle sat. I asked Warner what he'd done, and why.

"The green on the new view shows soft returns and the red indicates hard returns. That's how we know it's not a natural object down there. It's man made and tells me it's a vehicle," he said.

"Ah. Geez, it looks like a car, all right. Gotta be an older one with that longer hood, boxy shape," Weber said.

"That is a long hood." Mason shook his head then pulled his goggles over his eyes. "So you want us to take a closer look and report back, Tim?"

"That'd be good." Sergeant Warner pointed to the houses sitting at the top of the hill. "I wonder if one of them is missing a car."

I shook my head. "You'd think they'd notice."

Warner shrugged slightly then nodded at the divers. "The lake's about twenty-five feet deep where it's sitting, so at that depth you shouldn't need a safety stop on the way back to the surface."

"It's my turn to be the rescue diver. You'll have to control your descent with your buoyancy compressors. And be careful not to go too far down, or let your fins catch the bottom. If that silt is stirred up, you'll have zero visibility. Are we ready, team?" Mason said.

Weber and Carlson put on their goggles then the three of them affixed their masks in place. Their vests were equipped with regulators and inflatable options. The oxygen tanks would supply them for well over an hour, even if they overexerted, or got nervous and sucked in air faster than normal. Warner and I helped guide them over the side of the boat then they dropped in the water. The two of them dove under the surface, and Mason stayed on top.

We watched them on the sonar; an educational first experience for me. When my cell phone rang a minute later, I looked at the display then hit the talk button. "Hey, Smoke."

"Are they in the water yet?"

"They are. I'm on the boat with Warner and we're watching them getting close to the sunken treasure. It appears it's an old car, all right. I'd say about the same vintage as mine."

"What in the heck? I'll head out there shortly."

"See ya." I hung up and refocused on the divers. They were making their way around the car, brushing the windows, looking inside. Weber lifted his arm and Carlson started his ascent. When he surfaced, he gripped the side of the boat with one hand and lifted the breathing mask from his face with the other. His face was reddened from the cold water and camouflaged the freckles on his drawn face. He was panting when he delivered the news. "It's an old Dodge Charger. We don't have a clear view, but there are two bodies inside, from what we can see."

"*What?*" Warner and I said together.

"And I've never seen anything like it. Real, but not real, like they're coated with wax," he added.

I leaned closer to Carlson and studied his face. He wasn't kidding. The normal dancing twinkle was absent from his blue eyes. He looked like he'd seen a ghost or two, all right.

"Damn," Warner said and stared at me like I should know what to say.

"You call Sheriff Twardy, I'll call Detective Dawes," finally came out of my mouth.

"Damn," he repeated and took another moment. "Carlson, we'll need to figure out how to proceed with a recovery. In the meantime, get some shots from every which way you can down there." Warner retrieved an underwater camera and waited while Carlson repositioned his mask then accepted the camera.

When Carlson dove back in, Warner and I kept our eyes fixed on the vehicle that had come to rest on the bottom of Whitetail Lake and the deputies who were investigating it.

Warner phoned the sheriff, but it went to voicemail. "Sheriff, we're sitting on top of a possible crime scene on Whitetail Lake. There's an older car on the bottom, and it appears there are human remains inside of it."

Per department policy, the sheriff was notified of any unnatural or suspicious death in the county. Human remains in a vehicle submerged in a small lake fit both of the criteria.

Warner hung up. "Sheriff must be away from his desk."

"Are you going to try his cell phone?" I said.

He shook his head. "The sheriff will get back to me when he's clear. I ran into him earlier when I stopped by the office, and he made some noise about needing to spend the morning catching up on paperwork. He might be with a citizen, or in the biffy."

I nodded and phoned Smoke. "I'm just about there," he said.

It was better to deliver the big news in person. "I'll see if Warner can pick you up on shore." Warner nodded. "He says yes."

"Thanks," Smoke said and disconnected.

"Mason!" Warner called out. "We're running in to get Detective Dawes on shore and will be back shortly."

Mason gave him a thumbs' up sign.

"From the way Carlson described the way the bodies look, it can't be easy working down there," I said.

"No." Warner turned on the engine and shifted into low gear to safely clear the area, then steered toward the north shore. He eased against the landing area.

"Sometime back the sheriff mentioned purchasing those diving helmets with the communications capability built right in, depending on how much they cost. They'd be handy about now," I said.

Warner puffed out a breath. "That's an understatement. That'll be the next big purchase for boat and water, especially if we start finding a shitload of stuff with this sonar system.

Problem is, having more to investigate will mean more dive time. That might be a tough sell."

I pointed at the vehicle stopping by the side of the road. "Smoke's here. Man, his day just got a lot more interesting."

Warner's lips twisted. "Surprise, surprise, surprise."

Smoke got out of his car and jogged to the boat. He was long and lean and the best-looking man on the planet as far as I was concerned: angular face, long dimples, strong chin, full lips, and sky-blue eyes. His dark brown hair was sprinkled with some gray. He was wearing a light tan jacket over his shirt and tie, brown pants, and brown shoes polished to a gleaming shine. Not the usual fishing attire. But this wasn't a normal expedition. "What's up?" he asked. I leaned over the boat and offered my hand to help him in. "You guys look like cats that swallowed a bunch of canaries."

"It's bigger than that," I said and took a step back to give Smoke a place to stand.

He gave my hand a squeeze then released it. "How's that?"

"The guys found human remains in the submerged car," Warner said as he backed the boat away from shore.

"It was an *occupied* vehicle?" Smoke pointed at the steep hill that rose up from the lake on the south side. "How in the hell would they have driven in the lake from over there? It's not like the cases we've heard about where a guy is driving too fast down a road, loses control, and then winds up in a body of water. There's no road even close on that side."

We all agreed on that one and neither Warner, nor I, had an answer. We reached the site and Warner killed the engine. Smoke planted himself in front of the sonar's screen to watch the action. The divers rose to the surface. Carlson swam to the boat and lifted the camera. Warner bent over and scooped it up. The other two treaded water while Carlson climbed the rope ladder up to the boat, and then they followed suit.

We were hovering over the burial grounds of two unknown people. The momentary hush in the air was our unspoken way of showing some respect. When Weber and Mason were on board, the divers pulled off their masks and shook their heads. Warner clicked on the pictures captured by Carlson. We all packed in behind him to see.

Looking at the clouded images of the bodies inside the vehicle, I was both intrigued and repulsed by them. I'd seen bodies in various stages of decay in my career, due to a variety of circumstances, but none that looked like these bodies. It was like they'd been mummified and then had a waxy coating applied.

"Nineteen sixty-six Dodge Charger?" Smoke said, and the blood drained from his face. His voice was quiet and a little shaky. "This can't be. Back when I was in high school two of our classmates, friends of mine, went missing on Homecoming night. Toby Fryor and Wendy Everton. Toby's folks had given him their old Charger to run around in. And we thought the two of them must have run away together in it."

The air sucked out of my lungs when Smoke said their names. I reached over and touched his arm. "I remember my mother telling me about that, how they were never heard from again. Nobody knew what happened and the whole class felt the loss."

Smoke nodded. "We all ran around together. Oak Lea was a smaller school back then."

"How long ago was that?" Warner finally said.

"Our senior year, thirty-three years ago."

The unexpected twist left Weber, Carlson, and Mason speechless.

Smoke and I fixed our eyes on each other. My mother thought Toby and Wendy were star-crossed lovers who'd decided to run away for reasons known only to them. I knew Smoke had dated Wendy for a short time. She was the one who'd helped him earn his nickname in the incident that took him from his given name of Elton, to his nickname of Smoke, in one fell swoop.

2

"Geez, Detective, let's hope that's not your friends down there," Weber said, and the rest of us muttered words of agreement.

There was a chance it wasn't them.

"Wouldn't you think they'd be skeletons by now? These two in the car—from what it looks like are a male and a female—and still have tissue and skin," Warner said.

"Bodies can stay pretty much intact for years, even centuries, under the right conditions. Cold water being one," Smoke said.

"And inside a car like that, no fish or other lake creatures could get at them," Warner said.

We were quiet for a moment then Mason said, "We need to get them out of here. But we've never had a vehicle recovery in this deep of water before. In my time here, anyway."

"It'd be safe to say we've never had one in the department's history, period," Warner said. "Whitetail's about as deep as they get in Winnebago County, and what further complicates things is having no road access on this side of the lake."

Weber looked at Warner. "Geez, Sergeant, that car would've been down there another who knows how many years, maybe forever, without you and your fancy new device."

"Apparently no one thought there was a reason to dredge the lake back when these people went in," Mason said.

Smoke released a short puff of air. "Back then? No, apparently not. Well, whether they're our classmates or not, they've been down there long enough. Let's get them out, and figure out what we're dealing with." He pulled his cell phone out of its holder. "Anybody get a hold of the sheriff?"

Warner shook his head. "I left him a message on his office phone, but he hasn't called back."

"I'll try his cell. We'll need a tow truck with what, about a hundred yards of strap?"

"About that. The divers will have to use extra caution after they get the vehicle hooked on. It'll be a dangerous operation," Warner said.

"No doubt." Smoke looked at the divers. "When we recovered that truck from Bison Lake last year, the one that went through the ice, were all three of you involved with that one?"

"Yeah. That was a much easier deal, by far. It was only twenty-five or so feet out from shore in ten feet of water," Mason answered for the group.

"That turkey shoulda known better than to park there with that ice getting as thin as it was." Weber was referring to the owner of the truck.

Smoke hit a couple of numbers on his phone. "Sheriff, it's Dawes. Call me a-sap. We're about to launch a recovery of a vehicle on Whitetail Lake, and there are remains of at least two victims inside." He disconnected. "Huh, Sheriff must be in an important meeting. I'll have Communications locate us a tow truck with extra strap and connectors." He made the call, told Officer Robin what he needed then answered her questions about what we had found.

A few minutes later, she called back and said both Kyle and Ted, the owners of KT Towing, would be en route as soon as they loaded their rig.

We all waited impatiently in the boat, taking turns staring at the photos of the older-model Dodge and what we could see of its occupants. Whether or not it was the missing couple from Smoke's class, it had served as a burial ground for some time. The combined nervous anticipation warmed the air around us. Between that and the waterproof wetsuits, the divers all had beads of sweat on their brows.

Three cars—two squads and a sergeant's personal vehicle—arrived on the scene in so many minutes. Word had spread from Communications to the patrol deputies like a hayfield on fire in the middle of a drought.

"Nothing like this kind of a mystery to bring out the troops," Warner said.

Deputies Amanda Zubinski, Joel Ortiz, and Sergeant Leo Roth got out of their vehicles and gathered at the water's edge.

"You need another diver?" Roth called out from the shore. "I got my gear in my car." Roth was off-duty, dressed in jeans and a sweatshirt.

Warner didn't hesitate. "Yeah, suit up," he yelled back.

"Tim, when you go in to pick up Roth, I'll get off the boat so Zubinski and Ortiz can go out on the next run. I'm sure they're dying to see what you and your sonar discovered," I said.

"I'll do the same," Smoke said.

Warner raised a hand. "Why not? This is not your run-of-the-mill find."

He trolled the boat in. Roth had changed in his SUV, and got out of it carrying his fins, face gear, and tank. When we reached the bank, Smoke threw the rope to Ortiz who tied it on the post. Smoke climbed out of the boat and turned to help me get on shore. "Mandy, Joel, your turn. Hop aboard."

Neither would have asked for the chance to view the find themselves, and their faces brightened like kids seeing lights on a Christmas tree for the first time. They nodded, and climbed into the boat before Smoke changed his mind. Roth was right behind them.

Smoke looked at his watch. "Where in the hell is the sheriff?"

"Call Dina, maybe she knows." I loosened the rope on the boat, and threw it to Weber who caught it, and pulled it inside.

Smoke withdrew his phone and dialed. After a two-minute conversation, he hung up. "She has no idea, and that is not at all like our little mother hen, Dina."

"No it's not. I'll call my personal mother hen and ask her."

"Yeah, if Dina doesn't know, Kristen should."

My mother and the sheriff were engaged to be married sometime down the road. I figured they were waiting until all the stars and planets were perfectly aligned, whenever that might be.

"Kristen's Corner, may I help you?"

"Mother."

"Oh, Corinne, hello. What are you up to on your day off?"

"I'll tell you about it later. Mother, do you know where the sheriff, where Denny, is?"

"Denny? Why are you looking for him?"

"We're trying to reach him, and thought maybe you knew his schedule, like if he had any appointments."

"Why, no I don't. He should be at work at this time of day. I talked to him earlier, and he didn't say he had anything special planned," she said.

"I'm sure he would have, if he did. No biggie. We figured he's tied up in a meeting. I've gotta go, so I'll catch you later."

"'Bye, sweetheart."

"Later, Mom." I pushed the end button. "Mother doesn't know either."

Smoke scratched his cheek. "I don't think I'll bug Dina again. She gets pretty worked up when it comes to keeping the sheriff healthy and safe. I'll get Cindy to do a little checking. If she can't locate him, I'll see if I can raise him on the radio." Cindy was one of the administrative clerks, next in line behind Dina.

An uneasy feeling danced through me. "I hope he's all right."

Smoke's eyes captured mine. "Me, too."

He phoned Cindy, and was still talking when the towing team pulled up in their rig. The earth rumbled around us and the smell of diesel drifted through the air when they pulled to a stop and let the truck idle. Kyle and Ted climbed out and hurried over to us. Kyle was the half of the team who did most of the maintenance, and had grease permanently embedded in his cracked, beefy hands. He was taller and heavier than Ted who was more on the wiry side. Ted responded to the majority of the calls and gave the impression that time was money, and the faster and more efficiently he got the job done, the better.

I pointed to where Warner and his boat crew were anchored. "That's where that car is sitting, believe it or not."

"Damn, that'll be about the biggest challenge we've ever had, wouldn't you say, Ted?" Kyle said.

Ted didn't answer right away. He was deep in thought as he looked from Warner's boat to the surrounding shoreline. "I'd say, all right. And there's no good spot for us to pull in to get any closer. How in the hell did a car wind up over there?"

Smoke finished his call and put a hand on Ted's shoulder. "That is the great unknown. But we figured you could handle the job, if anyone could."

"We'll do our best, Detective," Ted said. "Kyle, jump in the truck and I'll guide you to where you'll need to stop."

"There's not much of a landing here," Kyle said.

"Nope, but it's what we got," Ted answered.

"Detective Dawes, on two." It was Sergeant Warner telling Smoke to switch from the main radio-band channel.

Smoke plucked the radio from his belt, turned the knob, and depressed the call button. "Go ahead on two."

"We'll wait 'til KT is in position before we come in."

"Copy."

People driving by slowed down to check out the happenings on Whitetail Lake. Others that had no pressing deadline, or particular schedule to keep, pulled off County Road 35 onto the shoulders of both sides of the road.

"This is turning into a three-ring circus," I said.

Smoke shook his head slightly. "Barnum and Bailey."

"The Ringling Brothers," Ted added and smiled, surprising me. He'd never given any indication he had a sense of humor before. He moved over to guide his partner.

"People must be thinking there's been a drowning," I said.

"And they are most likely right. When the drowning occurred is yet to be determined," Smoke said.

Kyle backed the rig closer to us, and Ted jumped to attention. He held his left hand up and bent his fingers over and over in a "keep coming" motion. Then gave him the halt sign.

"I hope you got good brakes on that thing," Smoke said.

"Something we test all the time," Ted said.

Smoke's phone rang. "It's Communications," he said when he glanced at the display. "Hey. . . . Just tell them we found an object on the bottom of the lake and we're retrieving it. . . . Yup. . . . Thanks." He pushed the end button and replaced his phone. "They're getting flooded with phone calls from people wondering what we're up to."

Kyle joined us by the water's edge as Warner and company reached the landing. "Detective?" Warner said to Smoke.

"I'll defer to you and your divers, and the towing guys here, to make the calls," Smoke said.

"Excuse me, but can you tell us what's going on here?" A middle-aged man, with skinny legs and a round belly, inched near the front of the tow truck, and pointed to one of the houses at the top of the south side hill. "I live up there and own part of this lakeshore."

"Sir, our water patrol spotted a large object on the bottom of the lake with his sonar, and we're here to recover it. I'll need you to stay clear of the area." Smoke looked around at the other people crowding in, and added, "All of you."

The group shifted over to the guardrail on the inside edge of the road's shoulder for a box office view of the action.

Smoke focused on the crew in the boat. "Ortiz, Zubinski, change of plans. I guess I'll need you to do crowd control."

They nodded, got out of the boat, and walked to the front of the tow truck. "It was fun while it lasted," Ortiz muttered under his breath.

Smoke lowered his voice to avoid being overheard by any of the bystanders. "Okay, Ted, Kyle, there's an old Dodge down there. And as much as we've been able to see, it appears it's been a coffin for a pair of individuals for a long time."

Kyle did a double take. "What'd you say?"

"Robin didn't say there were people in there." Wiry Ted rocked onto his tiptoes.

"Unfortunately, there are, and it's not a pretty sight," Warner said.

"If it weren't for that, we might not have made the decision to try this risky of an operation. And we want to keep quiet about the bodies, for the time being," Smoke said.

Kyle's face was solemn when he nodded. "Understood. We should have plenty of strap, and we'll get them in."

Ted bounced from one foot to the other. "Why don't you secure the D-Ring shackle in your boat, and we'll unwind the strap as you drive."

"After we're set up, I'll put a diver on each side of the vehicle, at a safe distance, to keep watch. And the rescue divers will follow behind, close to the surface. It'll be a slow process, but we'll take as much time as we need," Warner said.

Smoke inclined his head toward the boat. "Corky, you go out with Warner. I'll work on this end of it."

I gave him a nod and climbed into the boat. Kyle turned on the hydraulic winch, and slowly unrolled the strap. Ted grabbed it and walked it over to the boat. Weber took the strap and shackle from him, and held on.

"How much power does that baby have?" Weber asked.

"Pulling power of twelve thousand pounds," Ted said.

"Whoa, no shit." Weber turned to Warner. "Sarge, how many pounds you figure that car full of water down there weighs?"

Warner plopped a hand on his opposite forearm and tapped his fingers like he was counting. "Well. The car would be around four thousand pounds, two tons. Maybe a little less. The water and silt inside of it? I'd guess there's around five hundred gallons of water. No good idea about the silt, so let's stick with the water weight. Who's good at math?"

"Mason is," Carlson said.

"A gallon of water weighs about eight point three pounds," Warner said.

Mason nodded. "Right around forty-one hundred."

"So we're looking at less than ten thousand pounds of combined weight for the vehicle and the water."

"We're okay then. We want the strap to have a little stretch, but not a lot. We'll have some resistance from the lake itself. The test will be when we pull it up on shore," Ted said.

"Let's do it," Warner said.

Smoke released his hold on the boat's tie rope. Warner gave the boat some gas and moved slowly toward the site. The strap unrolled from the winch as he did. When the car came into view, he cut the engine.

"Okay, Weber and Carlson, I'll have you get her hooked up. Attach the shackle to the tie rod, as close to the center as possible, then slip on the loop of the strap, and secure it. Signal when you want us to start tightening the strap. When it's taut, give us the stop signal. Then get into position, far enough away, in case she snaps loose.

"We'll wait until you're out of the way before we start the tow. Roth you're with Weber, Mason you're with Carlson. Signal us to stop if you notice any part of the operation going south. The car is facing west, so we'll need to get it turned to the north. Any questions, comments, concerns?" Warner said.

"I got a concern. When they turn the car, it's going to stir up that muck on the lake's bottom," Mason said.

"Good point. We'll go as slow as we can to minimize that. Okay, Carlson you take the south side of the car, the driver's side. Weber, you take the north. Let's get this operation underway."

The four of them pulled on their face masks and jumped in. Weber took the strap, and Carlson took the shackle. The divers lowered themselves into the water, and we watched the action on the screen. Weber and Carlson worked for a while to attach the strap. When it was secured, Weber gave the sign to start tightening the strap.

Warner depressed the talk button on his radio. "Six eleven, Three forty on two."

"Go ahead on two," Smoke answered.

"The strap's in place and we're ready for a slow and easy shortening of the line."

"Copy."

"I'll put my arm up when it looks like they're getting close and drop it when the divers tell me to stop," Warner added.

"We'll keep a close watch."

I held my breath and kept my eyes peeled to the screen. When it appeared the strap was losing the last of its slack, Mason waved his hand back and forth as a "slow-down" signal. Warner stuck his hand in the air then dropped it like a lead balloon when Mason's hand shot up to stop. Ted's reflexes were spot on. He halted the winch's pull, but there was a slight jerk on the car nonetheless.

Weber and Mason joined their partners, and Warner spoke into his radio. "Six eleven to Three forty."

"Six eleven?"

"Let's get the vehicle turned a quarter turn to the north. Nice and easy."

A sharp, involuntary sound escaped from my innards, making me feel like I was the tensest one on the scene. Watching deputies work in risky situations with a high probability of personal injury was burdensome for me.

When the car moved, the dark, cloudy bottom of silt rose and surrounded it, then hung in the water like a dense fog. Ted had the hydraulic winch moving at a snail's pace, and it took a few minutes before the car was in a north-facing position. I glanced up at Warner. Lines of sweat were running from his temples down the front of his ears to his neck. His jaw was set, and his eyes were intently focused on the sonar screen. I wasn't the only one on pins and needles.

"Breathe," I said.

"Huh?"

"That's what I have to tell myself when I'm tied up in knots."

He nodded, sucked in a breath then held up his hand for Kyle to proceed. He said, "Nice and easy," into his radio.

"Nice and easy," Smoke repeated.

The silt continued to be stirred along the way as the hydraulic winch was tightened, and the old Dodge inched its way toward Whitetail's north shore. Warner trolled behind and we maintained a close watch on the operation, especially on the divers who were visible even when clouds from the rising lake bottom surrounded them. Despite the slow pace, it was still only a matter of minutes before the car reached the shoreline.

The divers surfaced, and Warner steered the boat to the west of the car. "So far, so good," Warner said. "Bottom here is right around eight feet."

Smoke and Ted moved to the water's edge and looked down. Kyle jumped off his flat bed truck and joined them. He craned his neck both right and left, assessing the situation. "I'd feel better if we'd get some guiding straps around it. It'll be less likely to twist and turn, and maybe even flip over."

Ted agreed. "You divers okay with that?"

They were.

Kyle fished around in a large stainless steel storage bin in the back of the truck and found the equipment he needed. He carried two straps and shackles to the edge, then said, "Heads up," and dropped them on the ground near Ted's feet.

Ted picked up a strap by the shackle at the end and handed it to Mason. "Attach this to the undercarriage behind the left front wheel." He gave the second set to Weber. "And this one to the right side." The two deputies went underwater with the straps, and completed their task in no time. Ted gave Kyle the loose ends which he fed into two smaller hydraulic winches on opposite sides of the truck bed. He wound them until they were taut and ready for tugging action. Then he hit the pause button to halt the winches.

My stomach muscles were as tight as the towing straps when Ted said, "We're ready to bring her out. I need everyone to move to either side of the truck when she reaches the surface. We've never had a strap break, and she should be fine, but a guy can never be too careful in a deal like this."

Kyle nodded, and waited for the four divers to get out of the way before he continued. He fussed with the settings on the winches then started them up, from one to the next, in a seamless move. Warner turned his video camera on the landing, and hit the record button.

Smoke was standing as close to the edge as possible, and was hopefully safe. He looked at me with what seemed like a pleading expression, and I knew he was convinced his missing friends from all those years back were about to be found. I managed a weak smile and folded my hands. He blinked his eyes in response then turned his attention back to the vehicle that was emerging from the deep.

3

When the car was freed from the lake that had held its secret for too many years, every one of us released noisy exhales. We couldn't help ourselves. Warner reached over and grabbed my forearm. But I didn't take my eyes off the old blue water and silt-filled Charger that surfaced, aided by the best equipment available. When most of the vehicle had cleared, water and muck began draining out as it was guided onto the bank.

My attention was drawn back to Smoke, and his reaction. He closed his eyes, bent his head, and stroked his forehead with the fingers of one hand for a moment. Maybe he was saying a prayer. I had been praying myself throughout the operation.

Kyle stopped the winches and Smoke, Ted, and the divers slowly approached the car, knowing it was a coffin holding human remains. They cautiously peered in the car windows, dumbstruck. They all stared, and not a word spilled from their mouths. We had been cautioned to keep quiet about the discovery for the time being, but that's not why they were mute.

From what I saw in the photos, the bodies did not look real. They more closely resembled ancient, deformed, clay statues. They had not decayed in ways we were accustomed to.

"Let's dock," Warner said in a whisper. He pulled up to shore and signaled Weber who was closest to the landing post. Warner threw him the rope, and when the boat was secure, we climbed out.

My legs were shaky, like I'd been on board for days. I wobbled over to Smoke's side and caught his hand in mine, offering a brief, comforting touch.

"This is definitely a first for us." Kyle was the one to break the silence. It was a first for every single one of us there.

More people arrived and moved near the front of the truck, craning their necks in an effort to see what they could before Ortiz and Zubinski directed them to get back. Someone standing by the guardrail yelled they had a good vantage point, and the newcomers moved over there, making crowd control an easier job for the team.

I leaned over and stared into the Charger. I had my second involuntary gasp of the morning. It was one thing to see the photos of the victims; it was another to see them in person. Two grotesque-looking bodies were in the front seat of the car. One was partially lying on the other, making it appear like he was shielding her. If the crash hadn't killed them, they must have embraced after the plunge into the lake, when they knew they were trapped. But more likely—since there was no evidence of attached seats belts—the bodies had ended up that way as they settled. Plus, the move to land may have shifted them somewhat.

I followed Smoke as he began a visual tour of the rest of the vehicle. "Smoke?"

"I am ninety-nine point nine percent certain this is Toby Fryor's Charger." His face was solemn as he leaned closer to the passenger window and squinted against the sun.

I bent over, close to Smoke, so I could talk quietly. "Mother is going to freak out if it turns out to be your friends. And she'll have a very good reason, for a change."

Smoke lifted his eyebrows, wrinkling his forehead. "No doubt. Think of their families who have wondered all these years." He straightened up and so did I.

"I know. I can't even imagine." Having a loved one disappear, never to be heard from again, was one of the worst things for a person to cope with. I glanced around at the sheriff's department personnel who were on the scene and it brought to mind the one who wasn't there. "I'm surprised the sheriff hasn't shown up."

"Cindy hasn't been able to locate him just yet."

That didn't seem possible. "Really?"

"She called me during the towing process to let me know. Truth be told, it's got me a little concerned."

His words made shivers run quickly up my spine. "He must have a good reason for being wherever he is, as strange as it is he didn't tell anyone."

Smoke's shoulder lifted a couple of inches in response then he went back to his perusal. The other deputies made quiet comments about the car, the bodies, and the possible circumstances. All were wondering how in the hell the car had ended up in the lake in the first place, without anyone seeing it go in. Or at least noticing damage the tire tracks would have caused on the hill, and on the bank of the lake, after it did.

I walked over to where Zubinski and Ortiz were stationed and called them aside. "I'll cover here so you two can go over and have a look. It's something we'll never see again in our careers, at least I hope not. Be prepared for the condition of the bodies."

They murmured their thanks and joined the others who were looking at the interior and exterior of the car from all angles. Mason had gotten his camera and was capturing the scene in still shots. The man who had asked Smoke for information earlier walked over and said, "How long has that car been in Whitetail? And how did it get there in the first place?"

"What's your name, sir?" I said.

"Harry Gimler."

"Mister Gimler, we don't have any information on that just yet."

"People are wondering if there are bodies in that car, since the deputies keep looking inside like there is," he said.

"They are doing a good visual sweep, and then we'll take the car to our crime lab and see if we can get good answers of when and why it went down."

"I've lived here for years, and you're telling me all this time there was an old car sitting on the bottom?" he persisted.

"We'll do our best to figure all that out. In the meantime, if you'd be so kind to watch from over there." I pointed to the guardrail. "It sounds like they're ready to load the car on the flatbed."

Gimler's eyes darted from me to the Charger, like he was considering whether or not he could make it to the car for a sneak peek before he was apprehended. Instead, he followed my directive and joined the group who was watching from afar.

When Zubinski and Ortiz returned from their viewing, they maintained poker faces, but I knew them well enough to know they were affected after seeing the remains in the car. I nodded then walked back to check on the loading process.

Kyle pushed wheel ramps from the truck bed to the ground, and Ted adjusted them. "Let's move the side winches back to get them out of the way," he said, and Ted jumped up on the truck to help him. They loosened the straps enough so they could accomplish the task. After the equipment had been repositioned, Ted got off the truck and the Charger was pulled up the ramp and onto the truck's bed in no time, leaving more muddy water behind on the way.

Smoke addressed Warner. "Are you going out for another look around the lake?"

Warner blinked, and his lips turned down at the corners. "Hmmph, I hadn't planned on it, but as long as we're here, it's not a bad idea." It looked to me like it he was ready to get *off* the water, and the sooner the better.

Smoke waved his hand at the lake. "I was thinking you and the divers should go back where the car was sitting, check for any other evidence. Most likely there's none after all this time, but who knows?"

Warner nodded and called out to the divers. "I'll need two of you to stay behind, in case we need to employ your diving skills again."

Mason and Weber volunteered to be the two. Then we watched as the tow truck company prepared to set off on their journey back to the county's evidence garage shop where the victims would be freed from the Dodge Charger, at last.

Smoke walked over to Kyle's driver's side window. "I'll meet you at the evidence garage."

No one from the crowd of spectators moved until the tow truck was heading east on County Road 35. Harry Gimler puffed his way over to me. "Will you let me know what you find? I mean, that car was technically just off my property line, from the looks of it."

"I will do that. We'll probably be talking to all the neighbors," I said.

His eyebrows squeezed together. "So you're saying there was something notable in that car. Or someone."

I smiled at his doggedness, despite my intention not to. "Mister Gimler, I'm not at liberty to say anything. The investigation has barely begun."

He gave me a once over, taking in my street clothes, the Glock in its holster on the right side of my belt, and my sheriff's badge clipped on next to it. "You look too young to be a detective."

I opted not to tell I wasn't that young, nor was I a detective. "I'm Sergeant Corinne Aleckson." I fingered my county identification badge and lifted it so Gimler could read it.

"That's why you looked familiar. I've seen your picture in the paper."

There was something off with him that I tried to put my finger on. He wasn't creepy, exactly. He struck me as cagey and secretive more than anything, enough to prompt me to want to look him up in our department arrest records, and calls for service files, when I had a minute. "If you'll excuse me, I need to shove off," I said.

I caught up with Smoke who was giving instructions to Zubinski and Ortiz. "You can get back on the road as soon as all the snoopers leave."

"Will do," Mandy said.

I nodded at the two deputies. "Thanks, Mandy and Joel, for doing crowd control."

"You bet," Joel said, and Mandy nodded.

I turned to Smoke. "I'll meet you at the garage."

"It's your day off, little lady."

"Not anymore."

Sergeant Doug Matsen, head of the newly expanded Winnebago County Crime Lab, was waiting with the overhead door of the evidence garage standing open. KT Towing's flatbed truck was backed up close to the garage, ready to unload the Dodge Charger. Smoke and I joined the group, and we all squinted against the blinding rays of the late morning sun reflecting from the glass and metal on the vehicles. Even with my sunglasses cutting out most of the glare, my eyes still closed halfway from the assault.

Sergeant Matsen was in his late thirties, seven or eight years older than me. He had been on the wild side in his early days with the department, pushing the limits of what he could legally do to solve crimes. Word had it that it kept Sheriff Twardy on edge, wondering if Matsen might cross the wrong line at some point. But Matsen had determination and dedication, and was an astute road deputy. When he put in for the crime lab's supervisory position, he had strong support from the majority of the department.

"Back far enough into the garage to unload this precious cargo," Smoke said.

Kyle got back in the driver's seat and did just that. "Say when," he yelled out his open window.

Smoke, Matsen, Ted, and I went into the garage to monitor the process.

"That's good," Smoke called out, and the truck came to an immediate stop.

Ted walked around to the back of the truck. "Okay, Kyle, let's cut this baby loose."

Kyle joined his partner and they disconnected the strap then safely shook the vehicle from the truck's bed onto the garage floor.

"If this don't beat all," Matsen said as he snapped on latex gloves and stared into the Dodge Charger he'd been gifted with. "When you get out of bed in the morning, you never know what the new day will bring."

"That's a given," Smoke said.

It most certainly was.

Smoke honed in on Kyle and Ted who looked like they were settling in, prepared to stay for the duration of the investigation. "Thanks, guys. We need to get to work, and I'm sure you do too," he said.

The towing team took the non-subtle hint and left with a wave and a nod.

Matsen frowned as we bent over and stared in the windows. "Two victims from what I can see. I've seen bodies fairly well-preserved under the right conditions, but never to this degree. That waxy look must be from the formation of adipocere."

Smoke cleared his throat. "I guess that's why they call it grave wax. When I was working up north for Cook County, I had a case where a guy was found in a pond in early spring. He was similar looking to these two. You're correct about having the right conditions to be preserved like that. And if they're who I think they are they've been down there a hell of a long time."

"What do you mean?" Matsen said.

"I'd be willing to bet I know who owned this car and that he's one of the victims. And the other victim is his girlfriend."

Matsen straightened and studied Smoke like he was a specimen under his microscope. "You're serious?"

"This would not be a time I'd be kidding."

"No. No, I guess not. Who are they are?" Matsen said.

"Toby Fryor and Wendy Everton. They disappeared Homecoming night, thirty-three years ago." He paused a moment. "It seemed to all of us here in Oak Lea like they fell off the face of the planet."

"Thirty-three years ago? Damn, that is an old case. And you knew them?"

"Yup, they were my classmates and my friends."

"And my mom and dad's, too," I added.

Matsen seemed to have forgotten I was there until I spoke. He looked at me and nodded then said, "That's got to be a shock. Sorry." He shook his head then took another look inside the Charger. "And they did a thorough investigation at the time?"

"Yeah, it sure seemed like it. Back when, after the sheriff's department had hit enough dead ends, the sheriff called it. That file is pretty thick, and I had a look at it myself after I started with Winnebago."

Matsen frowned. "What did they think happened to them when they disappeared like that, some kind of foul play?"

"No. They figured they ran off together, maybe eloped. There was no evidence to suspect anything else." Smoke paused, lost in thought for a moment. "After they disappeared, everyone who knew them was questioned, including me. And Corky's parents too, of course. The class sizes were smaller then and we all knew each other, at least to some degree.

"The detectives—and there were only two of them in the county in those days—were trying to find at least one person that Toby or Wendy had talked to about plans they might have had, including running away together. But they never found anyone who had. The detectives also had zero success locating Toby's vehicle anywhere in the U.S. Now we know why."

Matsen swiped his forehead with his sleeve. "What a hell of a deal. The car is shifted into drive so what are we looking at here, an accident, or a homicide-suicide? That's what we'll try to find out."

Smoke drew his eyebrows together and sucked in a breath. "No, that's what we *will* find out. Now that we know where they ended up, we have a starting point anyway."

"It's good to have a starting point," Matsen said.

"Smoke, are their parents still around?" I asked.

"Yeah, as far as I know. Damn. You know, I've thought about Toby and Wendy from time to time over the years—wishful thinking really—wondering if they'd come back with a pack of kids and prove to everyone they had been meant to be together after all."

"This is a much sadder ending, but at least their families will finally have answers," I said.

Smoke nodded.

"There won't be any fingerprints on anything in the vehicle itself, of course. The water would have dissolved them within the first month," Matsen said, enlightening me on that detail. "What time did you phone the medical examiner?" he asked Smoke.

"As soon as the divers said we had human remains. Doc Bridey Patrick was tied up, finishing an autopsy. When she called me back, she said she'd meet us here." Smoke looked at his watch. "And it should be shortly."

"Good. I've dealt with bodies in all kinds of conditions, but like I said, never anything close to this," Matsen said.

"If I would have had to guess, I'd have thought there'd be nothing left but bones after all this time," Smoke said.

Matsen wiped his brow with his sleeve. "I'll get some more shots of the car and the contents."

The contents.

Smoke's phone rang. He pulled it out of its holder, looked at the display, and pushed a button. "Cindy. What have you got for me? . . . Hmm, his radio? And his car is gone from the parking garage? . . . . Okay, well thanks. Keep me posted." He hung up and caught my eyes with his. A slight shake of his head told me there was still no word from the sheriff, and that he had driven somewhere. "His portable radio is sitting on his desk."

A growing sense of agitation tickled my nerve endings. It was completely out of character for the sheriff not to answer his phone, or to at least let his staff know where he was going if he left in the middle of the workday. Not taking his portable radio with him was unheard of. As the chief law enforcement officer in the county, Dennis Twardy was always on duty. Always. Yet there we were, sitting with evidence of a very old, unsolved mysterious disappearance of a young couple— something he'd want to know about—and he was nowhere to be found.

"I'm gonna give Kenner a call, see if the sheriff stopped by to see him. And maybe has a dead cell phone," Smoke said.

Chief Deputy Mike Kenner was on medical leave for a few days, following a minor surgical procedure.

"You're looking for the sheriff?" Matsen said.

"Yeah, nobody seems to know where he is," Smoke said.

"I saw him in the break room getting a cup of coffee first thing this morning," Matsen said.

But where did he go after that?

Smoke phoned Kenner, checked on how he was doing, and learned Kenner had not heard from the sheriff at all that day.

Sergeant Matsen spent the time getting photos of the car from every angle.

"I'll try one last thing. Denny took his car, so he's got that radio, if he's still driving." Smoke pulled out his radio. "Three forty to Three oh one, on two." When there was no response, he repeated the call, but still no answer. He shook his head and his shoulders lifted in a slight shrug.

As Smoke turned to me, Doctor Bridey Patrick from the Midwest Medical Examiner's Office opened the inside entrance door and walked toward us with purpose in her step. She was short and squat and had spiked gray hair. Patrick was wearing a white top and tan pants. She gave Smoke a look of noted appreciation, and greeted us with a simple, "Morning," then turned her full attention to the Dodge Charger and its "contents."

Doctor Patrick shook her head back and forth a number of times. "This is my first experience with remains that have been submerged in a vehicle for many years, possibly decades. It's something that most medical examiners won't see in an entire career. I've had a number of victims whose bodies were preserved by adipocere, however."

Matsen turned his head to the doctor. "What exactly happens to cause that?"

"Adipocere? The short answer is it's fat decomposition. It's formed when adipose tissue—fatty tissue—undergoes a slow hydrolysis caused by anaerobic bacteria. Ideal conditions for the transformation of body fats into adipocere would be in a cold, wet environment where there is little oxygen. In this case, in a car at the bottom of a lake."

I'd learned about adipocere a couple years before when we'd worked on another case where a dog brought home the unwanted gift of a woman's dismembered leg he'd found in their lake.

Doctor Patrick couldn't take her eyes off the bodies in the old Dodge. "Without a doubt, this is one for the record books. My two assistants are on their way with gurneys and body bags."

"The team assigned to Major Crimes this week happens to be two of the guys that got called out on the dive. They'll get here before long," Matsen said.

"Mason and Weber?" Smoke said.

"Yes. You might want to put on coveralls. I got a good supply of the impervious ones that will protect your clothes from possible contamination," Matsen said to Smoke and me.

"I'll get into mine," Doctor Patrick said.

Smoke and I followed Matsen to the supply closet on the back wall of the garage. He handed each of us a plastic bag containing a coverall, booties, protective gloves and glasses. We tore into the bags, withdrew them, and put them on. When we were all outfitted, Smoke, Matsen, and I moved in then stopped some feet behind the doctor who had donned her own gear. She turned and visually surveyed us. "Are we ready?"

I was touched by the significance of it all. "Smoke, they were your friends. Maybe you should do the honor of opening the door."

Doctor Patrick frowned, and Smoke explained.

She nodded. "By all means, that is certainly fitting. Go right ahead, Detective."

4

The Charger was a two-door model with push buttons on the handles, similar to the ones on my GTO. Smoke tried to push the button of the driver's door with his thumb, but it didn't budge. He put more weight into it, but it still didn't move. "I guess we need to try a spray lubricant and some tools. If that doesn't work, we may have to break the window."

"I've got some spray, and a screwdriver, and hammer right over there. We'll give it a shot." Matsen went to get the supplies. When he returned he handed Smoke the tools, and then aimed the nozzle of the lubricant at the area around the opener, and gave it a generous shot of spray. When he finished, Matsen took a step back.

Smoke stepped in, set the screwdriver against the button, and tapped it with the hammer. After a few tries, it went in. "Bingo," he said. He handed the tools back to Matsen, depressed the button, and pulled the door open.

I braced myself for whatever stench the vehicle might release. A fishy, lake and mud smell spilled out. I was used to similar odors from many hours of fishing with my gramps, and since it was tied to great memories, I didn't find it unpleasant. When the car dried out, any number of other smells would likely make themselves known. Leather, mildew, rust. From the car itself, and from the shoes, clothing, and other belongings left behind by the victims.

"Do you recognize them, Detective?" Matsen said.

Smoke stared for a time then shook his head. "No, not from the way they looked in life and how they look now. There should be some IDs on them. I see a purse and what looks like the sleeves and part of an old letter jacket on the seat."

Doctor Patrick got a phone call from her assistants saying they were outside and requested that we open the garage door. I jogged over and pushed the automatic opener. Doctor Calvin Helsing, assistant medical examiner, and Karen Sherman, a pathology assistant, were waiting with the necessary equipment. They were wearing the same type of coveralls we had on, with elastic closures at the wrists and ankles. They pushed in the gurneys that were laden with supplies, and body bags atop.

I'd met both of them the previous fall at the autopsy of a woman we'd worked diligently to identify. It was a couple of days after I'd met Doctor Patrick. We'd called her to the scene where a female victim was found lying on the floor of a wooded area. It was another death outside the realm of usual or expected, and the cause and manner took investigative work from both the sheriff's, and the medical examiner's, offices.

Dr. Helsing was dark and striking and around my age. His pupils dilated when his eyes met mine, like they had the first time we'd met. It seemed he found me attractive. I felt complimented, but wasn't certain how I'd respond if he ever asked me out. Karen was a few years older, on the plump side, with a flawless complexion that no makeup could further enhance.

Helsing and Karen greeted all of us, and joined their boss on the driver's side of the car. Smoke and Matsen went to the passenger side and opened the door using the same spray-and-pounding method. With both doors open, it was easier to view and assess the inside and its contents. Matsen snapped another series of photos, and I captured image after image with my mind's eye.

The more I was around the bodies, the easier it was to observe them and the state they were in. Some of their clothing had disintegrated, but other articles were still largely intact. The male had jeans on, and it appeared the female had been wearing lined pants because what remained was a thin, shiny polyester-looking cover on her legs. Neither had shirts on, but the female was wearing a bra. A large leather purse was lying on the back seat bench.

Smoke pointed to the seat on the passenger side. "I'd say that's what's left of Toby Fryor's school letter jacket. He was a standout athlete who lettered in football, basketball, and baseball."

Dr. Patrick nodded. "The jacket was lined wool, no doubt, with leather sleeves. Wool and cotton fabrics disintegrate over time in water. But tanned leather, denim, and polyester are more water-resistant. That's why the victims are still partially clothed," Dr. Patrick said.

Doctor Helsing rolled a gurney close to the vehicle. "If we move the seats back as far as possible, it'll give us more room to work," he said.

"Good plan," Smoke said. He struggled for a moment with a lever under the driver's seat, and when it finally depressed, he held it down with his right hand and pushed the seat back with his left.

Doctor Helsing worked on the passenger seat and got it moved further back. Karen opened the body bag on a gurney, readying it to receive a body.

Deputies Todd Mason and Vince Weber walked into the garage quietly, observed for a minute the progress we'd made, then helped themselves to coveralls.

"Anything else of import turn up on the bottom of Whitetail Lake?" Smoke asked.

"Nope. Warner took a couple of laps to be sure he didn't miss anything," Mason said.

"He's kind of itchin' to get out on some of the other lakes, after coming upon that major find." Weber nodded at the Charger.

"Mason and Weber, why don't you help Doc Helsing there? If that's okay with you, Doc Bridey?" Smoke said.

"Certainly," she said.

"This will be awkward, but if one of you can assist, we'll get the victims out and onto the gurneys," Helsing said.

Weber and Mason glanced at each other, and by silent agreement decided Mason would be the one to do that. Mason had a slighter build than Weber, and wouldn't take up as much space next to Helsing.

They worked slowly and carefully, and I was again struck by how intact the bodies were. "Once adipocere is formed, it's quite firm," Dr. Patrick said, like she had read my thoughts.

Captain Clayton Randolph, next-in-command after Chief Deputy Kenner, who was next-in-command after the sheriff, paid the investigative team a visit. He watched the progress, but stayed in the background.

Before he went back to his desk, the captain sidled over to where Smoke and I were standing. We talked about the impact of finding the Charger with its human remains for some minutes then he changed subjects. "No one seems to know where Denny Twardy disappeared to. It is the damndest thing. It's been four hours since anyone in the office has had contact with him."

Smoke's face tightened. "Something's not right."

Randolph nodded. "I'm going to have Communications send a message to all the road deputies asking if they've seen his car parked anywhere."

"Good idea," Smoke said.

Randolph looked at me. "You've talked to your mother about it, Sergeant?"

"I did, a few hours ago. I just asked if she'd heard from him. She must be really busy at the store, because she hasn't called back to check if I'd talked to him yet."

"Captain, have you sent someone to check Twardy's home?" Smoke asked.

"Yes, with no luck." He shook his head. "We know what to do if we hear from our sheriff," Randolph said then left.

We needed to communicate the news to the rest of the department.

Deputies and other sheriff's department personnel came into the garage to see for themselves the historical find. Pulling an old car out of Whitetail Lake was not a secret, but who it belonged to, and who may have been inside of it, was to be kept as quiet as possible until the victims were identified and their families were notified.

After the victims' bodies had been safely removed and were on their way to the Midwest Medical Examiner's Office in Anoka County, our team vigilantly worked to remove items, mucky or not, from the inside of the car, including the glove box and the trunk. It was painstaking.

Smoke picked a man's wallet out of the glove box. After he worked it open, he found what he was looking for: Toby Fryor's driver's license. "Thank God for plastic. It's about the only thing left in here," he said.

At three o'clock, Captain Randolph phoned Smoke to tell him he had ordered pizzas, and we all needed to take a break. I hadn't even thought about eating since the granola bar and yogurt I'd had for breakfast, and the mention of food made my stomach rumble in response.

"You guys go ahead. There are only a couple more things to mark. We'll keep this cart full of items secured and drying in here," Matsen said.

"I can help you finish up," Mason told him.

"And if someone would hang a 'Do Not Enter' sign on both the outside of the garage doors and on the inside entrance, that'd be good," Matsen added.

"Will do," Weber said.

Smoke and I got out of our coveralls. Then I followed him to his desk and waited while he gave the sheriff's cell phone another try. "I know Randolph has half the county looking for him, but I keep thinkin' he's gonna answer one of these times."

"Should I call my mom again?" I said.

He nodded. "Maybe you should."

When Mother answered the phone, she sounded flustered. But it wasn't because she hadn't heard from Denny

Twardy. "Corinne, people are flocking in for the winter clearance sale. I haven't had a chance to catch my breath all day. I should have scheduled one of my helpers to work, but I never dreamed I'd be so swamped. It hasn't been busy enough to keep two of us here lately."

"I won't keep you, but just checking in again to see if you've talked to Denny or if you remembered he had something after all."

"Oh my goodness, no I haven't. And I was going to call him but got too busy. Is something wrong?"

"We don't know that anything's wrong. But we've got a big investigation going on here, and we don't know where he is."

"Corinne, I can hear the concern in your voice. Now you've got me worried."

"Mother, no don't. Take care of your business, and if Denny calls or stops in, tell him to call the office. Okay?"

"Okay. But Corinne—"

"I have to go and I'll talk to you later. 'Bye." I hung up before she pumped me for more information and then shook my head at Smoke.

He bounced his fist on his desk. "He's driving an equipped Ford Taurus which is pretty easy to identify by just about anyone, unmarked or not. And our deputies certainly know his vehicle."

"And Randolph said they checked his house."

"Yeah, but it wouldn't hurt to check again." Smoke phoned Captain Randolph. After they'd talked for a minute, they disconnected and Smoke shook his head. "He was just about to track me down. Ortiz did another check of Sheriff Twardy's place and took a look through his garage window. It seems Denny switched vehicles. His department vehicle is in the garage and his Buick is not."

"Really?" I said.

"I don't know what to think, but it's got me a little worried."

I tried to think of why he'd switch vehicles. "Maybe he had a medical appointment he didn't want to talk about," I said.

Smoke shrugged. "Let's get some nourishment, and then we'll decide on our next course of action."

"I'd like to review the original missing persons file."

"Sure, and we need to talk to Toby's and Wendy's families before rumors start floating around. That's a given." He paused. "I'd like to run over to Ramsey to see how Doc Bridey Patrick's team is doing on that end. But since there are only so many hours in a day, that's not going to happen."

"True."

Smoke put his hand between my shoulder blades and gave me a mild push. "Let's go scarf down some pizza."

While we were eating, about a dozen sheriff's department personnel stopped by the break room to hear all about the recovery of the old Dodge Charger from Whitetail Lake and the shocker of finding two fairly well-preserved bodies in it. We relayed the details between bites and swallows of a late, lukewarm lunch. Finally, Smoke and I broke away and headed to the records room.

I unlocked the door, stepped in, and scanned the letters on the drawers. The files were stored in mammoth, horizontal file cabinets.

"I wouldn't be surprised if the files have been archived by now. I'll check to see if they've been moved to a storage box." Smoke sat down at the computer and typed in Toby Fryor's name. I resisted looking over his shoulder, so while he pulled up the information, I checked my phone for messages.

"Yeah, they were moved to the archived-files store room since the last time I looked. In box number seventy-three dash ten." He logged off the computer, stood up, and pulled a set of keys from his pocket.

I followed him next door and waited while he keyed in. The storeroom was about twenty feet by thirty feet and held cardboard boxes on shelves that started from a foot off the floor to a foot from the ceiling. We located the one we were looking for on the west wall, about six feet up. I grabbed the ladder that was equipped with wheels and rolled it to the shelf. Smoke jumped on the first rung, climbed up a few feet then hooked his hand on the opening in the front of a box and pulled it toward him. He held it in one hand and climbed back down. I took it from him and carried it to the table in the center of the room.

"This is heavy," I said as I heaved the box onto the table.

"The Fryor-Everton case alone must weigh a few pounds."

Smoke lifted the cover off the box, and after a quick glance found what he needed. He reached in with both hands and pulled out the twelve-inch expandable file that was filled to the limit with papers. He set it on the table. "Divide and conquer?" he said.

I moved the box on the floor, giving us room to spread out the papers as needed. "Holy man, where do we begin?"

Smoke made a little clicking sound with his tongue. "Same as always, one step at a time, one page at a time." He scooped up the top half of the pile, then lifted the first sheet and handed it to me. "Here's the confirmation. Proof positive it's Toby's car we recovered, all right."

He handed the paper to me. I looked at the vehicle description, including the license plate number that matched the one on the old Charger in the sheriff's evidence garage. I handed the paper back. "Yeah."

The next two pages were photos of Wendy and Toby. I held them up and studied them a moment. "Good-looking kids, both of them."

Smoke nodded. "It's hard to believe the bodies in the Charger once looked that fine."

I cringed, knowing I would carry the images of their remains with me forever. I set the photos aside to make copies of them. I liked keeping victims' photos close at hand. It kept me focused and reminded me for whom I was working and why.

I reached over, slid the bottom half of the pile down a ways then sat on a chair behind it. A chilled sensation ran through me, and it wasn't because it was a cold case. It happened more often than not when I worked to solve a mystery, and most notably, a crime. "Someone in here, who was interviewed at the time, must have known something."

"That would not surprise me. We just gotta figure out who it is." He paused a minute. "After we talk to the families about what we got so far, we'll need their help in the identification process."

"Besides DNA, I'm wondering about dental records. The dentists might still be around, but probably wouldn't have the records after all these years. Do you remember the legal requirement for a dentist to keep them? Is it six years, seven years?" I said.

"I remember from a past case that it's six years after a patient's last visit. But I know a few of the old docs never throw anything away."

"We'll get the families' DNA samples for comparison, for positive identification."

Smoke smiled. "We've come a long way, baby."

His phone rang some time later. "Dawes. . . . Huh. Well then, I'll be right out to see him."

"Who?" I asked when he'd disconnected.

"It was Cindy saying Darwin Fryor—Toby's dad—is at the reception window and wants to talk to me."

"Man, I guess word zips around pretty fast."

"With or without social media. I'll go meet him and take him back to my cubicle. We'll have a little privacy there, and it'll be less formal than an interview room. Wanna join us?"

I stood up. "Sure." I picked up Toby's and Wendy's photos and put them in my breast pocket.

Smoke headed to the front entrance. I headed down the hallway and waited in the corridor outside Smoke's cubicle. When Mr. Fryor walked toward me, I was caught slightly off-guard by his appearance. He was around Gramps Brandt's age, but looked even more feeble than Gramps. He was bent over at the waist, and his spine was twisted so one hip had a forward tilt and the other leaned more to the back. He swung his right leg in a painful-looking way when he walked.

After introductions, we settled in around Smoke's desk. I flinched while Mr. Fryor lowered himself onto a chair, seeing how much of a challenge it was for him. He let go of a drawn out "Ahhh," when he was finally seated. Smoke sat behind his desk, and I pulled up a chair by Mr. Fryor's side.

"I got a call from a friend of mine who said the sheriff's department pulled an old blue Dodge Charger out of Whitetail Lake this morning. Is it true? Could it be Toby's?" Darwin Fryor leaned in and rested his elbow on the desk. A dozen wrinkles fanned out from his milky, brown eyes.

Smoke gave the top of his desk a single tap with his pointer finger, seemingly as a subconscious confirmation. "I wish I could say it wasn't, but we verified a little while ago that it's the same license plate as Toby's." He paused. "There were two bodies inside, a male and a female. I can't tell you how sorry I am."

"Bodies?" Fryor lifted one hand and dropped his forehead into it. After a moment, he let his hand fall and raised his head. There were tears on his lower lids when he pulled a handkerchief out of his pocket and wiped his nose. "Those kids drowned in a lake not two miles from home, and all this time we thought they'd up and run off?"

"It's about impossible to comprehend," Smoke said.

Fryor seemed to be studying the pile of papers on Smoke's desk then he finally looked up and shook his head. "That Wendy sure had a way of turning a boy's head when she wanted to." His eyes landed on Smoke. "Well, I guess I don't have to tell you that, Elton. She caused a problem for you too, and a pretty big one, as I recall."

Smoke shifted in his chair, clearly uncomfortable the attention had switched to him and a past indiscretion. "That's true enough." He cleared his throat. "Mister Fryor, my sincere apologies you tracked us down before we paid you a visit to let you know we'd recovered Toby's car."

He nodded. "You know, Toby disappearing like that caused a rift between the missus and me that we couldn't mend. I tried, but she didn't seem to want to. Less than a year later, she moved out and left me with the younger two boys. She was living over in Emerald Lake until last month—" He quit talking and his eyes teared up again.

"Where'd she go?" Smoke said.

"Passed on. Here she's barely gone, and they find Toby after all these years."

"I hadn't heard," Smoke said.

"If she'd a held on a little longer, at least she would have known what happened to her son. Back in those days, she'd go off by herself every now and again, for a day or a weekend, for what she called some meditating time. It really stung that she shut me out of her life, wouldn't let me help her. I was hurting too.

"But Toby was her baby. They had about as tight a bond as you can imagine. You try not to favor one kid over the next, but she couldn't seem to help herself. It was pretty obvious to the other two boys, so I did what I could to be fair and loved each one as much as the next."

What my mother had told us is that she loved my brother John Carl and me the same, but liked us for different reasons. That made sense to me.

"We used up a lot of our savings trying to find Toby. But one day Adela—that's my wife—she said we'd spent enough on the two private detectives we'd hired and needed to save some in case we ever had to help our other two boys down the line."

"How long did you work with the PIs?" Smoke said.

"Six weeks. I knew we'd used up a lot of our savings, but I was surprised she'd made that call, is all. She'd been so obsessed about finding out where they'd gone. I figured Toby and Wendy would tire of each other one day, and they'd come back. Anyways, I agreed, and we called off the search. I know the folks here at the sheriff's department did what they could to find them. Now come to find out why it wasn't meant to be."

"People disappear way more often than you could ever imagine," Smoke said.

I thought back to the case we'd had the previous November and the staggering statistics I'd read about missing people and unidentified remains. If I had a loved one that disappeared, I would never give up hope until I was positively convinced there was none.

"Mister Fryor, to help us in the investigation, we'd like to collect a DNA sample from you to help the medical examiner make a positive identification," Smoke said.

Darwin Fryor swiped at a new tear. "You never really get over a thing like this. This is probably going to sound strange, especially now, but I still think of Toby being alive out there somewhere."

Self-protection was a natural mechanism when a tragedy occurred, I'd learned during my years with the department. It was difficult for most, and impossible for some, to accept the worst.

My personal cell phone rang, and when I glanced at the dial, I decided it was important to answer. "Excuse me." I slipped out and found a semi-private corner. "Hi, Mom."

"Corinne, I'm worried sick. After you called me that second time looking for Denny, I've tried his phone a dozen times, and he hasn't called me back. It's not like him to not return a call after so many hours."

I searched for encouraging words to reassure her. "We found out he switched vehicles at his house and took his Buick. I know it seems odd, but I also know there must be a good reason. The patrol deputies are keeping an eye out for him, and we'll find him."

"You sound so certain."

"I am." I counted on the fact that the sheriff was a resourceful man with years of experience in any number of dangerous and unusual situations. "Mother, sorry, but I have to cut this short. I'm in the middle of something right now. Hang in there and I'll call the minute we get word about Denny."

"All right. Thank you, dear."

I hung up and it took me a minute to steer my mind back to the investigation at hand. When I returned to the cubicle, Smoke was in the middle of collecting DNA from Darwin Fryor. He swabbed the inside of his mouth, dropped the sample in a sterile bottle, and sealed it.

"We'll keep you in the loop, Mister Fryor. We haven't talked to Wendy's folks yet, and we'll be heading over to their house after a bit," Smoke said

Mr. Fryor shook his head. "My, my, my. You'd a thought we might have kept in touch better than we have, living in the same town, losing our kids at the same time. But whenever we'd run into each other, it seemed to make the bad memories even worse."

Smoke nodded. "I can understand that. We'll work to get answers for you, do all we can to piece together how this happened."

"I can't figure out how the car could have ended up in Whitetail Lake." Fryor rubbed his forehead then his cheek.

"It's a real puzzle to be sure," Smoke said.

5

Smoke escorted Darwin Fryor out, and I stopped by the squad room, scanned and printed the old photos of Toby and Wendy, then returned to the archived files storeroom. I was replacing the original photos in the file when Smoke joined me.

"You come across something troubling in there?" he said.

My expression had given me away. "What? No, I'm thinking about the sheriff. Mother was the one who called. She is a nervous wreck, of course, because that's who she is. And in this instance, it seems like she's got a good reason."

"I'm with you on that one."

"I hate to say this, but what if someone lured Denny out to some remote location, took control of him somehow, and is planning to hold him for ransom. Or something equally crazy," I said.

Smoke's eyebrows shot up and his lips formed an O. "Whoa, little lady. You do have a vivid imagination at times. I can't picture the sheriff falling for anything like that. On the other hand, the whole thing is definitely worrisome. We got a bunch of deputies scouring the county for him. Captain

Randolph is checking with every county employee to see if anyone saw him leave this morning. We're bound to learn something before long."

I nodded, and as much as I wanted to believe that, I wasn't convinced. I knew Smoke wasn't either. "One thing I'm sure of, we can trust our department to be thorough," I said.

"That's a truism. In the meantime, we've got our work cut out for us on this case." He sat down at the table and moved a pile of documents closer to himself. "So is there a golden needle in this haystack that will give us a clue, or not?"

"Give me the skinny, the events of that night."

"The skinny, huh? Well, we won the football game against Little Mountain, a very sweet victory I might add. Then, I think just about everybody went to the dance in the gym. A bunch of us noticed that Toby and Wendy weren't there, and that was strange, especially since Wendy was crowned as one of the princesses at the Coronation. We figured they were doing a little private celebrating and would show up at one of the after-dance parties. But they never did."

"Was one of the after-dance parties at the Williams' farm?"

"No, not that I heard of."

After reading and taking notes for a while, I said, "It sounds like Toby was a bit of a risk-taker, which led some of his classmates at the time to support the theory that they had run off on some new adventure, new life."

"He was a risk-taker, and Wendy was too, I'd say. Not unlike a lot of teenagers I've known. Most of us feel immortal when we're sixteen, seventeen, even eighteen."

"I have to say I felt that way myself."

Smoke nodded. "Ditto."

"Even though most everyone thought they must have run off together, there were a number of Toby's friends who were surprised he'd do that. It looked like he had a promising future, either as a professional athlete or a coach."

"Yeah, when you get to my statement, you'll see I was in that camp. Toby was offered a full scholarship at three or so colleges. But he was also smitten—more like obsessed—with Wendy Everton. A lot of other guys were, too. Fortunately, I did not go too far down that road with her."

"From what I read in the statements, a few wondered if Wendy was pregnant," I said.

"That was the talk at the time. If she was, no one knew it for sure."

"After what Mister Fryor said, I'm trying not to dislike her."

Smoke reached over and squeezed my forearm. "Corinne, whatever Wendy was, or was not, is no longer an issue."

And she wasn't there to defend herself. "I know, and mostly I feel awful that her family—and Toby's family—have gone through agony for over thirty years."

"It is awful. But we can thank Sergeant Warner for picking Whitetail, of all lakes, to test his new sonar equipment. Now they'll be able to bury Toby and Wendy, hopefully work through it all, and come to accept it."

We pored through the documents for a while longer.

"Let's go pay Wendy's parents a visit before it gets any later. And then I'd like to examine the area where the car went in. Try to figure out what in the hell happened," Smoke said.

"What happened is right."

We gathered the papers, packed up the file, and put it back in its place in the drawer. It was 6:03 in the evening, and my mother phoned again from work. "Corinne, you haven't called and I thought maybe you got busy and forgot."

"I've been busy, but I haven't forgotten."

"So there is still no word on Denny?"

"Not yet, unfortunately."

"Where are you, anyway?"

I knew she was wondering why I hadn't stopped by to see her. "I got caught up in a case. A car was pulled out of Whitetail Lake this morning."

"One of my customers told me about it a little while ago. She happened by when they were loading it on a tow truck. I hadn't heard of any cars going in the lake, and the road is nice and straight along there. How did it happen?" she said.

Maybe if my mother had something else to think about, she'd worry less about Sheriff Dennis Twardy. "Brace yourself for this one. That car has been down there a long time—since you were in high school, in fact. It was Toby Fryor's Dodge Charger."

There was a clunking sound in my ear, and I realized Mother had dropped the phone on her counter. It took a few seconds before she was back. "What did you say?"

Smoke reached his hand out for my phone, so I passed it over. "Kristen, it's Elton. . . . No, it doesn't seem real. . . . No, they did not push the car in the lake before they ran off. . . . Because there were human remains in the car." Smoke put my phone against his chest. "I think she dropped the phone."

I took it back from him and waited until Mother said, "What?"

"I'm going to pick you up and give you a ride to Gramps' house, okay? . . . I'll be there in five minutes." And then I hung up.

"Your poor mom. We might as well take my car then I'll drop you off at yours when we get done for the day. Let's go rescue Kristen."

I nodded.

Mother was pacing outside her shop, and for the umpteenth time in my adult life, I was struck with wonder at how she managed to stay so young-looking despite her propensity to agonize over the darnedest things. She was trim with wavy blonde hair that touched her shoulders. Most people guessed she was at least ten years younger than her actual age of fifty. Smoke told me it was due to good genes. I agreed that played a part, and Mother had an otherwise healthy lifestyle besides.

When Smoke pulled up to the curb, I got out and Mother threw her arms around me and held on for dear life. I indulged her until my arms started to numb. "Hey, Mom, it's going to be okay. Like everything else, we'll get through it."

I felt her tears on my cheeks and fought the urge to cry with her. Smoke got out of the car and waited the minute it took me to nestle Mother safely in the front seat before I hopped in the back. Smoke closed my door because there wasn't a handle on the inside. The better to keep the arrestees secure.

Smoke was barely in the driver's seat before Mother asked his opinion on where in the world Denny might be. "Maybe I should go wait at his house for him."

"I think it'd be better to wait with Gramps," I said.

"I suppose." She was quiet for a few seconds then said, "How could Toby and Wendy have driven into Whitetail Lake?"

"Kristen, I can't tell you how many times I've wished for a crystal ball to help shed light on some of the tougher cases we've had over the years. Unfortunately, we have to be more patient than we think we're capable of most of the time. Whether it be Denny's unexplained absence, or what happened to Toby and Wendy back when, we'll do all we can to get answers as fast as possible."

Mother nodded and a small gulp of air, followed by a hiccup, slipped out. After a few minutes, Smoke pulled into my maternal grandfather's driveway and parked. He got out and opened both the front and back passenger side doors. I was out before Mother. She needed a moment to compose herself before she faced her father.

"Mom, will you be okay with Gramps for a couple of hours?"

Her face squeezed together. "You think you'll be gone that long?"

"Maybe," I said.

"The sun will be setting in," Smoke looked at his watch, "about ninety minutes. We won't be doing much outside after that."

I gave my mother a gentle pat on the back, feeling for a second like I was the parent. "We've got to get moving, so tell Gramps I'll see him later."

Mom looked like more tears were about to spill. She turned and headed into the house as Smoke and I pulled out of the driveway.

"Kristen really is a basket case. We need Denny to turn up sooner rather than later," Smoke said.

"I thought telling her about your classmates might distract her, but I think it just piled on more stress," I said.

"After all that time being single and finally finding love, I'm hoping against hope nothing bad has happened to her fiancé. She went through enough being widowed with two babies."

I prayed for Denny's safe return while Smoke drove us to Wendy Everton's parents' house. They lived in a two-story home in a nice neighborhood on the west side of town. It was the same place Smoke had picked up Wendy for the few dates they'd had. After she'd aided him in accidentally burning down his ice fishing house, he'd decided she was too hot to handle and their relationship had cooled.

"I had no way of knowing I'd ever have to give the Evertons this kind of news about Wendy," Smoke said. He turned off the ignition but made no attempt to move.

"I can take the lead on this one," I said.

He turned his head toward me. "I think that's a good idea. I'm feeling kind of strange. It brings me back to all those years ago when I was a teenager, and the future was one big unpainted canvas."

"That's almost philosophic, Smoke."

"Yeah, well, my philosophy on that changed quite a long time ago." We got out, and then Smoke followed me slowly up the sidewalk to the front door. I gave him a reassuring smile as I rang the doorbell.

A minute later, a well-kept woman around seventy years old opened the door and looked from me to Smoke then back to me. She kept her eyes on my face for what felt like a very long time. "You're Kristen and Carl Aleckson's daughter. It was very sad, about your father I mean, taken so young like that."

It seemed like a strange way to greet me, but I let it go. My father had been gone over thirty years, and people still referenced it from time to time. It was part of my identity. "Yes, thank you. My name's Corinne and I'm a sergeant with the sheriff's department."

She glanced down at my badge and gun, nodded, studied me some more, and then focused on Smoke. "And of course I know you, Elton. Aside from a little salt in your hair, you don't look much different from your high school days. This seems like an unusual visit."

"Missus Everton, there's something we need to talk to you about, if we can come in," I said.

Her lips pursed and her frown lines deepened. "Yes, come in. But I have to tell you you've got me a little worried."

"We'll talk inside," I said.

Mrs. Everton led us to the living room where her husband was sitting in a recliner with the television turned up to a volume my grandparents would appreciate but made my eardrums throb. When he saw us, Mr. Everton moved the lever in his chair and was brought upright. He retrieved the remote from the small table beside him, hit the off button, and the room fell silent.

"Clifford, this is Corinne Aleckson, Kristen and Carl's daughter. You know . . . we've seen her picture in the newspaper. And you remember Elton Dawes, of course."

Mr. Everton dug his hands into the arms of his chair and pushed himself up. It was a brief struggle for him to get stable on his feet, but he managed. He shook hands with Smoke. "It's been some time since you've been here, Elton." He turned to me and stared, much like his wife had done a moment before. "You look some like your dad, and some like your mom, like they did back all those years ago."

I smiled. "Thanks. Is it all right to sit in here, or would you rather go to the kitchen?"

Mrs. Everton's eyebrows lifted. "Oh, I haven't even cleaned up the supper dishes yet, so why don't we stay here?"

"What's this about?" Mr. Everton said as he settled back in his chair.

Smoke and I sat on the gold-and-red-striped couch, and Mrs. Everton took the coordinating, patterned chair next to it.

"Have you folks heard about the vehicle that was recovered from Whitetail Lake this morning?" I said.

"Why no, we haven't. Whitetail, you say?" Mr. Everton said.

"That's right. This is going to be difficult news to hear, but it turns out it was the Dodge Charger that belonged to Toby Fryor." I said the words slowly hoping they'd understand them.

"Say again?" Mr. Everton said.

I repeated myself.

Mrs. Everton grabbed her ample bosom. "How can that be?"

"Toby Fryor's Charger? How can you be sure?" Mr. Everton's face took on a reddish tinge as he held onto the arms of his chair.

"We verified the nineteen sixty-six license plate."

"So they left his car behind and hid it in the lake so no one would find it?" Mr. Everton said.

I shook my head. "Sadly, no, that's not what happened. There are human remains in the vehicle that we believe belong to your daughter and to Toby Fryor."

Mr. Everton dropped his hands in his lap then folded them. His chin bent down, nearly resting on his chest. Mrs. Everton appeared too stunned to do more than tighten the grip on her own chest.

"Are you sure?" Mr. Everton raised his eyes and his words came out sounding like a plea.

I nodded. "Reasonably sure. The two of them are with the medical examiner now."

"We should go where Wendy is," Mrs. Everton said.

"You certainly have that right. But if it was me, I'd want to remember Wendy as the beautiful girl she was in life." I gave them a moment then said, "The medical examiner will need DNA samples from you to compare with your daughter's, if you'd be so kind to provide them."

Mr. Everton nodded.

Mrs. Everton searched her husband's eyes with her own then moved them to Smoke and me. "I always believed in my heart that something bad had happened to Wendy."

"What do you mean?" I said.

"I knew she wouldn't run off and never come back, if she had anything to say about it. I was afraid Toby had done some kind of mind-control over her. I've seen that on television where a person will fill another person's mind with all kinds of lies about their family and friends."

Striving for complete control of a victim was a typical behavior pattern of an abusive person. Is that what the Evertons believed about Toby Fryor?

"We were worried she might be dead. And in the early days we called police departments all around the country whenever we heard a young woman's body had been found," Mr. Everton said.

"We sent her picture everywhere," Mrs. Everton added.

"What about Toby's dad? Have you talked to him yet?" Mr. Everton said.

"We have. If anyone can appreciate what you're going through, it's Mister Fryor," I said.

Mr. Everton nodded then rocked himself of out his chair and went over to his wife. He eased himself onto the arm of her chair, put one arm behind her shoulders, and placed the other hand on her arm. She reached up with both hands and grasped his. Their eyes filled with tears.

"Well, sweetie, here they were just a few miles away all this time," Mr. Everton said.

Mrs. Everton looked up at her husband. "Now that we've got her back, we can give her a Christian burial."

Before we left, we collected and secured the DNA samples. Then Smoke gave each of them a hug, and we quietly made our way out the door.

"Thanks," Smoke said when we were back in his car. "This whole thing is hitting me harder, now that we've been talking to Toby and Wendy's folks. I don't think I could have handled telling Wendy's parents as well as you did. Talking to Darwin Fryor seemed easier somehow."

"You're welcome. And I know your professionalism would have guided you through the visit as it has time and time again. And giving them each a hug was a nice touch, Smoke. It shows you care."

"Yeah, there are a lot of people who think a case is a case for us. They don't realize how often we are the deliverers of bad news."

All too often. "When did Doctor Patrick think they'd do the autopsies?"

"She didn't know for sure, but indicated it might be tomorrow. She said with the bodies being fairly intact, they should get good information." He glanced at his watch. "We have about forty minutes 'til sunset. Let's pay Harry Gimler a visit, that guy that showed up at the scene today. We'll get his permission to hike down his hill to the lake."

"Which house is his?"

"Not sure. It's one of the three on the dead end. In the interest of time, let's have Communications look him up."

It took Officer Randy about fifteen seconds to discover Harry Gimler's address was 1503 Burlington Avenue. Smoke drove up and parked on the circular drive in front of his home. It was in the middle, an upscale home flanked on either side by equally expensive ones. All three properties, including the surrounding grounds, were well-kept from what we could see.

"Now these guys know how to keep up with the Joneses," Smoke said.

We got out and made our way up the brick walkway to the house. There was a security-camera eye and intercom two feet above the doorbell. I rang the bell, prepared to identify myself. Instead, Harry Gimler opened the door, looking a little worse for the wear, or three sheets to the wind, as Smoke would say. The smell of an alcoholic beverage emanated from his person, and his lazy eyelids confirmed he'd been drinking.

"Come in, deputies. I have to confess I started the cocktail hour a little early. All things considered, with finding those people, this has been a difficult day."

"So you heard there were two victims in the vehicle," Smoke said.

Gimler nodded. "A friend of mine told me." Word leaked out, no matter what.

"Truth be told, no one wants a discovery like that on, or near, their property," Smoke said.

"No." Gimler took a step back. "Come in."

"Actually, we're on a bit of a race against time here. We're hoping to get permission to take a walk down to the lake from here," Smoke said.

"Oh. Well, that would be fine. I'll go with you." He shifted to steady himself.

Smoke shook his head. "That's not necessary. We're just going to have a quick look-see, try to do some calculations, and then we'll get out of your hair."

Harry was obviously disappointed.

"Mister Gimler, did you build your house?" I said.

"Well, I had it built, yes."

"How long ago was that?"

"Almost twenty years ago."

"There used to be an old farmhouse here. Did you have it torn down, or was it gone before you bought the land?" I said.

Gimler cleared his throat. "I had it removed. The farmstead belonged to my grandfather. He was in the nursing home a long time before he died. I always loved it here and was happy when he finally decided to sell. The house was in tough shape and wasn't worth restoring. Same with the barn. It was starting to collapse and getting dangerous. But I used some of the wood from it as paneling in my den. It's rustic and reminds me of the fun I had as a kid when we visited here."

"You're not from around here?" Smoke asked.

"No, I grew up in Swift County outside of Benson, about a hundred miles. When I was old enough, I'd help Grandpa on the farm here in the summers."

"All right, well, we might chat about that another time, but tonight we need to get a move on. Thanks for the info, Mister—"

"Harry. Mister makes me sound old, and we must be about the same age, Detective."

Smoke nodded. "Thanks, we'll be in touch." He pulled a card from his breast pocket and handed it to Gimler. "Call if you have any questions or concerns."

Harry's lips turned downward. The alcohol was taking more of a hold on him, evidenced when he grabbed onto the door jamb for support.

"Will you be all right?" I asked.

He blinked hard. "Yeah. I might just go to bed early." He closed the door, and I followed Smoke around the house to the back yard.

6

Harry had a massive multi-level deck system that was surrounded by patio stones on the lawn level. "Wow," I said quietly.

"You talking about the view?"

"That too. Wow. Can you imagine what it would be like drinking your morning coffee on that deck overlooking the lake?"

"It is breathtaking. Especially if you're afraid of heights."

I smiled and suppressed a chuckle.

"I didn't want to get into the party days at the farm here with Gimler. I was only here one time and never really thought about who even owned the farm. But thinking about it now, I can't imagine the old man letting a bunch of underage-drinking partygoers use his property," Smoke said.

"That is a discussion we need to have with Gimler on another day. Much earlier in the day, before the cocktail hour."

"You got that right." Smoke walked around, studying the ground. "Okay, if the farmhouse was on about the same spot as Harry's house is currently sitting, I'd say the barn was close to where the neighbor's house is now." He waved his hand at the house to the south of Harry's. "Let's hike down to the lake."

The soles of my boots had a little tread on them, but not enough for a good grip going down such a steep hill, still damp from the recently melted snow. I slid a short ways. "Behind you," I called in time for Smoke to turn around and act as a protective shield as I plowed into his chest.

"We should have stopped by your house for your hiking boots," he said as his arms closed around me and held on firmly.

As much as I liked being right where I was, anyone, including Harry Gimler may be watching and wondering what was going on. "Thanks. Maybe I should wait here."

"Nah, come on. Hold my hand."

"Aren't you worried what the *Joneses* will think?"

"No. I'm doing what I can to keep my partner safe, and they can think what they want."

Smoke grabbed my hand and we cautiously made our way halfway to the lake. We stopped where the mowed lawn ended. "Are you steady enough so you won't go sliding into the lake on me?"

"I think so." I dug my feet into the ground for the best possible hold.

Smoke let go of my hand and turned to look back at the house. "It's steep all right. Say Toby and Wendy got into his car, and Toby had had a few beers and got mixed up, turned the car the wrong way then there was no stopping it on this grade of decline. On the other hand, if he had applied the brakes, it might have taken some effort, but with a crank of the wheel, it seems he could have avoided plunging into the lake."

"Maybe he passed out and the car rolled down by itself," I offered.

"Poor Wendy." Smoke shook his head. "In any case, there would have been the tire tracks they created."

"They might not have noticed them, depending on where the house sat exactly, what their view was, and what kind of underbrush there was. If the ground was dry, the car wouldn't leave any real depressions," I said.

"That's true enough."

"But why didn't anyone hear anything?"

"When you're drinking, hearing is the first sense to go. A bunch of drunk kids can't even hear what anyone else is saying." Smoke shook his head. "Thirty-three years ago no one knew where Toby and Wendy had disappeared to. Hard to believe this is where they've been all these years. Old Whitetail was finally forced to give up her secret."

"I know this is hard for you, Smoke."

He held his hand out for me. "Another time, we might enjoy the colors of the sunset. But tonight it's reminding us nightfall is upon us."

I lowered my voice as I took his hand for the uphill climb. "Do you think we should let Harry know we're leaving?"

"You mean should we check on him?"

"Maybe." I raised my eyebrows.

Smoke spoke at a near-whisper. "Nah, let's leave him be for tonight. It sounds like he was going to retire the bottle for the night. And I want to get that DNA we collected checked into evidence, so they can get it to the lab first thing in the morning."

After Smoke dropped me off at my car, I climbed in and headed to Gramps' house. I gathered every ounce of optimism I could pull from within and put on a smile as I walked into his house. Gramps was in his usual chair watching a news show, and I heard Mother in the kitchen. I gave him a kiss on the cheek then checked on Mom who had thrown herself into cleaning out Gramps' refrigerator. She was setting the milk back on a shelf when I said, "I'm back."

She jumped half a foot and turned around. "Corinne! You know better than to sneak up on me."

"Sorry. I guess the TV was too loud for you to hear me."

Mother threw the dish cloth she was holding onto the counter. "It's so loud I can't even hear myself think." She shrugged. "Maybe that's not such a bad thing when I'm this worried, imagining the worst."

I put my arms around her for a comforting hug. "Don't make yourself sick over this."

"I called John Carl earlier, and he's worried about Denny too."

"Of course he is." I took a small step back. "What do you think, would you like to go home, or would you rather stay here?"

"Well, I guess I'll go home. In case Denny calls there."

"I'll run you home and we'll pick up your car tomorrow."

A puzzled look crossed her face. "That's right. I forgot I left it at the shop."

Mother put her arm around my waist and steered me into the living room, so we could say goodnight to Gramps.

When my mother was safely in her house, I drove home and rescued my energetic dog from her kennel. After she licked my hand and we'd run around the yard for a few minutes, I gave her the command to sit. Then I said, "Do you want to go for a ride, girl?"

She jumped up and moved her head back and forth telling me she did. "Okay, let's go." I opened the door to my GTO, and she hopped in the back seat like she'd been taught. "Good girl. You probably think we're going to Gramps' house, but I need to go over to Whitetail Lake for a while."

I drove the short distance, did a U-turn, and pulled to a stop on the north side of Whitetail Lake. I pulled the pictures of Toby and Wendy from my pocket and set them on the dashboard. In the cloak of night, with illumination from a half moon and twinkling stars, the houses on the far hill were visible but not well-defined. The middle house was dark, indicating that Harry Gimler had likely gone to bed after all.

I was lost in thought, studying the lake, when a car pulled up behind me and parked. I turned in my seat instead of relying on my rearview mirror. "Queenie, guess who's coming to visit us? Your friend, Detective Dawes."

Queenie yelped, and when Smoke opened the passenger door she barked some more. "Can I come in?" he said.

"I suppose."

"I get the feeling that Queenie is more excited to see me than you are." He reached in the back and patted her head.

"No offense, but I think that is probably true, given the fact that we were together all day, and my doggie hasn't seen you for a while."

"I'll give you that. So why are you here? Trying to pull information out of a lake that can't talk?" Smoke said.

"Something like that. I've driven by this lake probably thousands of times. We both have. It's not much of a swimming lake, since there's no beach. But there are fishers out in boats now and then, and no one knew what was sitting on the bottom."

"It's gotta be disconcerting finding out, especially when you live just up the hill."

"Yeah, I keep looking up there, where the car came down. It must have been moving at a pretty fast clip and gone airborne, or it would have gotten caught up in the brush at the edge of the lake," I said.

"Speed is a decided factor. Actually, those cattails may have helped slow it down so it didn't end up further out in the lake. And we come back to the big questions we talked about earlier. Why they went down the hill in the first place and why no one heard them or noticed the tracks they may have left."

"I'll have to ask Mother if she and my dad ever partied there."

Smoke rubbed his hand over his five o'clock shadow. "Maybe one time, if that. Your mom, dad, and I all had parents who kept track of us, and they'd surely have known if we'd been to a beer party."

I nodded. "So what made you stop here tonight?"

"I'd just finished up at the office and spotted you when I drove by. As nosy as I am, I thought I'd see what you were up to. Although I'd pretty much figured it out."

"I'm curious about the ME's report. I wonder if they can tell if Toby and Wendy died in the crash or drowned afterwards."

"You'd think. They weren't buckled in and I think there'd be evidence of blunt-force trauma. I'm hoping they got knocked out so they didn't know they were drowning."

I shivered at the thought. "You reminded me of why I don't like driving on the ice in the winter, even when it should be perfectly safe. There is always that minute chance . . ." I paused and smiled, "Especially if you burn your fish house down. That must melt the ice beneath it."

Smoke leaned in close to me, and I smelled cinnamon, probably from an herbal tea on his breath. "I wonder how many times that whole fiasco with Wendy is going to come up during this investigation?"

I resisted the temptation to close the small gap between our faces and kiss him. It was an exercise in self-control. I held onto the hope that someday he would realize that whatever barriers he thought prevented us from having an intimate relationship were not insurmountable. My grandma had told me that Smoke and I were intimate all right, just without the fun part. A little sad, and true.

I rubbed my nose across his in place of a kiss. "Old secrets have a way of bubbling to the surface when we least expect them to, my friend. I promise not to bring the subject up with anyone. And if the guys catch wind of it and try to pry it out of me, I'll send them your way."

He reached over and squeezed my hand. "Thanks. Yeah, every stupid thing we do in life seems to come back to haunt us at some point. But I sure never expected that embarrassing, not to mention costly, incident with Wendy to be brought to light like this."

Smoke gave my hand a final squeeze then turned and scratched Queenie's head. "You're reminding me I need to get home and take care of my own mutt. Rex is used to my unpredictable schedule, but I know he doesn't always like it." He opened the door. "Goodnight, you two."

"Goodnight."

Smoke got out and drove off a minute later. I needed a little more time at the lake, pondering the night's events from long ago. Whitetail Lake had been holding its secret for over thirty years—before I was born. The victims' families had a lot to cope with and work through now that they knew where Toby and Wendy had been all along. I drove home with a heavy heart, thinking about them, and the tragic ending.

After attending to Queenie's needs, I paced around my house to burn off some stress, wondering about the sheriff's whereabouts. My home phone rang and startled me out of my stewing.

It was my mother. "Corinne, I'll never be able to sleep tonight. Why would God send Denny into my life, only to take him away so soon?"

Oh, boy. "Mom, we have no real reason to panic yet. Do you want me to come over?"

"No, but thanks anyway."

"Have a nice tall glass of wine. Or warm milk."

"Maybe a glass of wine will help settle me down."

"If you need me, call and I'll be right over."

"You're such a capable woman, Corinne. It's nice knowing you're only a mile away."

"You too, Mom."

It wasn't long after we'd hung up that my best girlfriend Sara, a probation officer with Winnebago County, phoned. She was at a conference in northern Minnesota for the week.

"Corky, I'm gone for two days, and all hell breaks loose down there. Jon sent me a text, and then I read about it online." Jon was a fellow probation officer.

"It's been a crazy day, that's for darn sure."

We talked about the recovered Charger, Smoke and my mother's classmates, and the condition of the bodies. And then about Sheriff Twardy and how concerned we all were.

"Tell everyone to hang in there, and keep me posted," she said.

"Will do. Thanks, Sara."

"'Bye, Corky."

Chief Deputy Mike Kenner called a meeting for eight o'clock the next morning. Smoke phoned me at seven. "It's for all the command staff and supervisors," he explained.

"If it got Kenner out of his recovery bed, it must be about the sheriff," I said.

"Yeah, the media got wind of it and let's just say if—when—it gets posted on a social media site, it will go viral."

"I wonder if there's a big bubble somewhere I can put my mother in until Denny reappears."

"Corky, I know you do your best to protect your mother, and most of the time it's with good reason. But in this case she's gotta know what's going on so she doesn't get blindsided by a reporter calling her, or showing up at her door."

"You're right. I'll ask her to get one of her helpers to run the store today, and she can spend the day with Gramps."

"Or with you."

"*Me?*"

"Sure, why not? It might help her if we included her, like at the meeting." Smoke was a brave man.

"I guess I can see if she wants to. And you'll clear it with Kenner?"

"I will, and it shouldn't be a problem. Then Kristen can tag along when we head to the ME's office if she wants, maybe when we check how our team is doing with the Charger." A very brave man.

"You don't think it will bother anyone having my mother there, gasping for a breath every five minutes?"

Smoke chuckled. "You have a point. We'll start with the meeting and take it from there."

After we hung up, I phoned my mother who surprisingly did not ask a hundred questions and even agreed to ask a helper to run her shop. Her voice was shaky when she said, "Thank you for asking me to go to Chief Deputy Kenner's meeting with you. That means a lot."

"Sure. I'll pick you up at seven forty-five."

"I'll be ready."

I scrambled a bit, showering, dressing, and getting Queenie situated in her kennel. My mother was waiting on the front step of her old farmhouse when I pulled into her driveway. Every once in a while, in particular, I noticed how lovely she was. She could have been posing for a fashion shoot, wearing her mid-length, flowing navy skirt with a subtle ivory print, an ivory silk shirt, and a navy waist-length cardigan sweater.

She waved and attempted a small smile when I stopped. Then she jogged to the car, hopped in, and buckled up. "'Morning."

"'Morning. Did you get any sleep?" I asked as I turned my car around and headed toward town.

"A few hours. Corinne, I know I worry too much about you, and John Carl, and Gramps. And maybe some other things. But this is different."

"I agree, it is different. Denny has always been dependable and we're all feeling a little lost here."

When she didn't answer, I glanced over and saw her lip was quivering. It broke my heart to see her suffering. We didn't talk for the rest of the drive. After I parked in the sheriff's department lot, I turned to her. "You don't have to go to the meeting, you know."

She looked at me then patted her face with a tissue. "Yes, I do."

We walked into the office, and the staff did not hide their looks of curiosity when we passed by. The sheriff was missing and his fiancé was in the building. *Did we know more about the disappearance than we were letting on? Had the sheriff been abducted after all?* That's what seemed were the possible questions no one asked.

We reached the squad room that had been converted into a conference room for the meeting. A sign, "Private Meeting," was posted on the outside of the door. When we went in, Chief Deputy Kenner graciously captured one of my mother's hands in a warm embrace and put his other arm around her shoulder. "Thanks for coming, Kristen."

She nodded and tucked in her lips, like she was doing her best not to break down. Smoke came over, blinked his eyes at me, gave Mother a quick hug, and then steered her to a seat at the large table. He sat down next to her, and I mingled for a minute before finding a seat on the opposite side of the table.

Extra chairs had been brought in to accommodate the twenty-plus command staff, detectives, and supervisors. The temperature in the room was rising with the body heat of concerned deputies. Although I didn't often suffer from claustrophobia, I felt uneasy. Tense. Glancing around at the others, with all the body shifting going on, it was clear I was not the only one.

Kenner clapped his hands together for everyone's attention. "Okay. Let's get started. We're here about our sheriff, and I thought it'd be good to apprise you of where we're at in terms of the investigation."

My mother winced but remained dry-eyed and silent.

"First off though, I'd like to thank everyone who's been working on the Whitetail case that got dropped in our laps yesterday. Unbelievable. But what a good thing for the families to have closure after all these years. We'll keep working on that along with all of our other cases. Meanwhile, I think all of us can agree that our top priority is locating Sheriff Twardy."

That initiated a moment of quiet conversations.

Kenner continued, "So, what do we know so far? Somehow Twardy got to the parking garage without being seen. He drove his unmarked vehicle to his house and parked it in his garage. His personal vehicle is not in his garage, and the belief is he took it. Detective Conley couldn't be here this morning, or he'd give you his report himself. Anyway, I've had Conley check on both credit card transactions and also cell phone pings in the five-county region. Unfortunately, he's come up empty-handed so far, which we all know is extremely frustrating. On the other hand, we're hoping that no news is good news."

More rumblings among the troops.

Sergeant Warner was leaning against a back wall and took a step forward. "What can we do to help?"

"It's important for all of us to have the same story to give to the media, or to Joe Citizen, or what have you. Detective

Dawes and I put our heads together this morning and came up with a statement that is honest and hopefully not too alarming. Detective?" Kenner looked at Smoke.

He nodded and stood up. "We decided to follow the KISS method in this situation, so our message is simple: Sheriff Twardy left work of his own volition at around nine-twenty yesterday morning without sharing his plans with his staff. We haven't heard from him, but have no reason to suspect foul play at this time. And if anyone has contact with him, please have him call his office."

A few of the staff shook their heads and others nodded. It was a mixed bag of reactions. My mother sucked in an audible gasp. She couldn't help herself.

After a moment, Mother looked from Smoke to Kenner. "I've wondered about this, but I'm not sure if it's a good idea, or not," she said.

It seemed like her words drew everyone in the room closer to her.

"What's that, Kristen?" Smoke asked, and his voice was as gentle as a soft rain.

"Well, you know he has a brother."

A few deputies shrugged, like they may or may not have known.

"Oh, sure. Norman's his name. He's in a nursing home in Arizona, if I remember right," Smoke said. "I'm embarrassed that I kind of forgot about him."

Kenner chimed in, "The sheriff hasn't talked about him for quite some time. I'm not sure where he's at, medically speaking."

Mother raised her hand for the floor. "And that's just it. Poor man has dementia pretty bad, from what Denny says.

He's wanted to go visit him, but it's hard on him since Norman hasn't known him for so long."

"We'll contact the home; see if the sheriff has called there the last day or so," Kenner said.

There was silence for a bit then Mother said, "What else can we do to find him?"

Kenner focused his attention on her. "Kristen, do you have a key, or the code, to Denny's house?"

She nodded. "Yes."

"We haven't looked inside yet because we don't believe he's there. We checked the doors and windows, and there's an alarm system, as you know. Since you have permission to enter his home, I'd like you to go there with your daughter and Detective Dawes, take a look around, see if he left any indication of where he might be. Will you do that?" Kenner said.

"Of course. In fact, I need to." Mother found me across the table and I gave her a thumbs' up.

Kenner addressed the group. "We have every agency in the state keeping a watch out for him. Since it's been almost twenty-four hours with no word, we're going to issue a statement to the media—press, radio, and television—with the same message Dawes told you. If anyone tries to pump you for more information, refer them to me. We don't need all kinds of rumors flying around the county, or the state. Any questions?"

No one spoke up, and I figured everyone was as stunned as I was, under the circumstances.

Chief Deputy cleared his throat. "Back to the other matter; I want to thank Sergeant Warner for locating and recovering—with the divers' help—that old Charger from its decades-long burial at the bottom of Whitetail Lake. The story is gaining national recognition, as you all know. One of our residents has already posted the whole thing on YouTube. We're waiting to hear from Doctor Bridey Patrick's office on their findings and hope to get some word today. Suffice it to say, we have a lot going on. We need to keep doing our jobs to the best of our abilities, keep the faith, and I'm confident we'll hear from our sheriff before long. If no one has anything to add, this meeting is over."

I was thinking, "We just found two people who disappeared over thirty years ago, so how can you be so certain Denny will turn up anytime soon?" But out of respect, I held my tongue.

Kenner waited a few seconds, and when no one spoke up, he stood, patted a few guys on the back, smiled at my mother, then left.

7

Smoke hustled Mother and me out of the building to his car.

"I'll take the back seat," I said before my mother could argue that it was her turn.

We were on the road in no time. "I wish Denny had taken his squad car, so it'd be easier for people to spot," she said.

"You could make that argument, depending on where he is, and if people are paying attention," I said.

"His Buick does not exactly stand out in a crowd, to be sure. But the expanded media coverage will be a good thing. That being said, we all need to be prepared for the extra attention we're going to get," Smoke said.

Mother turned her head to stare out the side window. Sheriff Twardy lived five miles south of Oak Lea. The back of his property bordered the Swan River. He had a large rambler with spacious rooms. In the summer, he kept his yard looking like a park. It was early in the season, and no one, including the sheriff, had begun mowing their lawns yet. Smoke followed the long concrete driveway to the front of the garage and parked. Mother sat an extra second before she moved.

Smoke let me out of the back seat then walked to the passenger side of the car. "Kristen, if you'd rather Corky and I go in alone, we should be fine. As long as you give us permission, and let us in, that is."

Mother shook her head. "No, I need to go in. Maybe it will give me some sense of where Denny is." She pulled a ring of keys from her purse and located the one she needed. "We'll go in the front door, instead of the garage." She keyed in, and Smoke and I followed behind.

I had been in the sheriff's house a few times and admired how tidy it always was. He had someone clean it twice a month and managed to keep the clutter to a minimum, something I personally found a constant challenge. When Mom sucked in another one of her under-stress gasps, Smoke glanced at me and raised his eyebrows. I lifted my shoulder an inch and gave a slight nod, indicating she'd be fine with us there as back-up. I was more accustomed to her emotional reactions and idiosyncrasies than he was.

Mom punched in the security code. If someone had entered uninvited, the alarm would have summoned deputies there, and that hadn't happened. The foyer led into the living room that was in the center of the house, and featured a fireplace on the opposite wall. There were tall windows on either side of it. A peaked ceiling rose twelve feet high in the middle of the room. One of the things that had delayed my mother's marriage to Denny was deciding where they would live: Denny's house, Mother's house, or another one they built or bought together.

"We'll do a walk-through and see if anything seems out of place, or if there are any hints as to where he went," Smoke said.

"Mom, officially speaking, Smoke and I can't open drawers without a search warrant. But if you happen to see something suspicious, like if you're looking for something that belongs to you, then we can deal with it," I added.

My mother raised her eyebrows and said, "Oh. I didn't realize how that worked."

"We're limited to what's in plain view," Smoke said.

We followed her through the rooms of the house. She didn't think it was respectful to rifle through cupboards and closets, and that was fine with us. That is, until we went into the sheriff's bedroom. The closet door was open and so was the safe that sat on a shelf.

"What in the hell," Smoke said as we all stared at the contents inside, not wanting to touch anything.

"What all does he keep in there, Mom? Do you know?"

She drew in a quick breath. "Some documents, like his passport. And a lot of money." Mother reached in, withdrew some papers, and held up Twardy's passport. "This is here, but his money's all gone. What could that mean?"

He wasn't planning to flee the country if he'd left his passport behind. "Any idea how much cash he normally keeps in there?" I said.

"No, not exactly. But it's thousands, tens of thousands, I'm pretty sure."

"Tens of thousands?" Smoke echoed.

"Really?" I said.

Mother nodded. "He likes to deal in cash as much as possible. I was in here when he got some money out to buy a flat screen TV. He grabbed a stack of one hundred dollar bills and counted out ten of them. And it didn't take the stack down by much. I didn't question what he had in here, and I didn't even want to know the code."

"Hmmph." Smoke moved his face in close to the safe. "You're right, no money in there now." He turned and scanned the room. "And there are no signs of a struggle."

Tears formed in my mother's eyes. "Do you think someone's holding Denny somewhere, and they made him give them his codes to the door and safe?"

Smoke looked at her. "I don't know, Kristen. Nothing seems logical here. It looks like Denny took the money and ran, which certainly does not fit his usual behavior. He is one of the most predicable men I know. And I mean that in a good way."

"Smoke, do you think he left the door of the safe open to give us some sort of clue?" I said.

He lifted a shoulder. "Something to consider, all right. Why don't you two keep looking around? Corky, check all the doors, windows, see if we missed anything. I'm going to call the chief deputy then take pictures of this. I'll see about getting permission to dust for prints."

My mother took in another loud gulp of air, and Smoke drew his shoulders in, a sign he had tensed up. There was no argument that my mother was not cut out for police work. She wasn't fragile; she was emotional about certain things, and incapable of putting on a poker face.

I put my hand on the back of her shoulder and gave her a nudge. "Let's see what we can find, Mom."

I carefully checked the doors and windows, inside and out, and found no signs of a forced entry. Then Mother and I went into the garage, and I looked in the windows of the sheriff's department-issued vehicle. There weren't any papers, or anything else, lying on the seats or the floors. "Man, I think Denny is more of a clean freak than you are, Mom. He even keeps his car as neat as a pin, just like his home and office."

"He certainly is. And it's one of the things I really appreciate about him." Of course she did.

We completed our tasks in fairly short order, and Smoke found us in the garage. "Anything?" he asked, and I shook my head. "Chief Deputy said we'd need a search warrant to dust the safe for prints. And getting that might be difficult given the lack of evidence that anyone broke in and stole the money. He's posting deputies around the clock to keep watch here until the sheriff returns."

"Okay," I said.

"I guess we're done here for now. Deputy Ortiz pulled up a minute ago and parked back by the sheriff's lawn shed. He won't let anything get by him. Oh, and Sergeant Matsen phoned and asked us to stop by the evidence garage."

I nodded and turned to my mother. "You look worn out, Mom. Why don't we drop you off at Gramps' house and maybe you can take a nap."

"Corinne, you know I can't sleep during the day. But it's probably a good idea to go there, after all. Your grandfather is worried too."

We delivered my mother to Gramps' house then headed back to the sheriff's office to meet with Sergeant Matsen. Smoke took his eyes off the road for a quick glance at me. "I have a better insight on your mother, little lady. And a clearer understanding of what you've been complaining about over the years."

I gave him a short laugh. "When I was younger, all my friends told me she was the most protective parent on the planet, and I really had a hard time with that. Then I finally got to the point when I realized she is who she is, and she's not going to change. But amazingly, the one person she seems the most calm around is Dennis Twardy. So not knowing where he's at is like a double whammy for her."

"Kristen wasn't as high-strung in high school, and maybe it was because she had your dad. Losing him probably explains the main reason she's such a worrywart. I'm just not used to people, even under stress, gasping as much as she does."

I laughed again. "It takes some getting used to, that's for sure. When I was about ten I vowed would never—under any circumstances—make that sucking-in sound she does. It used to startle me, make me afraid that something awful was happening. Now I barely notice when she does it."

"Maybe I, too, will get to that point," he said with a grin.

"Maybe. You know, she's so preoccupied with Denny vanishing she hasn't started processing your friends' deaths at all."

"It's going to take some time for all of us to understand what happened to them all those years ago. And to figure out what that was in the first place. But at this point in time, finding Denny is a whole lot more pressing."

"Where in the world is he?" I said.

He tapped the steering wheel. "Truth be told, I have not a single theory I'd dare to say out loud."

"Will you whisper it, then?"

He gave me a half-smile and whispered, "I wish I knew."

"Very funny. I know the sheriff is always under pressure with criminal activity and investigations, personnel problems. But he also deals with the public and listens to all their questions and complaints. What struck me last night is what if he just reached his limit and had to escape for a day or two? As out of character as that is for him."

"I can't imagine him doing that."

"No."

When we arrived at the office, we headed straight for the evidence garage. Sergeant Doug Matsen set a small tool on a shelf. "Thanks for coming in."

"You working alone today?" Smoke said.

"For a while, anyway. Kenner has his hands full with Twardy disappearing and pulled the Major Crimes guys to help in that effort. Oh, and I got the DNA samples from the victims' families delivered to the regional lab this morning. The ones you left in evidence last night, Detective."

"Thanks," Smoke said.

I visually scanned over the recovered items. The back seat of the car was sitting on a pallet. There were four fans running at a medium speed some distance away. The smaller items we had helped remove from the vehicle were drying on a rolling unit with mesh shelves: the wallet, the purse and its contents, keys, some small tools, what was left of the various articles of clothing, including the letter jacket, and the tire iron from the trunk. A cement block sat on a paper on the floor.

"Where'd that come from?" Smoke pointed at the block.

"That's what I wanted to talk to you about. I wondered if you guys carried cement blocks around in your car in the old days, for any reason." Matsen said.

Smoke smiled at his friendly jibe then frowned. "I'll forget the 'old days' wise crack and answer your question. No one I knew drove around with cement blocks in their cars."

"I didn't think so, and that's what makes this one so suspicious. I found it wedged in under the front seat this morning."

"With the seats and carpet so soaking wet, I guess we didn't get that far before we left. It was wedged under the seat?" Smoke said.

"Yeah, under the driver's seat. It was stuck in there pretty good."

Smoke stared at the object in question. "Looks like the kind of patio block a lot of people used back then. And still do today, although they've gotten fancier, with different sizes and shapes. What are the measurements on this one?"

"Six inches wide, three inches thick, twelve inches long."

"And weight?"

"Twenty-three pounds."

Smoke nodded. "Fairly dense. A buddy of mine built an entertainment center of sorts with wooden boards and cement blocks similar to this one, but they were more decorative. Back in the *old days*."

Matsen raised his eyebrows and grinned.

"Seems to me that it'd be stupid and downright dangerous to carry something that heavy in your car. In the event of a crash, it'd turn into a heavy projectile that would do a whole lot of damage to a human body," Smoke said.

"People don't always think of things like that," Matsen said.

"Unfortunately, you are right on there. The question is why Toby would have one in his car."

"Maybe his dad was building a patio and sent him to get more of the same kind of blocks, and he forgot one in his car. It could have been on the floor in the back and moved during the crash," I said.

"That's a slim possibility. Knowing Toby, he'd have it in the trunk so it wouldn't mess up the inside of his car. And it's an easy enough thing to verify with his dad." Smoke pulled the memo pad out of his pocket and flipped through some pages. "I'll call him and ask." He picked up his phone, dialed, and waited. When he was connected, he said, "Hi, Mister Fryor, it's Elton Dawes. How are you doing today? . . . Yes, it will take time. Say, I'm sorry to bother you with this, but something came up that raised a question. We found a cement block in Toby's car and we're wondering if you'd have any idea why. . . . Wedged under the front seat. . . . No landscaping projects you were working on? . . . Okay, thank you. Be sure to let us know if we can help you with anything. . . . Goodbye." Smoke hung up and shook his head. "Poor guy. I hope he's going to make it through all this. And no, he has no idea why the block would've been there."

"Like I said, it's suspicious," Doug said.

"Yes, it is," Smoke said.

I pulled out my phone and snapped a picture of the block for future reference.

Smoke's phone rang. "The ME's office," he said, pushed a button, and put the phone to his ear. "Detective Dawes. . . . Yes, Doctor Patrick. . . . Say again?" Smoke's voice went up a few decibels. "I'm with Matsen and Aleckson, and I'm putting the phone on speaker so they'll hear this too." He hit the button and held up his phone. "Ready," he said.

Dr. Patrick's voice rang out loud and clear. "All right. We finished taking the X-rays on our lake victims a little while ago. We can rule out an accidental drive into the lake."

My heart picked up its pace. Matsen and I moved in closer. "What'd you find?" Smoke said.

"They both suffered gunshot wounds. There are shotgun-shell pellets in organs, and embedded in their bones."

The three of us looked at each other and shook our heads.

Matsen chimed in, "There wasn't a shotgun found anywhere inside the Charger. So that rules out the possibility of a murder-suicide."

A double homicide.

"I don't get it. Who in the hell would have killed them? They were just kids, probably partying after the big win on Homecoming night." Smoke's face colored and tightened.

"A real tragedy, and it's difficult to understand why things like that happen." Dr. Patrick paused a moment. "We're preparing for the autopsies, and we'll wait for your detectives to get here."

"We'll be on our way, momentarily," Smoke said and disconnected. "Well Doug, I think you have your answer of why that block was in the car."

Matsen nodded. "To ensure a successful plunge into Whitetail Lake."

"Since the car was in drive, the killer would have had to put the cement block on the gas pedal, and then shifted from neutral into drive."

"And then gotten the hell out of the way," Matsen said.

"I'll phone Kenner to let him know this just turned into a cold case murder investigation," Smoke said.

When they finished their conversation, Smoke said, "Kenner is way more easy-going than our sheriff at handling departmental issues. And he said that since Toby and Wendy were my friends, the two of you should sit in on the autopsies." He looked from Matsen to me.

Matsen nodded. "I'll lock up here and meet you there."

8

Smoke and I arrived at the medical examiner's office and hung out in the waiting room until Sergeant Matsen arrived. The woman at the front desk told us Doctors Bridey Patrick and Calvin Helsing were expecting us and directed us to go down the hallway to the first room on the right. Then she clicked the door lock open and allowed us access. When we reached the autopsy room, Smoke knocked on the door to alert the doctors, and then we stepped in. Patrick and Helsing were standing by a counter looking at some papers.

The room smelled like antiseptic and death.

The doctors were dressed in their protective gear from head to toe. Dr. Patrick's piercing brown eyes honed in on Matsen and me then settled on Smoke. She handed him the printouts of the X-ray images. Smoke held them so both Matsen and I could see. The areas where the pellets rested had been circled.

Smoke turned to Dr. Patrick. "So they were dead when they went in the lake, Doc?"

"That would be my supposition. They would have been very critically wounded by the blast and either died immediately or a short time later.

"Our male victim was shot in the back, further evidenced by the pellets in the bones. And to make it more curious, our female victim was shot in the front. From our observation of the damage caused, and the location of the pellets in their bodies, it's very likely a single shot killed them. They may have been embracing," Dr. Patrick said.

I touched the back of Smoke's hand with the back of mine.

Doctor Patrick let that settle in our brains before she went on. "The young woman was five six, and the young man was five eleven—"

"Five eleven? I thought he was about an inch taller than me, so that'd be six one," Smoke said.

The doctor shrugged. "Did he wear shoes with thicker soles, higher heels to give him more height, perhaps?"

"Maybe he did," Smoke said then laid the X-ray images side by side on the counter, lining up the victims' feet. I took a closer look at how the pellets in the bodies were the same approximate distance from the ground, and that the ones in the male were more on the left side of his body, and the female's were on the right side of hers."

"You may have something there, Doc," Smoke said.

Dr. Helsing nodded. "It appears the majority of the pellets passed through the male victim, with the exception of the ones that embedded in bones. There are more in the female victim. It makes sense that the pellets were slowed down somewhat, passing through the first body."

Doctor Patrick pointed at the images. "As you can see, our male victim has a total of seven pellets embedded in his bones, in the mid-section of his body. Two in thoracic vertebrae, three in ribs, and two in the left scapula. The thoracic area of the spine, ribs, and shoulder blade.

"Our female victim has ten pellets in her body. You can see how, overall, they are approximately five inches higher on her body than the male victim's. In addition to the ones in her heart and lungs, she has one in the first rib, two in the right mandible, and two in the right clavicle, and one in C-3." That translated to her rib, jaw, shoulder bone, and cervical spine.

Smoke, Matsen, and I were silent as we studied the evidence on the images.

"We'll measure the pellets after we remove them. But looking at the X-rays, it appears they could be between number three, and number four, buckshot. An educated guess," Dr. Patrick said.

Smoke moved his head right then left as he studied the images. "Could be."

"I've notified the Bureau of Criminal Apprehension. They'll run the tests to determine how far the shooter was from the victims," Doctor Patrick said.

Smoke drew in a quick breath through his nostrils. "Here are the two scenarios that come to my mind. The kids were threatened by someone with a gun, and the boy stepped in front of the girl to protect her. Or they were hugging, and got blindsided with a shot before they knew what was happening. But why?"

Dr. Patrick raised her eyebrows. "I don't think we'll get that answer today, but we will know more after we've completed the autopsies. Are we all ready to begin?"

"I'll be in the waiting room," Smoke said then left.

Doctor Helsing gave Matsen and me protective suits, and after we had donned them, we took our seats to witness the procedure.

Doctor Helsing had stepped out of the room and returned with assistant Karen and a gurney holding the male victim's body. I had prepared myself as best I could, but there was a long list of duties I'd rather do than witness autopsy examinations. I discovered that was especially true with bodies preserved by adipocere.

The doctors did an external exam of the body, noting the damage from the pellets and the discoloration on the body of where they'd gone in.

The doctors and Karen completed taking measurements and photos. Then Dr. Helsing did the Y-incision for the internal examination. That cut was the worst part of the autopsy for me. Matsen gave my arm a nudge, and I looked over at his drawn face. He was likely feeling about as squeamish as I was.

The doctors were deliberate and efficient as they removed and weighed each organ, making comments and taking notes. They removed the pellets and Karen determined they were number 3 buckshot by referencing a pellet-size chart. When they were finished with that portion of the exam, they stitched the victim back together. They retained the organs for further examination.

The doctors took a break between the autopsies, and Matsen and I went out to the waiting room to fill Smoke in on what we'd learned so far.

"Number three buckshot? We all know the twelve-gauge shotgun is the most popular, but they could have used a twenty gauge," Smoke said.

Matsen agreed. "Number three buckshot would be common choice for a twenty gauge. And it still has twice the power of a forty-four magnum."

"I didn't realize that," I said.

"Oh yeah, major stopping power." That I did know.

"Doug, how far away would you guesstimate the shooter was from the kids?" Smoke said.

"It depends on the barrel. A short eighteen to twenty inch, open-choke-cylinder barrel at eighteen feet would have a spread of about six inches."

"And refresh my memory, how many pellets are there in number three?"

"Nineteen, nowadays anyhow," Matsen said.

"There were seventeen pellets in the bodies," I said.

"I didn't find any in the Charger yet, but it's possible there's a couple in there. I'll sweep it with a magnet," Matsen said.

Not long after that, Sergeant Matsen and I were called in to witness the female victim's autopsy. The thing that struck me most during the exam was when Dr. Patrick said, "One amazing thing about bodies essentially mummified by adipocere: they often still have food contents in their stomachs." Who'd have thought?

It had been a long day by the time we left the medical examiner's office. Smoke left a message for the chief deputy informing him of our status then we got on the road heading southwest to Oak Lea. "I'm trying to get my mind around the reality that Wendy and Toby got shot. What kind of a monster kills a couple of teenagers, then goes to considerable effort to put their bodies in a car and then pushes that car into the lake?" Smoke said.

"A bad one. We should take a closer look at the interviews from all those years ago, see if anything new pops out, a guarded comment someone made."

"Yeah. Back then the investigation was focused on the belief the kids ran away. Obviously the killer, or killers, knew what really happened, but they somehow slipped by without being identified. Damn, they should have been rotting in prison instead of running around free all this time," Smoke said.

"Is there anyone in particular you knew of who hated either one of them, or would have had any kind of a reason—crazy or not—for hurting them?"

"I've been racking my brain since Doc Patrick dropped that bolt from the blue about them getting shot, and I can't think of a single one. Not every kid likes every other kid in the sandbox, but that doesn't mean you kill them."

"Smoke, what was Toby really like, your take on him? Could he have done something that set someone off? If alcohol was involved, things could have escalated for no good reason."

"Toby did have a temper that got him in trouble a time or two. You're right about alcohol making a disagreement that much worse. But bad enough that someone grabbed a gun, in this instance, and shot the kids? I don't know. Teenage boys with their overactive hormones do and say things that piss others off all the time. Mostly their parents, maybe teachers, other boys and girls, sure," he said.

"I've banished most of the bad behaviors of my high school classmates from my mind."

"Yeah, when you're in school, it's just part of life. What you have to put up with."

"This is going to be unfathomable news for Toby and Wendy's families. Yesterday was bad enough, but at least it gave them some closure."

"We'll run it by the chief deputy, but if it were up to me, I'd give it a day or so before we tell them. The ME's office gave us their initial findings, but they're not done with their tests or their reports. That will take a while. Plus the crime labs need to complete their tests, too. That buys us a little time," Smoke said.

And when the regional crime lab techs completed their tests, none of us could have guessed what they would uncover.

When we got back to the office, Smoke and I headed to the archived-files store room. Smoke located the old file once again and set it on the table. He picked out papers from the pile and scanned over a few of them. "We'll try to figure out who should have a second interview."

I took the sheets from him. "The question is, does anyone in here know something after all, or is it someone else who got overlooked in the first place?"

"You mean someone like Harry Gimler? Could be. The bodies were disposed of at his grandfather's farm. Harry's name didn't ring a bell with me, but there was another grandson who hosted parties there. What in the heck was his name?"

He paused then said, "There was no mention by anyone of partying with Toby and Wendy at the farm that night, so it never came up in the investigation. It'd be nice if Detectives Haldin and Brown were still alive so we could pick their brains." They were the two detectives who had worked the case.

"You're right. Smoke, have you thought of anyone who acted like they were keeping a deep, dark secret after that Homecoming night?"

Smoke hitched up a shoulder. "Call me oblivious. If we'd known the kids had been killed, everything would have been different. But there was no evidence of foul play at the time, and no one gave an indication anything bad had happened." He gave me the top half of the file. "We'll switch up what we read last time."

Smoke sat down and I stood, resting my knee on a chair from time to time to take the pressure off my back. It was sometimes easier for me to assess from that distance.

"Hmm, this is interesting," I said.

Smoke looked at me over the top of his readers. "What's that?"

"Dana English. You know her?"

"Sure, she's one of our classmates."

"Well, according to Dana, she said that Wendy must have run off with Toby, but she was a little surprised because she thought things were cooling off between the two of them."

Smoke held out his hand. "Can I take a look at that?" He read for a minute. "I must not have paid much attention to that comment when I skimmed over it. I know Dana and Wendy were not the best of friends. They were football and basketball cheerleaders together, but had a little rivalry going on."

"Over what?"

"Give me your number one guess."

"Boys?"

"You got it. Who knows, maybe Dana was putting moves on Toby, and she hoped things were cooling off between him and Wendy."

"The teenage years are tough, aren't they?"

"Tell me about it. Dana would be a good person to talk to." Smoke handed me two sheets of paper. "Here are your mom and dad's interviews."

I smiled when I took them. "Yes. I read them yesterday. I've only known my father through my mother and grandparents . . . and you, of course. Still, I often think of the two of them, young and in love, like the way they look in that photo, standing in front of the GTO on their wedding day."

Smoke put his hand on mine. "The worst news of my entire life was when I heard he'd been killed in the war."

I nodded.

"Your mother has said a hundred times how grateful she is to have you and John Carl."

I nodded again.

"And so am I." He gave my hand a squeeze then dropped it.

"Thanks."

I felt close to my father—a man I'd never met—when I drove his pride and joy: the classic red 1967 Pontiac GTO that Mother had allowed me to take out of storage and put back on the road. Sometimes, when I was troubled about this or that, I'd sit in the old car until I was grounded again.

Smoke and I studied the documents for some time. "Nothing is jumping out at me. Was there a party at the Williams' farm that night or not? Rudy, that was his name, Mister Williams' other grandson. If there was a party at the grandfather's place Homecoming night, Rudy must have been there. We'll ask Harry Gimler where his cousin lives now."

My phone rang at 5:32. I took a calming breath. "Hi, Mom. How are you and Gramps doing?"

She spoke quietly, probably so Gramps couldn't hear her. "Corinne, I can hardly concentrate on anything other than thinking about Denny. This is the most worried I've been since you went into police work."

I knew from frequent reminders that "most worried" said a lot. "Hang in there, Mom. We're bound to hear from him before long."

Her exhale sounded like "huh." "I need to believe that. Where are you now, are you still working?"

"Yes, Smoke and I are reviewing the files from when Toby Fryor and Wendy Everton went missing. I read what you and Dad said in your interviews back then." I hoped that would distract her.

Mother was silent was a moment. "Corinne, that was such a long time ago, but there are times it seems like yesterday. . . . I'm sorry I keep asking about Denny."

"Don't apologize for that, it's only natural. We're about ready to wrap things up for the day. Can I bring you and Gramps something to eat?"

"Thanks, but that's the main reason I called, to see if you—and Elton, too—want to join us for dinner."

My empty stomach rumbled. "Nice. Let me check."

When I asked Smoke, he didn't hesitate. "You bet," he said.

"I heard him. Come anytime and we'll eat about six thirty."

"Sounds good. 'Bye."

After we hung up Smoke said, "It may not be the best time to talk to your mother about Wendy and Toby, but I'm interested in what she has to say. Back when, she was more shocked than anything they had run away. And now, knowing what we do, maybe she has some other insight."

"If it takes her mind off Denny's disappearance for five minutes, that's not a bad thing."

"I agree."

Smoke and I drove our own vehicles to Gramps Brandt's house and met at the front door. When we went inside, the tantalizing aroma of roasting beef surrounded us like a low-hanging cloud, and I inhaled a big whiff.

"Well, that's the best welcome home I've had in a long, long time," Smoke said with a smile that deepened his long dimples.

Gramps waved at us from his recliner and muted the volume on the television. "Kristen has been jumpy all day. More than normal, that is."

Mother came out of the kitchen, her face flushed like she had literally been slaving over a hot stove for hours. "Your cupboards needed a good cleaning out, Dad." She waved her dishtowel. "I'm glad you're here, and the table's all set in the dining room."

"I'll help you dish up the food." Mother liked food served in bowls, family-style, and passed around the table.

We were all situated in front of our place settings in short order then Gramps said a prayer, asking God to bless our food and to bring Denny Twardy back safely. Mother had tears in her eyes when she raised her head and lifted the meat platter. She passed it to Smoke, the guest of honor.

"Kristen, you have created a feast. Roast beef, mashed potatoes and gravy, broccoli, fresh baked bread. There is nothing quite like a home-cooked meal."

"Of a good cook," I added.

"With your mother, that's a given." He raised his water glass in a toast.

We dished up our plates, ate, and talked between swallows, purposely avoiding the topic of the missing sheriff. And that wasn't easy. When we'd finished our meal, I helped Gramps get back to his recliner—the spot where he spent too much time. Even though he'd said, "My legs are all played out," on a number of occasions, I did what I could to keep him walking.

Smoke and my mother were clearing off the table when I went back to the kitchen. I joined in the effort, and the kitchen was spic-and-span in no time.

"Kristen, there's been a development in the Toby and Wendy case, if we can pick your brain for a few minutes," Smoke said as he hung up the dish towel on the stove handle to dry.

Mother's eyebrows lifted. "Oh?" She leaned her back against the counter, like she needed the support.

"Maybe you'll want to sit down for this," I said.

She studied my face for a hint of what Smoke might say but didn't move. "What is it?"

"This will be a shock, but it turns out the kids were shot and killed before they went into the lake." Smoke said the words softy and slowly, letting them take hold in her mind.

"*What*?" Mother's knees buckled, and I moved in, slipping my arm around her waist. "Maybe I will sit down," she said.

"That isn't public knowledge yet. In fact, we haven't told their families. We're waiting for the official report. Plus, we don't want the details of how they were killed leaked out, knowing their killer might still be out there somewhere," Smoke said.

I guided my mother to a chair. "Mom, can you take yourself back to that time when the investigation was going on?"

She nodded. "How can I forget it? Wendy and I had our differences, but we sat together for lunch one day that Homecoming week. She seemed happier than usual so I asked her about it. She giggled and said, 'I'm in love, really in love for the first time.' It made me wonder how Toby had suddenly won her over, because I didn't think she was all that serious about him. She liked to date a lot of different boys. Right, Elton?"

Smoke cleared his throat. "Right."

Mother leaned forward like she was about to whisper a secret. "I didn't say this back then in the interview, but I thought maybe she was pregnant. Wendy was on the wild side, and her parents were fairly strict. So it was the only reason I could think of why they'd run away. But now this . . . I can't believe someone killed them." She folded her hands and shook her head.

"Is there anyone you'd consider as a possible suspect, Mother?" I said.

She studied her hands awhile then looked up. "No. Toby was good-looking and a great athlete. We all knew he had something of a temper that got him benched a few times. And I heard he'd gotten into some fights, but I can't imagine anyone carrying that kind of a grudge."

"Unless he picked a fight with the wrong guy," Smoke said.

Mother frowned slightly. "And Wendy? She was fun-loving and self-absorbed, like a lot of teenagers are. Most of our classmates liked her just fine. Not everyone, of course."

"Anyone jealous of her, I mean especially so?"

Smoke and Mother exchanged a look I couldn't quite read then Smoke said, "Toby was the jealous one. After they started dating, he'd get peeved if other boys looked twice at Wendy."

Mother nodded. "That's true, he was possessive. As far as other boys or girls, I don't know of any who were especially jealous of her, per se. There could have been, of course."

"Dana English?" I said.

Mother's eyebrows lifted. "Dana? She and Wendy weren't that close. I know Dana had a crush on Toby for a while, but the girls seemed to get along."

"Anyone come to mind that acted hateful toward either Toby or Wendy?" I said.

Smoke and Mother looked at each other for an answer then each shook their heads.

"How long had Toby and Wendy been dating?" I said.

"Not long, maybe a couple of months. Toby had liked Wendy for a long time before that, but she had a babysitting job at her aunt's house the summer before senior year, and it was a few hours away. They didn't really start dating until after she got back home," Mother said.

"My last questions of the night, how often did they have parties at the Williams' farm, and do you know who the regulars were?"

"Your father and I heard about the beer parties every now and then, but we weren't all that interested in going. And we figured we'd get caught for sure if we did. I can't really remember anyone in particular who talked about it. They kept it pretty quiet so the teachers didn't find out."

"Do you remember hearing about a kid named Rudy, or Harry Gimler? They were Mister Williams' grandsons," I said.

"Rudy, yes I remember hearing that name. But Harry, that doesn't sound familiar," Mother said.

"He's living in a newer house where the old farmhouse sat," I said.

Mother lifted her eyebrows and nodded like it was news to her.

"We'll talk to Harry Gimler and track down Rudy, see if they were at their grandfather's house on the night in question. Two things are certain—Toby and Wendy did not shoot themselves, nor did they drive Toby's car into the lake," Smoke said.

"We know they went into the lake from the Williams' farm, but that doesn't necessarily mean they were shot there. What we need is an eyewitness," I said.

"What a horrible thing this has turned out to be," Mother said.

I nodded. "I'm not looking forward to giving their folks this big blow."

What we didn't know was we were in for a big blow ourselves the next day.

9

When I got to the sheriff's office the next morning, there were a number of conversations going on about Twardy vanishing. The air was electric with tension. I headed to the chief deputy's office and knocked on the door.

"Come in, Sergeant." Kenner looked worn out. His eyes were bloodshot and squinty. He had not fully recovered from surgery and should be at home recuperating. "I just talked to Ben at the lab. They've been running the DNA tests on the victims in the Charger and hope to have some answers soon."

"That's great, we were hoping for a fast turn-around," I said

"Dawes all but begged the lab guys to complete the tests as soon as possible, and I'm happy they're cooperating. And that nothing more critical has come in to bump us out of the queue."

"So far, so good." I sat down across from him. "Mike, I'm here about the sheriff. This is day three since he disappeared. No one has contacted us about him, and his car hasn't been found. What could possibly have happened?"

"I wish to God I had that answer. Nothing about it makes sense to me. Sheriff's happier now than he's been in years, thanks to your mother. I can testify to that. Since there was no sign of a break-in at his place, we can only assume, but not prove, he was the one who emptied his safe."

"If someone was holding a gun to his head, could that be why he left the door to the safe open, as a clue?"

"Let's hope not, but I have to admit I've thought of a number of bad scenarios. I'm meeting with Judge Adams when he goes on recess, around ten-thirty, to see if he'll agree to sign a search warrant. If someone managed to grab the sheriff and stole his money, my question is how did he know about the safe in the first place? I sure didn't. And what happened after that? I'm popping Tums like they're candy." Maybe Kenner wasn't as easy going on the inside as he appeared on the outside.

"I'm glad you're talking to the judge. Thanks for listening."

"Anytime, Corky."

I headed to the archived-files storeroom to shift through the file yet again, hoping something would jump out at me from the pages. I read statements for over an hour until Smoke phoned me. "Where are you?" he asked. When I told him, he said he was on his way.

The urgency in his voice made me curious, and when I saw the look on his face a minute later, I was gripped by a sense of alarm. "Did they find something out about Denny, something bad?"

"No, nothing on the sheriff yet, but it's something that is definitely not good."

"Put me out of my misery."

"Ben from the lab called. They ran a genetic test and Toby's dad's DNA does not match that of our male victim. He is not Mister Fryor's son."

"Are they sure?"

"Positive. And now with his mother dying, we can't check hers."

"What about his brothers?"

"Yeah, that'd be the next step, to check their DNA with the victim's. We're looking at a couple of different possibilities here, because I don't think Mister Fryor would have given us a sample if he knew he wasn't Toby's father. He'd have told us the scoop."

"So Mister Fryor either thought he was Toby's father, or the victim in the Charger is not Toby after all."

"Correct."

"Wow, oh wow. And Wendy?"

"She is the daughter of Mister and Missus Everton."

"This just got more complicated."

"A whole lot more complicated. And it's time to tell them how the kids died."

"Who should we visit first, Mister Fryor, or the Evertons?"

"Let's go with Fryor."

We settled in Mr. Fryor's living room and Smoke did his best to soften the news he was bound to deliver. Fryor's face went to the palest shade of white possible when Smoke told him that his DNA did not match the victim's. "I don't understand that at all," he said.

"This is a delicate subject, Mister Fryor, but I have to ask you. Do you have any reason to believe Toby had a different father?"

He shook his head back and forth slowly. "No reason at all. That's impossible."

My heart went out to the elderly man who had grieved for the boy found in the old Charger, who may not have been his son after all. I reached over and put my hand on his. "One way to confirm that the victim is not Toby is to collect a sample from one of his brothers. That would prove your wife was not his mother, either."

Mr. Fryor blinked away tears from his lower lids. "I just don't know what to think about all of this. If it's not Toby, then who is that boy, and where is my son?"

Those were two of the smoldering questions.

"We'll need to make arrangements for one of your sons to give us a sample for the genetic test," I said.

Mr. Fryor nodded. "As it turns out, David is flying in this afternoon from Houston. He had to tie up some loose ends at his computer software company. My other boy, Wade, has been laid up with a broken ankle. They're both awfully upset by all this. And now thinking Toby may be somebody else's son, well that's downright unbelievable."

Smoke leaned in closer and lowered his voice. "There is another thing we need to tell you before word leaks out about it. And you'll need to brace yourself."

"What is it?" Mr. Fryor's eyebrows drew together.

"The kids in the car did not die accidentally. The medical examiner discovered they had been killed prior to going in the lake. They'd been shot."

Mr. Fryor's eyes opened wider than it seemed possible. His tongue pushed against his teeth like he was trying to talk, but the words refused to leave his lips. I started counting the seconds, wondering if he'd be okay. Finally, he closed his mouth and his eyes and dropped his head into his hands. I glanced at Smoke who nodded that we should give him some time.

When Fryor finally looked up, Smoke said, "That is the most awful news. We're very, very sorry."

Mr. Fryor nodded, and continued to stare at us then finally found his voice. "They were shot? I don't understand."

"No, none of us do."

"Where?"

"We don't have that answer yet, but we'll keep digging," Smoke said.

"Mister Fryor, you were asked a lot of questions at the time Toby and Wendy disappeared, but the sheriff's department had very little to go on. Until now. Do you recall any mention from Toby that he was going to the Williams' farm that night? It wasn't in your interview," I said.

"No, I don't. There was the big football game and then the dance after. We were surprised when we found out the next day that Toby and Wendy hadn't gone to the dance, after all. And then they disappeared. Kids often had parties at someone's house after a game, but I don't remember him ever saying he'd been to Williams' farm. That's why I couldn't figure out a good reason his car had gone into Whitetail from the southeast side there."

"Yeah, that's the puzzle we're working on. Mister Fryor, another question: do the names Rudy—not sure of his last name—or Harry Gimler ring a bell?" Smoke said.

"Rudy. That does sound familiar, but Harry, no."

"Did Toby talk about Rudy?" I said.

Fryor shook his head. "I don't recall much of anything. Just remember hearing the name."

I pulled a business card from my pocket. "Mister Fryor, please give us a call when David gets here. We'll collect a sample from him to compare with the DNA of our male victim. Then we'll get that answer."

He took the card. "I'll do that. Remember that old show, *The Twilight Zone*, Elton?"

"Sure," Smoke said.

"That's how I'm feeling about now. Like I'm in the twilight zone, and it's a scary place to be."

"I can only imagine. Will you be okay until David gets here?" Smoke said.

Mr. Fryor nodded.

The visit to Wendy Everton's parents' house was even more eventful. When I broke the news to them, Mrs. Everton fainted dead away. She was sitting at the kitchen table when she toppled over. Fortunately, Smoke reacted quickly enough and prevented her head from striking the floor. Her husband was frozen in his chair and watched with his mouth gaped open. Mrs. Everton was unconscious for a few seconds, and when she came to we assisted her back in her chair, then I checked her pulse and looked at the pupils of her eyes.

Her face regained some color. "What happened?"

"You fainted," I said.

"I've never fainted in my life."

"A sudden shock can do that to a person. Are you feeling all right, or should we call an ambulance?" Smoke said.

She waved her hand. "No, I'll be fine. Just give me a minute."

Mr. Everton pulled a chair in close to her, sat down, and reached for her hand. "You scared me, Verna. I was afraid I was going to lose you, too."

Mrs. Everton looked into her husband's concerned eyes. "I've worried for years that Wendy had passed on. But I never imagined something that violent had happened to her. Our poor baby." And then she broke down and wept like one. And her husband did the same.

Smoke and I bided our time, waiting for them to regain some composure. Then Smoke said, "I read over what you told the detectives back then, that Wendy hadn't told you specifically what her plans were, for after the game and the dance Homecoming night. Have you remembered anything since then?"

Mrs. Everton shook her head. "No. That night is as clear as a bell in my memory. Wendy said she was going to stay with friends. She'd packed her overnight bag, but she hadn't taken things that were important to her, like her diary and her photo albums. So when she hadn't come home after a couple of days, and we feared she had run away, we didn't think it would be forever." Her words, and their meaning, choked her up.

"Wendy's purse was in the car, and her wallet was inside. But there was no overnight bag in there," I said.

"No, there wasn't," Smoke said.

"I wonder what would have become of it?" Mr. Everton said.

The killer probably knew that answer.

Smoke shook his head. "We'll be sure you get her purse back to you when the crime lab is done processing it."

Mrs. Everton clutched her chest. "Thank you."

"One last thing. Do either of you remember Wendy talking about boys named Rudy or Harry?" I said.

They each repeated the names then shook their heads.

"Again, you have our very deepest sympathies. We'll let you know when the medical examiner's office is finished on their end, so you can make final arrangements for Wendy," Smoke said.

The Evertons looked at each other and nodded.

Smoke and I were back in the car, out of the Evertons' earshot before we spoke. "Giving parents bad news about their children is always difficult," I said.

"You got that right. Even when they've been missing for over thirty years, makes no difference. Hearing the particulars was especially devastating for them."

"That was the first time someone's actually passed out on me like that."

Smoke gave me a nod. "I've had it happen a time or two."

"You did good, catching the poor woman before she cracked her head."

"Yeah, we need to stay alert every minute on duty, don't we?"

"Yup."

His phone rang. "Detective Dawes. . . . Hi, Mike, what's up? . . . Australia, really? . . . Well, you can't blame them. The sheriffs are in unique positions, and form some pretty tight bonds. Still no word that anyone's found him? . . . Right, thanks."

Smoke disconnected and glanced over at me. "Chief Deputy says all hell is breaking loose, between the recovered vehicle and its victims and the missing sheriff."

"What about Australia?"

"A news channel saw the video on YouTube and called to get all the details. The calls are coming in from all over, but that was the farthest away."

"To think that what is happening in our little piece of the world is picked up in other countries is something else. Sure, recovering an occupied vehicle from the bottom of a deep lake after all those years is big news, but what is it that makes things go viral?"

Smoke made a "heh" noise. "You are asking the wrong guy, little lady. It hasn't quite gone viral, but Denny Twardy's disappearance has got the whole state on alert. Actually, make that the whole country."

"We're bound to catch a break with so many people on the lookout," I said.

"Let's hope." Smoke rapped his palm on the steering wheel. "Change of subject, let's go see if Harry Gimler's home. Hopefully we'll get there before happy hour."

"Or in his case, unhappy hour."

Smoke's lips curled up. "Good one. I kinda have a feeling that's the way most of his hours have been since Whitetail let go of its secret."

Harry Gimler smelled of gin—like cologne splashed on a Christmas tree—making me lose the inclination to ever want another gin and tonic in my life. The odor was the only obvious symptom of alcohol consumption he displayed. He walked without staggering and talked without struggling, signs he was used to fairly heavy drinking.

"What brings the sheriff's department out here today?" Gimler asked.

"We're trying to put the series of events together from that October night thirty-three years ago. We paid visits to the families of the victims. And when we asked if they knew what the teenagers had planned for after the big Homecoming game, neither of them knew for sure. They were surprised they'd come here. Or more specifically, to your grandfather's place," Smoke said.

Harry raised his eyebrows. "Well I certainly don't know why they'd be here, if that's what you're getting at."

I shook my head. "No, we're not saying that. But we have a few questions you may be able to help us with. If we can sit down for a bit?"

Harry gave a reluctant nod. "All right, well let's go to the living room."

We sat near the expansive windows overlooking the lake and surrounding land. One could see for miles, and I reluctantly drew my eyes back inside and focused my mind on the business at hand. Smoke nodded at me to start the questioning.

"Mister Gimler. Harry. You told us that you spent time here in the summers. What about during the school year, did you visit your grandfather much?"

Harry looked at his hands and moved his fingers before he spoke. "My grandfather was living here alone and getting up in years, so my mother tried to get here once a month the last few years when I was in high school. Most times I came with her; sometimes I drove out myself for the weekend."

I nodded. "What did you do, activity-wise, when you were here?"

"My grandfather had wound down his farming operation by then, but he kept some chickens and a few pigs. Still gardened, more out of habit, I think, because he gave most of the produce away. He puttered around the place, and I puttered with him. And I fell in love with the area, the property."

"You have a cousin people remember as hosting parties here. Rudy. What's his full name?"

"Rudy, ah I have to think of his middle name. Peter, so it's Rudy Peter Medlin."

I jotted that on my memo book. "Where is he now?"

"I don't know. We lost touch years ago."

"Is he in Minnesota, did he move out of state?"

"I have no idea. Really."

"Who does?" I said.

"No one in the family, that I know of."

"Really. What about his parents, siblings?"

"His parents have both passed, and he was an only child," Harry said.

"What about the rest of your family?"

"On my mother's side, besides my sister, I have two living aunts, an uncle, . . ." He looked down at his hands, and used his right pointer finger to count on his left hand until he got to five then switched hands, ". . . seven cousins. None of them live in Minnesota."

"And no one has been in contact with Rudy?" I said.

"No. Not for twenty, maybe twenty-five years now."

"That's a helluva deal," Smoke said. "And not a one of you has tried to locate him?"

"Well sure. One of my aunts especially, but she finally gave up. I did some searching when the Internet came alive, but nothing panned out. Rudy could have left the country for all we know."

"Do you have a photo of him?" I said.

"No, I didn't get any of the old pictures, except the one of my grandfather and me that's hanging in my bedroom."

"What is Rudy's date of birth?" I said.

Harry knew the month and year, but it took him a minute to remember the day.

I wrote that down then said, "Tell me about Rudy. What was he like?"

"Rudy was one of those kids that got in trouble a lot. He was from St. Paul, and when he started getting involved with a gang, my uncle and aunt sent him out here to stay with our grandfather most weekends. He fell in with some kids around here, and they came up with an arrangement they all agreed on: if Rudy provided the place to party, they'd bring the beer."

"And your grandfather, he allowed that? It's a big liability to be a party to underage drinking," I said.

Harry shrugged. "It was a different world back then. Kids having keggers out in a farmer's field seemed to slip under the radar more than it does now. My grandfather didn't exactly know what was going on, I'm sure. He went to bed early, and was nearly deaf. So unless the kids were partying right under his window, he wouldn't have heard a thing."

"It sounds like you know that from experience."

Harry nodded slightly. "I was here during a few of the parties."

"And the night Toby Fryor and Wendy Everton disappeared? Was there a party that Friday night, October fifth?"

"I wouldn't know. I didn't keep a diary."

"It was Oak Lea's Homecoming. The kids would have been talking about that," I said.

"That doesn't ring a bell." Harry shifted and crossed his leg, appearing more uncomfortable by the minute.

"Did your sister spend much time at your grandfather's farm?" I said.

He shook his head. "She's four years older than me, and she headed out to Oregon for college after she graduated. In the early years she'd come back for the holidays, but that's about it."

Smoke leaned forward in his chair. "Getting back to Rudy. You said he fell in with some area kids. Do you remember their names, what they looked like?"

"I remember two guys. There was an Abe. He was tall, had reddish hair. And then there was Keith who was about average height and a little on the pudgy side." He moved his hand to his own pudgy side.

"Remember any last names?" Smoke said.

Harry scratched at his chin. "No. And that's all I can come up with right now. There were different kids who showed up here and there, but no one that sticks out my memory. I was a shy kid, and Rudy's friends were not my friends."

"Toby Fryor or Wendy Everton?" Smoke said.

He lifted a hand and shook his head.

I pulled out my phone, found the photo of the cement patio block, and passed it to Harry. "Your grandfather use any of these for a patio or other project way back when?"

Harry looked at it a minute. "Not that I remember, but it's possible. Why do you ask?"

"It was in the recovered Charger and we thought it was odd."

"Yeah," was all he said.

"Think about what we talked about tonight, see if any other details come to mind," I said.

Harry opened his mouth like he was going to say something in protest but apparently thought better of it.

I softened my tone for the next question. "You were home the day we found the vehicle in Whitetail, and you're home today. I'm curious about your work life."

"Oh well, I work from home most days. I'm a stockbroker, but I don't put in the hours like I used to. I don't have to."

I stood up. "All right, we'll be on our way. Call if something more comes to mind."

Harry gave a head-bobbing sort of nod and pushed himself up. He sidestepped a little before he steadied himself. The gin was having an effect on him after all.

Smoke stood and focused on Gimler. "One thing I've learned, Harry, is that alcohol only dulls the pain for a little while," he said.

Harry lifted his eyebrows a tad and cast his eyes downward, appearing offended. Smoke and I left on that parting note.

10

"Gimler likes his gimlets, it seems," Smoke said as we drove away.

"Or maybe it's the gimlets that like Gimler."

"That is entirely possible. We just met the man, so I'm wondering if the discovery on his property triggered his drinking binge or if it's a regular occurrence, and lucky for him, he works from home."

"Or he's feeling guilty about what happened here thirty-three years ago."

"That too."

"Can you figure out who those guys are that Harry named, Abe and Keith?" I said.

"From his description, I think it must be Abe Greer who was in the class ahead of us. I don't think he was interviewed back then. He lived with his mother in an apartment downtown, above the bank on the corner. It was Oak Lea Bank at the time. He was the only kid I knew who lived right downtown."

"And there were not that many apartment buildings in Oak Lea back then, or so my mother tells me whenever a new one goes up."

"Nope. Aside from the ones above businesses, there were maybe a half dozen smaller ones. I'll have to consult my school yearbook for Keith. We had a couple of Keiths in our class, and from what Harry said, I think it was Brady. I'll get on that tomorrow."

"Good. Now to locate Rudy Medlin."

"Given his miscreant behavior back then, it's possible he's in prison," Smoke said.

"And that's easy enough to check."

Smoke shook his head. "It blows my mind how Medlin used his grandfather, hosting those parties at his house. Not to mention how it set him up for possible liability had something happened to one of the partying kids."

"Something did happen to two of them. Something fatal."

"Lest we never forget. Of course the murders themselves may have happened somewhere else."

"True."

"Corinne, what's your take on Harry Gimler?"

"He's tough to read. He strikes me as very guarded and secretive on the one hand. And overly sensitive on the other hand, like life has handed him more than he can cope with so he drinks to forget. Maybe he witnessed the shooting of two young people one Homecoming night long ago, and it set him on a bad course."

"You gotta wonder." Smoke tapped the steering wheel.

"Where to next?"

"Let's go back to the office. When we hear from Fryor that his son is here, we'll swing over for his DNA sample. Dana

English bubbled to the surface when we were going through the files. It'd be good to talk to her, see what she has to say now that we know the kids didn't run away after all."

"And there may be others who have an opinion of why the teens were killed," I said.

"You make a valid point, and any number might contact us with those opinions. In fact, I hope they do, and it pushes the investigation forward so we can solve these dreadful crimes," Smoke said.

"The criminal cold case that was sitting on the bottom of Whitetail Lake for thirty-three years."

"I'm real interested in what Rudy Medlin has to say. That he dropped contact with his family twenty or more years ago adds yet another hurdle for us to jump over. And in the middle, correction, in the forefront of it all, our sheriff is missing."

"I manage to go sixty or seventy seconds at a time without thinking about him."

"Same here. And here's the thing, I'm feeling compelled to join in his search, see if I can add anything to the mix."

"You should do that, Smoke. You're our best detective, and finding Denny is number one. As far as our Whitetail case is concerned, I'll talk to Dana English and see if I can locate Rudy Medlin. And collect the DNA sample when Darwin Fryor calls."

Smoke nodded then squeezed his eyebrows together in concentration. It wasn't difficult to figure out what he was thinking. Where on God's green earth was Sheriff Dennis Twardy?

When Smoke and I parted ways, I headed to the sergeants' office and phoned my mother. "Hey, Mom."

"No word from Denny?"

"Not yet, but our guys are ramping up their efforts though, so keep the faith."

"I'm trying, dear."

"I know. Actually, I was hoping you could help me with the Wendy and Toby case. I'd like to talk to Dana English and thought maybe you knew where she is, if she's had a name change."

"Dana. Why yes, let me think back to when I helped send out the invitations to our last class reunion. Her married name is Smyth—spelled S-M-Y-T-H, and she lives in a metro suburb. Maple Grove. At least she did two years ago. I can find the address for you, and probably her phone number."

A project would occupy her for a while. "That'd be great. In fact, if you have the addresses of the rest of your classmates, I'd like to get a copy. If it turns out there are others we need to talk to, it would save us time tracking down their contact info."

"I'll do that right now, and I'll bring you the list. Where are you?"

Was it a good idea for my mother to stop by the sheriff's office, or not. Why not? "Thank you, Mother. I'm at the S.O. Come to the south side door, and call my cell phone. I'll meet you there."

"All right, it shouldn't take me long."

I figured I'd be able to get the contact information on Dana English Smyth faster than it would take my mother to deliver it, but besides keeping her busy, it supported what I'd told her a hundred times or more—that I spent the bulk of my time at work gathering information, one way or the other. It wasn't all high-speed chases and bullet-dodging.

I logged onto the Internet and began a search on Rudy Peter Medlin. I found a man who shared his name, but not his date of birth. I ran a criminal history check, and that came up dry also. It baffled me that even in today's world of free-flowing information people successfully disappeared all the time. If they were determined to walk away from one life to start another, they somehow managed to. I'd known of several who'd done just that.

Sheriff Twardy. No, I didn't believe he was one of them.

In the case of the two teenagers who had gone missing all those years ago, they'd disappeared against their will after suffering violent deaths. What had gone down between them and the person, or persons, who shot and killed them, loaded their bodies into the car, and then pushed it into the lake?

If it wasn't Toby Fryor's body that was recovered in his Charger, might it be Rudy Medlin's after all? It took me a few seconds to realize it couldn't be Rudy, or he would have been reported missing around the same time Toby and Wendy were, and not years later.

Back to the drawing board. The way Harry Gimler portrayed it, he had not been especially close to his cousin, supported by the fact he didn't even know within five years of how long he'd been missing. At least one aunt had tried to find Rudy. I'd get her name and contact information from Harry Gimler and give her a call.

My mother arrived at the sheriff's office some minutes later. I let her in via the back door and gave her a reassuring smile when I saw the strained look on her face. Her exhaustion and anguish were apparent.

She handed me the pages of the document. "Here you go. You wanted to make a copy?"

"Sure. Come with me, and I'll give you the original back."

Mother hesitated, like she was afraid to step all the way in. "I guess that'd be okay."

I took a different route so we wouldn't go past Denny Twardy's empty office. I used the copy machine in the sergeants' office, gave the original back to Mother, and laid the copy on the desk.

We left the office, and when I was escorting her back to the door, we ran into Smoke in the hallway. "Kristen, good to see you. As luck would have it, I just got a lead on Denny to share with you."

I thought my mother was going to jump into Smoke's arms. Instead, she grabbed his hands with her own. "What?"

Smoke moved his head from one side to the next. "It's a very small lead, but it means something. We just gotta figure out what that something is."

"Smoke," I said, urging him to spit it out already.

"A guy named Rod from over at Steven's Gas Station in Rockwell called not three minutes ago to tell us a man fitting the sheriff's description had gotten gas there day before yesterday. Tuesday, at about ten hundred hours." Less than an hour after Denny had left the office.

"And he just called now?" I said.

"He's fairly new to town and doesn't know the sheriff yet. He didn't put two and two together until he was reviewing the video tape, looking for a guy who drove off without paying for his gas."

"Rockwell, huh?" I said.

"Rod says the man looks a lot like the sheriff, and paid for his gas with cash."

"Looks like the sheriff? The uniform, and badge, and sidearm should have given that much away," I said.

"You'd think. I'm guessing the sheriff was not in uniform."

"Did Rod say whether or not he was alone?" I said.

"I didn't get into any questioning. I'm on my way down there to review both the tapes—of the counter inside, and the gas pump outside. Then we should have some answers," he said.

My phone rang. I picked it out of its holder and pushed the talk button. "Sergeant Aleckson."

"Sergeant, this is Darwin Fryor."

"Hello."

"My son David is home. We've been talking quite a while now. And he's willing to help with the, you know, the test."

"I appreciate that, and I'll be over in short order."

"We'll be here."

"Thanks." I hung up and locked eyes with Smoke's. "I'll be heading over to the Fryor home."

"Toby's house? Whatever for?" My mother said.

"His brother David just got in from Texas, and I need to talk to him." It was enough of an explanation.

"Oh," Mother said.

Smoke nodded. "Understood. Well, Kristen, I guess your daughter and I have some duties to attend to. And I'll let you know what I find out at the gas station as soon as I can."

"Thank you," she said.

We walked out to the parking lot together, got in our cars, and drove off in different directions.

I pulled into the Fryors' driveway and parked. I had DNA test kits in my trunk, so I opened it, picked one out of the box, closed the trunk, and then made my way to the house. Apparently the Fryors had been watching for me because the front door opened when I was still several feet away.

A man who looked like the photo of eighteen-year-old Toby Fryor, thirty years later, stood in the entry. "Come in, Sergeant."

I extended my hand. "David Fryor?"

He took my hand, shook it firmly, and nodded. "This is all so mind-boggling. Life has never been the same for our family since that Homecoming night." His voice held a hint of a drawl, no doubt picked up from his years in Texas.

"I can't even guess what you've been through. You were just a teenager yourself when it happened."

David let go of my hand and nodded. "I was sixteen years old, a high school junior. Like I said, life was never the same ATD."

"ATD?" I said.

"After Toby disappeared." He pointed to the plastic bag I held in my left hand. "When they say there is a first time for everything, you never think it might include something like this."

I shook my head. "No you don't. And if it wasn't important, I wouldn't be here."

"He's my brother, so I'll do anything I can. Come in." He took the few steps into the living room. "My dad is obviously distressed, and completely worn out. I convinced him to go lie down for a while."

"That's good. I'm sure he's relieved you're here with him. He told us your mother died recently. I'm sorry about that, too."

"Thanks. I think that's why all this happening with Toby has hit Dad especially hard. I bet he's said, 'I wish your mother was here,' a dozen times."

I nodded.

David lowered his voice. "He never got over Mom leaving like that. And now with this DNA thing, making him doubt that Toby really was his son, it brings up a lot of questions about my mother."

"Ones she can't answer herself."

"That's right. Of all the times I've been sad for him, and after all he's been through, this about feels like the worst."

"I can understand that."

"Where to?" he said.

"Right here in the living room is fine." I waved at the furniture. "Let's sit down. Besides collecting the DNA sample, I have some questions. But it shouldn't take long."

David nodded and took a seat on the couch, and I chose the same chair as the last time I'd been there. I put the DNA kit on the coffee table then pulled a memo pad and pen from my breast pocket. "I need some information for my report and for the test. What's your full name, date of birth, address, and phone number?" I jotted down the information as he gave it to me. "David, before I collect the sample, I'd like to ask you about that Homecoming night when Toby and Wendy disappeared."

"All right," he said.

"Tell me everything you remember about that night and the days or even the week before that."

David folded his hands then looked down and watched his thumbs move back and forth. "There are times when it seems like it happened last month. And other times it seems like it never happened at all. Before Toby disappeared, our family was like day. ATD, it seemed like it was always night."

Day and then always night. That gave me pause. Mr. Fryor had said his wife shared a special bond with Toby. Her sorrow may have cast added gloom on the family. I gave David an acknowledging nod. "You were interviewed at the time, but as a refresher, did you know of any plans Toby had for after the football game that night?"

David shook his head. "Like everyone else, I figured he'd be at the dance, at least for a while. We didn't hang out together socially—he never invited me along to parties, and with good reason. Toby wasn't exactly a rule-follower, but I was. The last thing I wanted was to get caught at a beer party and get kicked out of sports for a month."

"So you knew about the parties at the Williams' farm?"

His shoulders lifted. "To some extent. The kids kept them fairly quiet, but word got around school. I don't remember hearing about a party there that night, but there surely could have been. I knew of some of the other ones. Parties that were thrown by parents or at least with parents' approval. Dry ones, no alcohol."

"Did Toby talk about Mister Williams' grandsons, Rudy Medlin and Harry Gimler? Rudy was from St. Paul, and Harry lived in Benson. But they'd be out at the farm on weekends."

"Rudy and Harry? Now that you say his name, I remember overhearing Toby talking to Rudy on the phone once in a while. But I never met him, and when I asked about him, Toby said it was none of my business. Harry? I don't remember hearing about him," he said.

"Toby said Rudy was none of your business?"

David nodded. "It might seem strange, since he was my brother, but Toby liked to keep his friends to himself. Along with any plans he had. And a lot of the time I don't think he necessarily knew what they were ahead of time. Like other teenagers, they see where the night takes them."

That was true enough. "What was your first thought when you found out Toby and Wendy were missing?"

"That they must have run away. Not that it made any sense, but I couldn't think of anything else. Certainly not that anything like this had happened."

"Was Toby in any kind of dispute with anyone at the time?" I said.

"Dispute?" He frowned like he was thinking about it.

"Disagreement."

"No, not that he talked about anyway. I've been thinking about that since my dad told me that, that . . . the kids had been killed. Thinking about . . . trying to remember if Toby was having a major problem with anyone." He shook his head. "But I couldn't. He did seem more tense than normal for a week or so before, though. I thought it was all about the big Homecoming game and the pressure, you know, when it seems like the whole town was counting on our team to win."

People take their sports pretty seriously. "Did you ask him about it?"

"I said something like, 'Why are you being such a big crab lately?' And he said, 'Why are you always sticking your big nose in my business?' Then he gave me a little shove, and that was about the extent of it. So when he and Wendy disappeared, I figured that's what was bothering him. They'd been planning to run away after the game for some crazy reason or other."

"We'll keep searching for answers, David." I finished my notes, put my memo pad and pen back in my pocket, and reached over and picked up the DNA kit from the coffee table. I removed the swab and moved in an arm's length away from David. "Nothing too invasive here. Open your mouth, and I'll swab the inside of your cheek and then we'll be done."

David stared intently at my face while I collected the sample. When I'd finished and taken a step back, he said, "I have to tell you that your parents were great kids back in high school. I was in my sophomore year at college when I heard your dad had been killed. That was a blow—for our whole town really. I heard your mom was expecting a baby besides."

I inserted the swab in its holder, dropped it in the baggie, and nodded. "That was with me. And my brother was a baby, not even a year old."

"Your mother must be a very strong woman," he said.

"Thank God she had my grandparents' help. And I appreciate the kind words about my parents. I'll pass them on to my mother."

"I understand she never married again."

It struck me that David knew so much about my family. "Not yet, but she's engaged." *And hopefully her fiancé is safe.*

David stood up. "Well, that's good to hear. Give her my best. Now back to this genetic test. If my DNA matches Toby's then what are the chances that my father is also his father?"

"To be perfectly blunt, if the victim we found in the Charger proves to be your brother, the chance is zero that the two of you have the same father."

"As in impossible?"

"Yes."

David took in a quick breath then released it. "No wonder my dad is tied up in knots. If that's the way it shakes down, that means my mother did something I can't believe she'd do."

"I'm going to run this sample over to our regional crime lab, and we'll get the test results to you as soon as they're done." I fished a business card from my pocket and handed it to David. "Your dad has one, too, but here's another in case you have any questions or if you think of something else. Sometimes when we look back on events as adults—especially the traumatic ones—we have a different perspective and it helps jog a memory."

David took the card and read it. "If I think of something, I'll give you a call. Otherwise, I'll wait to hear from you."

11

I was on pins and needles wondering what Smoke was uncovering at the gas station, but I knew he'd contact me as soon as he could. I phoned the chief deputy and told him I was on my way to the lab with David Fryor's sample.

"Thanks for the update, Sergeant. You think we got enough balls in the air?"

"More than enough to keep us juggling, that's for sure. At least we know they'll all come down, eventually."

"You're right on there. I'll keep hoping that when they land, the outcomes will be good ones and give us the answers we need."

Twenty minutes later, when I was halfway to the crime lab, a message from Smoke appeared on the car's laptop screen. *My cell is charging. It's Denny all right, out of uniform, ball cap on. Got the photos and video. We'll talk later.* I reached over, hit the reply key, typed *OK*, and hit Send.

The sheriff had switched vehicles at his house. There weren't any obvious signs that he'd changed out of his uniform, but if he'd hung up his pants and shirt, or thrown them in the laundry, we might not have noticed that.

However, that begged the question, had he taken the time to remove all the brass—including his badge—that decorated his shirt and then put them away? Where did he store them? I kept mine on top of my dresser or in a drawer, if I was cleaning up. What about his duty belt, and side arm, and handcuffs, and radio? Where did he normally keep all those things?

Where are you, Denny? Mother needs you. Our department needs you.

I shifted my concentration back to driving and the conduct of the other drivers on the road. I arrived at the regional crime lab and submitted David Fryor's DNA sample into evidence. I ran into Ben, the lab's director, on my way out.

"Hi, Sergeant, any word from your sheriff?"

"Not yet. But Detective Dawes is chasing down a possible lead."

"I'll hold good thoughts."

"Thanks. I just turned in the DNA sample from David Fryor to compare it with the one from the male victim in the Charger."

"We'll start running the tests right away."

"Appreciate it." I lifted my hand in a small wave as I turned to leave. "See you, Ben."

Smoke phoned me from his office phone and asked me to meet him at his desk on my return. When I arrived at the sheriff's office, I headed straight to his cubicle. His appearance jarred me for a moment. His face was drawn, and his eyes looked weary when he glanced over the top of his readers. "It's a damn puzzle." He slid a number of photos to my side of the desk.

I sat down and picked them up. The first was of Sheriff Twardy standing by a gas pump, and the next one was him at the service counter handing bills to the clerk. He was wearing a tan T-shirt, what looked like his brown uniform pants, and a Minnesota Twins baseball cap. The other photos were shots of him entering and leaving the service station and taking money out of his wallet. I studied each one, hoping some explanation would jump out at me.

"Here's an enlarged photo." Smoke handed it over.

"That's our sheriff, all right. But he doesn't look like his normal self, at all. His expression is sort of stunned, yet blank-looking at the same time."

"I know. It's the way I think I'd look if I had a bomb strapped to my body. One that was about to go off if I made the wrong move," he said.

That image popped into my mind. "That's a terrifying thought."

"And over the top. Forget I said it."

Like I could do that. I continued to study the sheriff's face in the photo. "It's like he's on drugs, maybe a depressant of some sort. Or a psychotrophic."

"And why would he take either one of them?"

"No clue. Probably not by choice. He's on high blood pressure meds. Suppose he accidentally took an extra dose, it might cause some sort of negative reaction," I said.

"You'd think so. We'll check with his doc and his pharmacy on that one. Have a look at the surveillance videos." He hit a few buttons on his laptop computer then turned it so we could both view the screen. It showed the sheriff first at the gas pump. From what we could see, there were no passengers in his Buick.

"I wonder why he didn't pay at the pump?" I said.

"You'll see why in a minute. He made another purchase."

The video continued with the sheriff walking up to the counter. He pulled out his wallet and then pointed at something behind the clerk. The clerk turned around, selected what turned out to be a pack of Marlboro cigarettes, and laid it on the counter in front of the sheriff. He then paid the clerk, put his wallet in his pocket, picked up the cigarettes, and walked out the door. He got back in his car and drove away.

"That is too crazy. Denny doesn't smoke," I said.

"No, but he did years ago. I did, too. We used to be able to smoke in our squad cars back in the Stone Age. And some nights on dog watch that was about all there was to do."

"Really?" I tried to imagine Denny and Smoke driving around, puffing away. "But why would he be buying cigarettes now?"

"It's got me wondering if there is someone hiding in his car, someone who is holding something over him," he said.

"But what?"

"I have absolutely no idea whatsoever."

"I wish the camera had a wide enough pan to show which direction Denny headed when he drove away. Rockwell is southeast of Oak Lea but the question is, did he continue southeast toward Minneapolis or turn due south toward who knows where?" I said.

"Exactly. At least now we have a new photo of the way he looks out of uniform, wearing a ball cap that we can circulate."

"When are you releasing it to the media?"

"The chief deputy is taking care of that. It should be shortly," Smoke said.

"You haven't called my mother?"

"No, I was waiting on you. Maybe we can get her take on why Denny bought cigarettes."

"That's probably a better question coming from you than from me."

"Maybe so. Change of subject. Did the lab give you any idea when they could run Toby's brother's DNA sample?"

"They were going to get right on it. The nice thing about delivering a cheek swab from a known person is all the time it saves."

Smoke nodded. "That's a given. Way faster than when they have to extract a sample from who knows what and maybe separate it from another person's DNA that might also be present. It can take weeks to get the profile. I would never have the patience those analysts have."

"Me either. It's too painstaking."

"So the test is in the works. Good. When you met Toby's brother, how did he strike you?" Smoke said.

"David? I like him. He's sincere, concerned. It sounds like he didn't do a lot of things with his brother—"

"Not all that unusual in high school, speaking from personal experience." Smoke had two brothers, also.

"He and his father are obviously anxious, wondering what the latest tests will show."

"Of course. Speaking of anxious, I best call Kristen, like I told her I would."

As it turned out, Smoke was the better one to have the conversation with my mother. She made him promise to get a copy of Denny's photo to her as soon as possible. When he asked if Denny had taken up smoking again, her denial was loud enough for me to hear on the other side of his desk. When they'd disconnected, Smoke shook his head. "That did not go very well."

My cell phone rang and when I saw Mother's name on my dial, I answered as cheerfully as possible. "Hi, Mom. You heard from Smoke?"

"Corinne, what on earth could possibly be going on with Denny? Elton told me that he bought a pack of cigarettes at a gas station in Rockwell. *Cigarettes. In Rockwell.*"

"It's strange, all right. But Denny's the one who's driving his car, so we've got that much." I let that sink in. "Mom, I have a question for you. Do you know what med Denny is on for his high blood pressure?"

"As a matter of fact, I do. Why?"

"It's a possibility that his leaving so unexpectedly might be related to the med he's taking."

It took her a minute. "Well yes, I guess it could be. I picked up his prescriptions a few months back, and you know how I remember words once I read them."

It was best, and far faster, to let her work through her explanations without rushing or interrupting her. "Yes, you are gifted that way. You said prescriptions, so there is more than one?"

"He takes two. One is clonidine and the other is metoprolol tartate. They're both for his high blood pressure."

"Can you spell those for me?" I grabbed my memo pad and jotted down the letters as she recited them. "Any idea of what kind of dosages he was on?"

"No. That I didn't pay attention to."

"Okay, well it helps to know what the drugs are. Smoke and I wondered if he could have taken an extra dose by mistake, and it caused his unusual behavior."

"Oh my, that would be a good question to talk to his doctor about."

"What's his doctor's name?"

"Dahlgren."

"Sure, I know him." I'd worked with him on another case a while back.

"How about his pharmacy?"

"Butler Drug Store. But wait a minute. I don't think he could have doubled up on his medications because he has those daily-dose containers, one for morning, and one for night."

"Do you know where he keeps his meds and the containers?"

"They're in his kitchen cupboard, next to the sink."

"Smoke told you that Denny wasn't wearing his uniform. Do you have any idea where he puts his belt, his gun, and all of his brass when he's off-duty?"

"I know he hangs his belt on a hook in his closet. I guess we should have noticed it there." Mother may not have, given her emotional state, but Smoke and I probably would. "And he has a dish for his badge and things on the shelf, right under where the safe is." I mouthed Mother's answers to Smoke as we went along.

We would not have missed a dish full of brass. "Okay, Mom, I have an assignment for you. You have a key and permission to enter Denny's house, so I'd like you go over there and check out his medication situation. Look at the dose containers and his pill bottles. Then double check to see if you can find his uniform and equipment."

"Oh dear, you wonder if his uniform is missing, and you think he took too many pills. I'm worried someone is threatening him, making him do things he wouldn't normally do."

"We don't know that. We're just trying to find out what's going on."

"I'll go over there now. Wish me luck."

"Luck, Mom, and thanks."

I pushed End on my phone, and Smoke closed his laptop. "Maybe one of us should go with Kristen. She might freak out if she finds something," he said.

"I think she'll be fine. She has a specific assignment to concentrate on, and that will keep her imagination at bay," I said.

He moved his head left to right and back again like he did when he considered options. "Ah, hell, I'm going out to the sheriff's. I'll wait outside with the deputy, but will be close by if Kristen comes up with anything."

I smiled, reached over, and gave his hand a squeeze. "Thanks. I'll see if I can get hold of Doctor Dahlgren."

Dr. Dahlgren was gone from the office for the day. I left a message with the receptionist, asking that he call me as soon as possible. She asked if it was an emergency, and I mentally threw the question around in my mind. "No, but it's important."

I phoned Butler Drug Store next, and when I got their voicemail saying they closed at 6:00 p.m., I realized it was getting late. Another day was winding down. The sheriff's name on the letterhead of a sheet of stationary caught my eye. I took in a deep breath then let it out slowly. The videos of him buying gas—and cigarettes—gave us a sense of renewed hope, as strange as it was. We knew he was alive and driving his Buick two days before. I had to believe he was safe, wherever he was.

I bent over and retrieved my briefcase from the floor and set it on the desk. Earlier in the day, I'd stuck the list of my mother's classmates, and their contact information, into a side pocket. I found the pages and pulled them out. Lots of familiar names, some I knew from growing up in Oak Lea. Others were friends my mother kept in touch with and talked about, and still others were from their official interviews after Toby and Wendy disappeared all those years ago.

The list wasn't complete, according to Mother. There were members of the class who had moved away after graduation and had never returned to Oak Lea to anyone's knowledge. I found Dana English Smyth's information at the bottom of the first page. I tried her home phone and a woman who sounded like she was smiling answered, "Smyth residence."

"Hello, is this Missus Smyth? Dana?"

"Yes it is. Is this a sales call?" she said.

"No, ma'am. I'm Sergeant Corinne Aleckson with the Winnebago County Sheriff's Department."

"Oh sure, Carl and Kristen's daughter." The identifier I could count on from those who knew my parents.

"Correct."

"You sound just like your mother."

"I do?" Maybe the way she sounded when she was younger.

"Oh my gosh, Corinne, Winnebago County is all over the news. And Toby's Charger getting pulled out of Whitetail Lake has gone viral on YouTube."

"I've heard that."

"I can't believe it. I've talked to a few of our old friends, and none of us can believe it. Not one of us."

"It falls in the realm of the unbelievable, that's for sure."

"And so tragic," she said.

"It is. Dana, I was wondering if you have some time, either tonight or tomorrow, when we can get together and talk." Smoke was watching over my mother, so I had no immediate worries there.

"Can I ask why?"

"We're going over the old files, sorting things out, and touching base again with some of the classmates and friends."

"I don't know what more I can tell you now than I told the detectives back then."

"The information is different now. We actually have some."

"I suppose that does change things. All right, well sure, I'm free for the rest of the night. Tomorrow is busy with work, and then I have an evening meeting."

"Tonight works for me. I can be there in forty minutes, or so."

"Are you in Oak Lea now?" she said.

"Yes, at the sheriff's office."

"I hate to make you drive all the way to Maple Grove. We could meet somewhere in between."

"Thanks, but it's just as easy for me to drive there. I'll see you soon."

"Okay."

After I hung up, I phoned Smoke. "Anything happening out at Twardy's place?"

"Not yet. I just got here and Ortiz, the deputy keeping watch, tells me Kristen went into the house four minutes ago," he said.

"Good. I couldn't get hold of either the doctor or the pharmacy, so looks like it'll be tomorrow when I talk to them."

"We don't know that Denny's behavior has anything to do with his meds anyhow."

"True. I did talk to Dana English Smyth, and I'll be on my way shortly to meet her."

"That was quick. Good, and say 'hi' for me."

"The way you lowered and softened your tone tells me she was more than just one of your high school classmates," I said in a teasing tone.

"No, she was very cute, and I may have had a crush on her for a couple of years, but that's the extent of it."

"All righty then, I'll be sure to send her your love."

"Sometimes, little lady." He tried to sound upset, but I knew there was a smile on his face.

We hung up, and I felt a stab of jealousy. Not because of the girls Smoke had liked, or dated, or loved, or the ones who'd pursued him in the past. What bothered me was I felt cheated out of all the years he'd lived before I'd known him. I couldn't imagine what my life would be like without Elton Dawes.

I was nearly to Maple Grove when Smoke called me back.

"Your mother is a basket case. After she got done exploring the sheriff's house, I followed her to your gramps' house to be sure she got there safely."

Oh Lord. "So it didn't go so well at the sheriff's?"

"Suffice it to say what she found was as puzzling as what she didn't find."

"Smoke—"

"Okay. First the meds: his pill bottles were missing. They were not in the cupboard he keeps them in, nor were they in any of the other cupboards, or drawers in the kitchen, or bathrooms, or bedrooms. His daily-dose containers, however, were in the cupboard and they were empty. Kristen saw me sitting in the driveway and waved me in. I helped look, and even checked the trash containers, but there was no sign of the bottles anywhere."

"What does that mean? That someone really did abduct him, but he somehow convinced them to let him get his meds first?"

"I don't know. The video at the gas station indicated Denny was alone."

"Maybe someone *was* hiding in the back seat of his car, or in a nearby car, watching him. Maybe he did have a bomb strapped to him."

"Slow down here. We know the chance of that is slim to none. But let's say Denny had someone nearby somehow controlling his actions, what would be their reason to do that? It'd have to be very compelling."

"We'll have to think more about that one. Back to what Mom did, and didn't, find."

"Meds, no. Med case, yes. His uniform, duty belt, sidearm, and brass, no."

"Really? It looked like he was wearing his uniform pants. But what could he have done with the rest of his things? Especially his Glock?"

"I talked to Chief Deputy Kenner, and he's finishing writing the search warrant he started this morning. After seeing the video of the sheriff, and his odd behavior at the gas station, not to mention the open safe minus the money, and now the latest on the meds and missing uniform, he got a hold of Judge Buchanan who agreed to sign it."

"Buchanan?" I said.

"Yeah, since he lives in Oak Lea. Kenner was supposed to meet with Judge Adams this morning, but Adams had to cancel. Adams lives an hour away, and Kenner decided time is of the essence."

"No offense to Kenner, but it's about time."

"I couldn't agree more. I'm pulling into the office parking lot now, and I'll likely be the one who runs over to Buchanan's house for the signature. Then I'll head back to Twardy's house with a couple of deputies."

"All right, I'm almost at Dana's house, and I'll check in with you when I'm done there."

"Copy that."

12

Dana Smyth looked several years older than my mother, most likely from spending much more time in the sun. It was impossible she could be more of a worrier. Her hair was its natural color, and the short cut, silver-gray frame around her face was becoming. Before I set foot in the door, she drew me into her arms like we were old friends. "Don't tell your mother, but you are even more gorgeous than either of your parents. It must be the combination that makes you so striking."

I didn't think of myself as striking and certainly not better-looking than either my mother or my father. Still it was a nice thing for her to say. "Um, I won't. Thank you."

"Come in and have a cup of herbal tea. I have some steeping."

I smiled. "That sounds good."

"My husband is playing racquetball at the club, so we've got the house to ourselves."

I followed Dana into the kitchen and she directed me to sit down while she poured tea in my cup. The smell of fruit tickled my nose. "Blueberry and pomegranate," she said.

That sounded like a health drink to me. "Thanks."

"I know you have some questions, but I've been wondering since you called what it's like for you, working on a case of something that happened before you were born."

I thought back to another, not-quite-as-old-cold case we'd solved a few years earlier. "There's not an easy answer to that. I feel driven to get answers, mainly so the families have closure. It's like all our cases, all the crimes we try to solve. The time that's passed with this case puts us at a major disadvantage. It's tough to locate key people. Some have moved away, others have died."

"I can't imagine. So tell me what's it like working with my old friend, Elton Dawes?" she said.

I hadn't expected that. "Detective Dawes? What can I say? He's the best."

Dana studied my face. "Hmm. The way you said that makes me think you're referring to more than just your working relationship."

I was under Dana's microscope and squirmed ever so slightly. "No comment."

"Smoke broke some hearts back when. If he still has the power to turn the head of a young woman like you, I'd say he's still got it."

Dana's observations warmed me by several degrees. "I've noticed he does turn women's heads, older ones, younger ones, and in-betweeners."

She giggled. "I understand, Corinne. And you don't have to say any more."

My shoulders lifted in a small shrug. "We're not dating, each other, or anyone else." Why was I over-explaining?

Dana raised her eyebrows and nodded. "I'm surprised he never married. A shame, really. It seems to me he's still looking for the right woman."

He thought he'd found the right woman years ago, but she wouldn't commit. "I almost forgot, he said to say 'hi' to you."

She smiled and a day-dreamy look crossed her face.

It was time to redirect the conversation from personal to professional. "Dana, the reason I wanted to talk to you is we're trying to get some answers about what happened the week or so before Homecoming."

"The week before?" She frowned and gave her teacup a swirl. "Let me think. There were all kinds of activities. Like a dress-up day, different contests. Of course the Coronation was the night before the big game. Like what kind of information are you looking for?"

Anything and everything, like the Coronation. "Tell me about the king and queen candidates."

"You know your parents were crowned, right?"

"I do." Mother had once told me how surprised my dad was getting crowned, and how debonair he looked that night.

Dana wiggled her shoulders. "Elton and Wendy were the first prince and princess."

Several of the classmates had noted that Wendy had been a princess when they'd been questioned at the time of the disappearance. I remember looking at the photo of the royalty in my mother's yearbook when I was a kid, but until I read classmates' comments in the file I'd forgotten who the runners-up were. I'd known who Smoke was growing up, but had only seen him a few times prior to starting my career with Winnebago County eight years earlier.

"I was named second princess, and a boy named Ron Hanken was second prince."

It was easy to picture Dana as a bubbly, popular teen. "What about Toby Fryor? I wonder why he wasn't selected as one of the royalty. By all accounts he was a star athlete, popular."

"He was one of the candidates, but he wasn't crowned," she said.

"Mmm, yet his girlfriend was. How do you suppose that sat with a guy who was known to have a temper?"

Dana's frown lines deepened. "I'm sure with his ego he thought he had it in the bag. He'd be king and Wendy would be queen."

"A big disappointment for him, I'm sure."

Dana tapped her finger on her saucer for a moment, then leaned her face in toward mine like she was about to share a secret. "There is something that happened the weekend before Homecoming that I wondered about at the time. And to tell you the truth, I pretty much put it out of my mind."

"What was that?"

"I saw Wendy with a boy from the cities. She was flirting with him."

That drew my attention. "Where'd you see them?"

"Downtown Oak Lea, at the old soda fountain. Back when Butler Drug had one."

"Can you tell me more about that?"

"I'd stopped by the drugstore to pick up a few things and spotted Wendy sitting at the counter, so I headed over to say 'hi.' Right about then, she reached over and gave the boy's hand a squeeze, and that kind of surprised me."

"Because she was dating Toby?" I said.

"That, and the fact that I'd never seen the boy before. I wondered who he could be. And there Wendy was, acting like she and the boy were close, like they were there together," Dana said.

"Did you talk to her?"

"Sure, and she introduced me to the boy, but I can't remember his name. It might have been Sean. No, it seemed like it was more different than that. I shouldn't even say. Anyway, he was a friend of another boy from the cities who used to come out to Oak Lea to stay with his grandfather. . ." Dana's face lit up like someone flipped on a switch, "who lived on Whitetail Lake. Oh my gosh!"

My heart picked up its pace. "Do you remember the grandson's name?"

"That I do remember, it was Rudy something or other. Oh no, do you think Toby and Wendy were at a party at the old farmhouse on Homecoming night, and accidentally drove into the lake?" Her eyebrows lifted.

"No, I'm sure that's not what happened. We know Toby's car went down the hill from that farm into Whitetail Lake. But we also know the kids did not die accidentally."

Dana reached over and grabbed my hand. "Get out of here! Then what happened?"

I spoke in a gentle tone. "This hasn't been released to the public yet, but they were victims of homicide. Their bodies were put in the Charger, and then the car was pushed into the lake."

Dana's hands flew to the back of her neck, planted there, and then her fingers dug in and massaged it. "They were *killed*? Like murdered?"

"That's the way it looks," I said.

"That's the saddest thing I've ever heard." Her voice cracked.

I gave her a moment then said, "Dana, back to Wendy and the boy she was flirting with. I've gotten some information about Rudy, but this is the first I've heard of another boy from the cities, a friend of Rudy's. Did you talk to Wendy about him, ask more about him?"

"No. She was a pretty big flirt, and I thought I'd leave well enough alone. I didn't say anything to anyone about it, actually."

"Did you hear about a party at the Williams' farm on Homecoming night?"

She shook her head. "No I didn't. I was at the farm with friends a couple of times before that though. But we never stayed long. I didn't like beer. Still don't."

I glanced up at the clock on the wall. It was closing in on seven thirty. "It was good meeting you and I appreciate the information. If you think of anything else, you'll give me a call?" I pulled a card from my pocket and put it on the table.

"Of course. Oh, and I wanted to tell you, I hope your sheriff is okay. When it hit the news, someone told me Kristen was dating him."

"Mom is actually engaged to Dennis Twardy, so she's pretty distraught at this point."

"Kristen's engaged?" She paused for a few seconds. "Oh my gosh, she must be frantic wondering what's happened to him."

"Definitely."

We stood up, and Dana gave me another hug. "You give that mother of yours my love, and tell her I hope her fiancé will return home safely very soon. It's been a lifetime since your dad died."

Longer ago than *my* lifetime. "We've got a good team working to find him. Including Detective Dawes."

She smiled. "And as for Elton, give him an extra squeeze."

I nodded and didn't ask for clarification about the "extra" part.

After I'd gotten in my car and started the engine, I pulled out my phone to see who had called me when I was meeting with Dana. The two I'd expected: Mother and Smoke. My mother most likely would need a more in-depth conversation, so I phoned Smoke first.

"I have the warrant in hand, and I grabbed Weber and Zubinski, since they were both available. We'll be at Twardy's house in six, seven minutes."

"Thank you, Judge Buchanan." I spoke my thoughts out loud. "Smoke, have you talked to Mom lately?"

"Nah, I want to keep her in the loop, but not in too tight."

"I totally understand. She's my next call, so we'll see how that goes."

"And how was your meeting with Dana?" he said.

"Productive. She remembered something that she didn't think to tell the detectives back then: Wendy was flirting with a friend of Rudy Medlin's at Butler's the Saturday before Homecoming."

"Wendy was flirting? That's not much of a news flash."

"No, but—"

"It's a friend of Rudy's and another possible lead. Did Dana know his name?"

"She couldn't remember it. She said maybe Sean, but that didn't seem right to her. She thought it was more unusual than that."

"An unnamed friend of Rudy's."

"And since Rudy is missing and Wendy is dead and we don't know the boy's name, we can't ask him if there was anything special about the encounter at the drugstore."

"We'll ask our new best buddy Harry Gimler if he remembers him."

"Right."

"Dana said Toby thought he and Wendy would be crowned king and queen. And he didn't get picked for anything."

"If you're thinking Toby was mad at your dad, or me, or Ron Hanken for winning something he wanted, I sure didn't know about it."

"Any idea where Ron is now?"

"It's been years, but last I heard he was in Minneapolis."

"Okay, he'd be a good one to talk to. Oh, and Dana asked me to give you something."

Smoke didn't answer right away. "Really? Good or bad?"

"I'd like to think it's good."

"But you're not going to tell me?" he said.

"I'll give it to you when I see you."

"I'm pulling into Twardy's driveway, so I'll catch you later."

After we hung up, I drew in a cleansing breath and dialed Gramps' home number.

"Hello?"

It caught me by surprise to hear Gramps' voice instead of my mother's. "Oh hi, how is everything?"

"Just fine, fine. If you're looking for your mother, I sent her to bed. She was plain tuckered out but nervous as a cat, so I gave her one of those sleeping pills my doctor gave me. Don't tell him I did that though. I don't think it's legal."

"Okay." I was still processing that Gramps had "sent" my mother to bed and she had actually gone.

"She's in there snoring away," he said.

"Mother doesn't snore."

"Stop over, and hear for yourself."

"I believe you."

"I wouldn't be surprised if she sleeps for twelve hours."

"That'd be a very good thing. Thanks for taking care of her, Gramps."

"No need to thank me. She'll always be my little girl, no matter how old she gets."

"Do you need anything?"

"I don't need a thing. Oh, and I prit' near forgot. Your Grandma Aleckson called. She and your grandpa are closing up their Arizona home for the summer and will be on their way back to Oak Lea. With all this hoopla going on, they said they'd rather be here. They should get here by Saturday."

Hopefully the sheriff would be back by then. In any case, it'd be more support for Mother. And for me. "I'm glad. Thanks, Gramps."

"You're welcome. Good night, Corky."

I drove back to Oak Lea mulling over the things that had fallen in our laps, from the recovered vehicle holding the remains of two young people missing for all those years, to the surprises the investigation had uncovered so far. And worse yet, the sheriff had gone missing the same day as that discovery. He'd emptied his safe and bought cigarettes at a gas station. Even though he didn't smoke. Were his unusual actions a way of leaving clues for our detectives to figure out? But why, and how?

When I got to town, instead of heading home, I drove south to Sheriff Denny Twardy's house. I waved at the deputy standing by his car, keeping watch over the place. Three Winnebago County squad cars—two marked and Smoke's unmarked—were parked in the driveway. Light spilled out from the windows in the main area of the house. I picked my portable radio from the center console and depressed the call button. "Six oh eight to Three forty."

"Three forty," Smoke said.

"I've arrived at your location."

"Copy."

I wasn't on-duty, but telling him over the radio alerted both Smoke and Communications of my whereabouts at the same time. I got out of my car and took in a whiff of the cool, calm air. There was a faint odor of dry leaves burning, a familiar smell in both autumn and spring, and one I'd relished since childhood.

Vince Weber met me at the front door. "Hey, Sergeant, do you work around the clock nowadays or what?"

I said, "Or what," and gave his bicep a light jab.

"Figured as much. Dawes and Zubinski are in the garage searching the sheriff's squad car with a fine tooth comb."

Weber and I headed to the attached garage. The trunk and all the doors on the sheriff's unmarked Ford Taurus were wide open. Amanda Zubinski was standing near the trunk, and Smoke was using a lint roller on the leather of the back seat.

He glanced at me over his readers and held up the roller. He hadn't collected much of anything that I could see. "The man is immaculate. If anything has been in the back seat of this car since it was cleaned—anything at all, much less a person—I'd be very surprised. We haven't picked up one single hair, as impossible as that seems."

"I know he has it detailed regularly," I said.

"He's got a topnotch detailer, that's for damn sure." Smoke eased out of his bent-over position, stood up straight, stretched his shoulders backward then released them.

"It's safe to say no one was in either his front passenger seat, or the back seat, since Sheriff had it cleaned," Zubinski said.

"So no one besides the sheriff was in this car when he drove it home and switched to his personal vehicle?" I said.

Smoke nodded. "That is the way it appears."

"What about in his house, did you uncover anything new?"

"We didn't find anything that would indicate he was being threatened or was taken against his will. We dusted his safe for prints, and it looks like they all belong to the same person, but we'll get that verified. And we've got a few phone numbers to check out. Mandy?" Smoke said and looked at Zubinski.

"Yes, we checked his Caller ID from the past two weeks and wrote down all the phone numbers. Most were eight hundreds. Then on Tuesday, there were a ton of calls from people in the sheriff's department and from your mother, Sergeant. Then there were three others we had questions about. We'll find out who they belong to and why they called," Zubinski said.

"Good," I said.

"We took a look at his laptop, and I don't think he uses it much. Nothing oddball showed up in his search engines. Some sheriff's association stuff, that's about it," Weber said.

"Our sheriff has a love-hate relationship with computers, and the world wide web. No surprise that he doesn't spend much time on search engines." Smoke scanned the garage then brought his attention back to the vehicle. "We can close her down for the night."

We all pitched in, shutting the doors and trunk of the Ford, then Smoke turned off the garage lights as we headed into the house. Zubinski held up an empty evidence bag. "The good and bad news is we didn't find anything to put in here."

Smoke nodded. "Well, thanks team. You can take off, and I'll lock up."

Weber and Zubinski said their goodbyes and left. I stayed behind to update Smoke, but Dr. Dahlgren phoned me before I did. "Sergeant, I just picked up my messages," he said.

"Thanks for calling me back, Doctor. It's about Dennis Twardy. I'm sure you've heard he's missing."

"Yes, of course."

"I have a medication question, and I know you're his prescribing doctor."

"Maybe the best way to handle this is if you ask the question first, and I'll determine if my answer would violate HIPAA laws."

"Doctor, this is an open investigation so I think you'd be fine, but you know more about that than I do. Detective Dawes is here with me, and I'd like to put you on speaker phone, if that's okay."

Dahlgren cleared his throat. "That's fine."

I hit the speaker button and positioned my cell phone so both Smoke and I could hear. Then I continued, "Our question is . . ." I pulled my memo pad from my breast pocket with my free hand and located the page I needed. "Oh, and I should tell you the reason for my question first. We know that Sheriff Twardy is taking clonidine and metoprolol tartate, if I'm saying them right. His pill bottles are missing from his house, but his dose containers are still there. He has one for the morning pills and one for evening. Both of them are empty.

"Anyway, we found out today that the sheriff stopped for gas in Rockwell about an hour or so after he was last seen in his office. We watched the video of him there at the pumps and in the store. He didn't look like himself. It was like he was drugged. Plus, he bought cigarettes, but he doesn't smoke. So here's the question, if he had taken an extra dose of those drugs, what effect would they have on him?" I said.

"Generally—not specifically speaking about one particular individual—when patients take such medications, they build up in their systems over time. What that means is an overdose the first week of being on them may be more serious than after they'd been on them for years." He paused for another brief throat-clearing. "What happens in a clonidine overdose? Depending on the level, it depresses the central nervous system to a degree, causes drowsiness. The person's reflexes would decrease; he'd be weaker."

"That sounds a lot like how the sheriff acted. What about the other one?"

"Metoprolol tartrate is a beta blocker, and an overdose would cause bradycardia—"

I interrupted, "Which is?"

"A very slow heart beat. Also, hypotension, the opposite of hypertension, and possibly cardiac failure."

"So an extra dose of either, or both, drugs is not a good thing," I said.

"No."

Smoke chimed in, "Doc, would you take a look at the video of the sheriff and give us your opinion of whether you think he might have done that?"

"I'd be happy to, but even without medical treatment, an extra dose would be out of his system long before now."

"And he should have been back to normal when it was," I said.

"I'd say so."

"I still think it'd be good if you'd have a look-see when you can," Smoke said.

I mouthed the words, "I can email it to him," to Smoke and he nodded.

"Doctor, our sergeant here will send you the video, if we can get your email address."

"My, well, I guess that makes it easy." He rattled off his address, and I jotted it down then repeated it back to him to be sure it was correct. It was.

"It'll be just a few minutes," I said.

"That's not a problem. I'm home, and I'll turn on my laptop."

"Thank you. Will you give me a call after you've watched it?" I said.

"I'll do that, Sergeant." Then we disconnected.

I checked my phone for the time. "No wonder my stomach has been talking to me. It's almost nine."

Smoke tilted his head. "Yeah, another late dinner of canned soup. Maybe."

I accessed my email account on the phone and forwarded the video attachment I'd downloaded earlier to Dr. Dahlgren. "Hope the doctor has some insights for us after he sees this."

"That'd be mighty fine. Corky, getting back to that boy, Rudy Medlin's friend that Dana saw with Wendy. That must have struck her if she brought it up now."

"I agree. I hope Harry knows him and remembers his name."

"Yup. You said Dana had something for me."

I let out a joking chuckle, and before he could stop me, I slid my arms under his, and drew him close to me in as tight a hug as the gear on my service belt would allow. "There you go, that's from Dana." I started to pull away then I felt Smoke's hands pressing into my back.

"Somehow, it will all work out," he whispered into my hair, close to my ear. Then he released his hold.

I stepped back and studied his face, sensing he was referring to something more personal than the two cases we were working on. I wanted to believe it was an indication I was breaking down his defenses after all. The glint in his eyes, before he blinked and looked away gave me a glimmer of hope.

13

I was driving home when Dr. Dahlgren got back to me.

"Sergeant, from what I observed, it is possible Dennis Twardy took an extra dose of his medications. His affect is rather flat, and that's consistent with a depressed central nervous system. Since he doesn't smoke, all I can think is that he bought the cigarettes for someone else," he said.

But who would that be? "So, it's your opinion he could have overdosed on his meds?"

"It's possible, but there again, it's only an opinion based on a minute or two of him captured on camera, and not examining him in person."

"I understand, and I really appreciate your help, Doctor."

"Sure. Let me know if there's anything else I can do."

After we'd disconnected, I phoned Smoke with the doctor's report, and then continued on my drive home. I lived only a few miles from the office in downtown Oak Lea, but it seemed to take forever to get there. As I passed Gramps' house, I noticed it was dark inside and prayed Mother and Gramps would get the long, quiet rest they needed.

Queenie barked from her kennel when she heard the garage door open. She was used to my oddball schedule, and had developed patience for the times I was gone, but when I returned, the dickens came out of her for those first minutes.

The previous autumn, I'd had a fenced area added in the back of the garage, with a doggie door that opened to her outdoor kennel. I found a heated dog house that not only kept her warm in the winter, but also gave her a comforting shelter, despite the weather. Not that I liked spoiling her or anything.

Queenie was giddy with joy when I opened the gate on the kennel, and I reminded her not to jump on me. She'd snagged a couple of my uniforms and a few other pairs of pants in the past. Instead, I knelt down and gave her a big hug. She whimpered with delight as I scratched behind her ears.

"Race you to the end of the driveway?" Queenie barked and waited until I stood up, maybe thinking she was giving me a fighting chance. Between my fairly heavy gear, work shoes, and exhausted body, I'd need a better head start than that.

My driveway was a tenth of a mile long, and Queenie reached Brandt Avenue before I was three quarters of the way there. She ran a few circles, and jumped around like she was cheering me on. When I caught up to her, she took off for the house, leaving me in the dust. It was dark, the moon a mere sliver in the sky. A few stars twinkled between clouds. The run toward the road, with the light from the house on my back, felt safer than the other way around, and I nearly beat Queenie in my sprint for the safety of my home.

I pushed the button to close the garage door, and as I stepped into my kitchen, my work cell phone rang. "Sergeant Aleckson."

"Hi, Corinne, it's Dana Smyth."

"Hello."

"Ever since you left my house, I've been going over and over the afternoon in Butler's Drug. You know at the soda fountain with Wendy and that boy? I finally did a meditative thing and let my mind completely relax. And I remembered the boy's name. Shelly. I knew it was different."

"Shelly."

"Short for Sheldon. When Wendy introduced us, she said this is Sheldon, but then she called him Shelly after that."

"That's a big help, thank you. But no last name?"

"No, not that I recall. But I'll work on it some more. Maybe I can coax it out of this old brain of mine."

The next morning dawned clear and bright, and I woke up feeling rested. I stretched and smiled then a heavy cloud descended when I remembered our missing leader. I tossed back the covers, and Queenie sprung up from her rug beside my bed.

I bent over and ruffled her fur. "I need to go on a long run, further than you can manage yet, but you can come with me for the first part." I pulled on running gear while Queenie sat by patiently, wagging her tail. After I'd let her outside to take care of business and run off some energy, I grabbed my Smith and Wesson and cell phone, and clipped them to the waistband of my pants. I'd carried a compact .38 caliber S&W Special revolver with me on runs since I'd been attacked, kidnapped, and almost killed two years before. I didn't live in fear that anything close to that would happen again, but having a weapon on my person gave me the assurance that it was there if I needed it.

Minutes later we were jogging down Brandt towards Gramps' house, and when I said, "Gramps," Queenie strained at her leash to get there faster. "Hey, slow down or I'll run out of gas." I gave her leash a gentle tug.

When we arrived at the house, Mother and Gramps were sitting at the kitchen table drinking coffee with the leftover remnants of their breakfast in front of them.

Gramps' face lit up when he saw Queenie. "There she is." Queenie trotted over, happily accepting his attention. He shared a special bond with my dog.

"Hi, dear, hi, Queenie," Mother said. Her face was serene, and not what I'd expected.

"Hi, Gramps. Mom, you looked relaxed."

She smiled. "I'm at peace."

Okay. "You're at peace?"

"Yes, when I woke up this morning I felt at peace with whatever we need to face."

The woman looked like my mother and sounded like my mother, but I'd never heard the words, "I'm at peace," leave her lips in the middle of a crisis. Or at any other time that I could remember. Last night she was a wreck, and now she was at peace. If it was the sleeping pill Gramps had given her, then my vote would be for her to get the same prescription. I didn't want to break the moment, so I smiled.

"Can I make you some breakfast, Corinne?" she said

"Thanks, no. I'd like to go for a run, and I was hoping my doggie could hang out here."

Gramps gave Queenie a small piece of buttery toast. "That's just fine," he said.

I sat down across from Mother. "We've gotten a little more info about Denny."

She tensed a bit. "What is it?"

I told her that a search of the sheriff's vehicle and a deeper look at the things in his house had all but ruled out that he'd been taken against his will. Then I shared Dr. Dahlgren's opinion that Denny may have taken an extra dose of his medications, and that's what had caused his strange appearance at the gas station.

Mother pursed her lips then relaxed them. "That's why I have to trust God in all of this."

I reached across the table and laid my hand on hers. "So what does your day look like?"

"I'm going to the shop. Working is good therapy for me. And Gramps needs a break from me."

Gramps lifted a hand and waved it back and forth. "Now, now, Kristen, that's not true."

"Oh, and I met Dana Smyth last night. She sends her love," I said.

Mother's lips turned up a bit. "How is she doing?"

"Good, as far as I know. She told me something curious. A week before Homecoming, she saw Wendy at Butler's Drug with a friend of Rudy Medlin's. A boy by the name of Sheldon, Shelly for short. And they were acting pretty friendly, from what Dana said."

"A week before Homecoming? If Wendy was with a boy besides Toby, I'm surprised it wasn't all over school," Mother said.

"Dana said she didn't talk to Wendy or anyone else about it. She'd basically forgotten about it."

"I can see Dana keeping something like that to herself. She never was much of a gossip. One of the things I always respected about her."

"So you don't remember a boy from the cities named Shelly hanging around?" I said.

Mother shook her head. "No."

I stood up. "I better get moving so I can get ready for work myself."

"If you want to leave Queenie here for the day, that'd be fine with me," Gramps said.

I gave him a hug. My own doggie daycare. "That'd be great. I've been working some long hours, and she would love spending the day with you."

I left Gramps' house and continued my run down Brandt Avenue. After I reached County Road 35, I turned left. As I approached Whitetail Lake, I saw a late-model Mercedes sitting on the shoulder with what looked like a lone occupant in the driver's seat. When I got closer, a man got out and hung his arm on the open door.

It was David Fryor. "I thought that was you, Sergeant. You're an early morning exerciser, I see."

"Sometimes, at least. I've got to work it in when I can." I pointed at his car. "Nice ride you've got."

"It's a rental I picked up at the airport. But it's what I drive at home, and I find it easier knowing where everything is," he said.

"I get that. Are you here thinking about your brother?" I said.

He nodded. "I watched the clip on YouTube of Toby's Charger getting pulled out. A buddy told me about it. I've just been sitting here, thinking about the circumstances. If someone had seen the car go into the lake back then, the last thirty-some years would have been very different for our family. My parents probably would have stayed together. And the sheriff's department might have had a chance to solve the murders."

"David, it's true that solving the crime after this much time is a long shot. But we're working on it, and something may pop."

He thought a moment and nodded. "How's your mother doing?"

"Better. Actually, she said she woke up this morning feeling more at peace. I hope the sheriff turns up soon so we can all feel that way."

David smiled. "I hope so."

"And what about your dad?" I said.

"He's putting up a brave front. Wade, my other brother, has been trying to decide if he should try to make the trip home or not. He broke his ankle a while ago, and it's been giving him problems. He had trouble navigating at the airports when he came back for our mother's funeral. But he talks to Dad a few times a day and offers support from afar," he said.

I smiled. "Well, I better get moving."

"Have a good run."

I fell back into my jogging pace and was about half a mile from Smoke's driveway when the man himself pulled over and parked. He rolled down his window, and I halted my run once again.

"You're full of energy this morning, little lady," he said.

"It helps that I slept like a rock. And so you know, Dana Smyth remembered Rudy's friend's name. Sheldon, but he went by Shelly. Dana called me last night when she thought of it."

"Sheldon, but no last name to go with it?"

"No last name. Maybe Harry Gimler knows."

"You're being optimistic."

"Hopeful. I'm planning to pay him another visit this morning. He may come through with something one of these days."

"Eternally optimistic."

"Ha. I just had a chat with David Fryor. He's sitting by Whitetail Lake in a Mercedes."

"Well, I may have to stop by, see how he's doing."

"I'm sure he'd appreciate it."

"Back in high school, he was a nice kid and a fine athlete in his own right."

"He gives off good vibes, probably one of the things that helped him build a successful business," I said.

Smoke nodded. "His dad said it was software, right?"

"Right. Are you on your way to the office?"

"Yeah, I want to get a jump on the day. That and I couldn't sleep thinking about Denny and his odd behavior. I'm going to spend some more time on the gas station video, see if we missed anything."

"See you later then."

It took some seconds before I hit my stride again. I ran another half mile then turned around and crossed the road for the return trip. There was a vehicle parked by Whitetail Lake, and it was not one I recognized. If Smoke had caught up with David, it couldn't have been a very long visit, because neither one was there now. As I got closer, I saw it was a white midsize Chevy SUV with one person in the driver's seat. Either he was about to go fishing, or he was one of the scores who had come to stare at the spot where two kids had been buried for all those years.

My eyes naturally moved to the house on the hill, and I thought of the man who lived there. Harry Gimler was a key to the past, but the information he'd so far provided was sketchy at best. I had more questions for him with the hope he had the answers.

As I passed the Chevy, the driver turned and looked at me. His eyebrows went up, like he recognized me, but then he turned away without further acknowledgment. I would have described him as either an old hippie, or the stereotypical mountain man. Bushy gray beard and longer hair pulled into a ponytail. He was wearing glasses. There was something vaguely familiar about him, but I couldn't place him. I'd dealt with countless people over the years, and some were more memorable than others.

An hour later, I sat across from Harry Gimler in his living room and studied his reaction to my questions. And that brought more to mind.

"Harry, I've got a name to run by you. I talked to someone yesterday who mentioned a friend of Rudy's who had been in Oak Lea the week before the Dodge Charger plunged into Whitetail Lake from your grandfather's farm here."

He noticeably flinched then blinked. "Oh?"

"Sheldon."

A muscle twitched under his eye. "Sheldon?"

"Also known as Shelly."

Harry's eyebrows joined together in a frown. "I met him."

"Tell me about that."

"Not much to tell. He was here one weekend with Rudy. Seemed like a nice enough guy."

"Just one weekend?"

"That I know of."

"The weekend before Homecoming?"

"I couldn't say."

Couldn't or wouldn't? "Did Sheldon live in St. Paul?"

"Probably, if he wasn't from Oak Lea."

"But you don't know that for a fact."

"No."

"So tell me, what high school did Rudy go to in St. Paul?"

"Highland Park Senior High."

"But you don't know if Sheldon did?"

"No."

After jotting Highland Park in my notebook, I looked up. "You mentioned your one aunt did most of the searching for Rudy. What's her name, her contact information?"

"I don't think she can help you much."

"We won't know that until I talk to her."

He reluctantly said, "Annette Jenry, like Henry with a J. She lives in South Dakota." Then he gave up her phone number.

I settled in at my desk in the sergeants' office armed with more ammunition than I'd had the day before. I phoned Harry's aunt, but there was no answer and no voicemail. So I tried the regional crime lab and asked for Ben.

"Sergeant Aleckson, we're making progress on the DNA test," he reported.

"That's good to hear. It's a lot to ask, but I was hoping to have an answer for the Fryors before the weekend."

"The test is with the reviewer now."

"That's amazing."

"Genetic testing is generally a faster process, as you know. It saves a good week when we don't have to pull a sample from a piece of evidence. That's why we were able to get those other profiles done in less than forty-eight hours. After the case turned into a double homicide, and the twists that the male victim is not related to Darwin Fryor, we moved it up in the queue. We all appreciate what it means for your office—and the family in particular."

"That's for sure. It's not easy for the Fryors, wondering whether or not the boy is really their son, their brother."

"That'd be rough. We didn't rush the tests, of course, but things went smoothly. Extracting the DNA from the rest of the cell took about an hour, cleaning it was two, and the next four steps took a total of just under ten hours. One of our techs starts at six in the morning, and she finished the analysis and interpretation this morning. So it's almost a wrap. I'll call you when the reviewer finishes up."

"Kudos to you and your staff."

"Thanks, I'll pass that along to them."

14

I tried Annette Jenry's number again. There was still no answer, so I looked up Highland Park Senior High School and was speaking with Marge in the office a minute later.

"You're looking for a student that attended here thirty-three years ago?" she said.

"Yes, as part of a homicide investigation." I told her about the recovered vehicle and the human remains inside.

"Of course, I saw it on the news. Did you say *homicide* investigation?"

"Yes ma'am."

"And you think students from *Highland* were involved?" she said.

"Not necessarily, but we're checking out everyone we know who had a connection to the farm where the vehicle entered the lake. I'm trying to locate a friend of one of your students from back then. The student's name was Rudy Medlin. I don't have his friend's last name, but his first name is Sheldon."

"Sheldon, hmm. Not overly common, at least. Let me check on it, and I'll get back to you. But it'll be this afternoon because I'm going into a meeting in a minute. And you said the other boy was Rudy Medlin?" she said.

"That's correct. His cousin told me Rudy got into some trouble back then. Since you're pulling records, it'd be helpful if you'd take a look at Rudy's file, see if there is anything important to note."

"I'll do that, Sergeant. What's a good number to reach you at?"

I gave her my cell phone number, thanked her, and we said our goodbyes. The third time I phoned Annette Jenry was a charm.

I was greeted by a cheery, matronly voice. "Hello?"

"Hello, Ms. Jenry. This is Sergeant Corinne Aleckson with the Winnebago County Sheriff's Department, in Minnesota."

"Who is this?"

After I repeated myself, she said, "Winnebago is my home county. I grew up on a farm outside of Oak Lea." Was it possible she hadn't heard the news? I found it difficult to believe Harry Gimler hadn't told his uncle and aunts about the vehicle recovered from Whitetail Lake, especially since it had gone in from their home place.

"Yes, I understand that. I've been talking with your nephew, Harry."

"Harry? Is everything all right?"

That was a loaded question. "Harry seems to be okay. But this is actually about another one of your nephews. It's about Rudy."

"Rudy? Don't tell me you have bad news," she said.

"No. I'm hoping you can help me locate him."

"Oh my, we lost track of him many years ago. Twenty-seven, to be exact." Harry had been off with his time estimate.

"That's a very long time. Why do you think he dropped contact with your family?"

"Why? Well, I think he got into some trouble. Like he was prone to do, I hate to say. The last time I saw him was puzzling, and it still troubles me. He came out here to South Dakota to visit, and he seemed scared."

"Scared in what way?" I said.

"Like he was in trouble and was running away from it. I asked him if the law was after him, and he said, 'Maybe.' So I said, 'What kind of an answer is that?' And he said he'd done something he shouldn't have and said some things he shouldn't have, and it was bound to catch up with him. He told me he was going to be laying low for a while."

"But he didn't tell you the reason why, or where he was going?"

"No. Of course I told him he should go to the police if he was in trouble, he should turn himself in. But Rudy said he couldn't do that. He gave me a big hug before he left and that was the last I saw of him, or even heard from him again."

"You must have had a special bond if he traveled out there see you. It almost sounds like it was to say goodbye."

Annette sniffled on the other end. "I know he got into trouble when he was a teen, but he was the sweetest little boy, and I always believed he'd grow up to be a good man."

"What did you think it was that caused him to cut himself completely off from the family?"

"The only thing I could think of, and I can't tell you how much I hate to say it... Well, here goes. I think he might have killed somebody."

My heart ping-pinged in my chest. "Really, killed someone? Any idea who that could have been?"

"No I don't. But I think he must have turned himself in to the police, and he didn't want any of us to know that his father was right about him, after all." Her voice cracked.

"Right in what way?"

"He told Rudy, more than once, he was a good for nothing that wouldn't amount to a hill of beans."

"Pretty harsh for a dad to say to a kid."

"It broke his mother's heart, and mine too, when my sister told me. I think Rudolph must be in prison, but I didn't have the heart, or the stomach, to find out for sure. I've wanted to tell him I love him no matter what he might have done. But if he's too ashamed to let us know where he is, then I finally decided I'd better leave well enough alone."

Rudolph. "Ms. Jenry, I appreciate you talking to me. If you'd grab a piece of paper and a pen, I'll give you my contact information." I started a search on Rudolph Peter Medlin while I waited, starting with the Department of Justice's federal inmate locator. When Annette was ready, I spelled my name and gave her my phone number. The computer worked while she was writing on her end. By the time she had finished, so had my search. No one with that name had been in a federal prison facility since the database was started in 1982.

"Thank you for calling, Sergeant. Maybe we'll talk again," she said.

"That'd be good." Because that would mean one of us had new information.

"And when you talk to Harry again, tell him not to be such a stranger."

"I'll pass that along."

Since there wasn't a database that listed inmates incarcerated in each state's prison system, I checked Minnesota first then Wisconsin, Iowa, South Dakota, and North Dakota on the chance Rudolph would give me what Rudy hadn't. To check all fifty states would take time.

I jotted Rudy's name and date of birth on a piece of paper, and tracked down Dina at her desk. It sat directly across from Sheriff Twardy's office, and I took a few seconds to glance inside at the empty space. Dina was responsible for monitoring a number of activities, mostly of the citizens who stopped by to talk to the sheriff about this or that.

"Any word yet, Sergeant?" she said. It was the same question we continually threw around the office, longing for an affirmative response.

I shook my head. "Dina, this is about the Whitetail Lake case. I'm hoping you and your staff can help me by checking the prisons in forty-five states to see if this guy's incarcerated anywhere." I handed her the paper. "Rudy has a possible connection to Toby Fryor and Wendy Everton. And he vanished twenty-seven years ago."

"Another missing person." Her voice was flat, like she expected defeat before she even went into battle.

"I can ask Cindy."

That perked her up. "Oh no, I didn't mean to put you off. Sorry." She read the paper I'd given her. "Did you say forty-five states?"

"Yes, I already checked Minnesota and our borders."

Dina put on her professional face. "All right. We'll get on it today."

"Thanks."

I made my way back to the sergeants' office, and switched my thoughts to the two boys Harry Gimler had identified as friends of Rudy's who'd partied at the farm. I pulled out my memo pad for their names. Abe and Keith. Smoke had said Abe was probably Abe Greer who had been in the previous graduating class. He had planned to look him up, but no doubt put it on the back burner when he was reassigned to the sheriff's case. I went to the archived-files store room, for what seemed like the tenth time, to search through the interviews. I'd remembered reading one with a Keith, but it must not have stuck out in my mind as significant. And it may not have been the same Keith.

There were two interviews with boys named Keith. Keith Dumont had moved to Oak Lea right before school started that year and stated he didn't really know either Wendy or Toby or why they'd disappeared. I remembered reading that now that I saw it again. Keith Brady was the one Smoke figured was the right Keith, and he had about as many words. "It seemed like Toby had everything; why would he give that up?" Why indeed. Keith said he knew Wendy, but not well enough to even take a guess why she'd run away with Toby.

Ron Hanken was another one I was interested in. He was also a football player, and one of the boys who had bumped Toby out of the royalty court when he was crowned prince. I found his interview, and he said he couldn't understand why Toby would run away in the middle of the football season, especially after the big win Homecoming night.

I scanned through more interviews once again, looking for a key word or phrase that revealed someone knew something about the secret in Whitetail Lake. I zeroed in on what the teachers had to say. Their observations were different than those of the teenagers' peers, but no more revealing. The teens' parents and Toby's brothers had been completely baffled and obviously very distraught by their disappearance.

After two hours of reading, I came up short once again. No one had indicated either Toby or Wendy was in any kind of trouble. Would their answers have been different had they known the two had been killed, and they hadn't run away, as they all seemed to presume?

I wrote down Keith Brady's and Ron Hanken's names and went back to the sergeants' office to uncover what I could about him. I found the reunion list my mother had provided in my briefcase. Keith and Ron were both listed, thankfully. I picked up the phone and dialed Keith's number first. It went to voicemail, so I left a message explaining who I was and requested that he call me. Then I did an Internet search and learned Keith served as a township board officer in neighboring Meeker County. I considered his service a good sign. Plus, in his position he was under the scrutiny of the public.

I phoned Ron Hanken and he answered right away. "Sergeant Aleckson, Carl and Kristen's daughter," he said. His voice was husky and his breathing was labored.

He couldn't see me, so I rolled my eyes. "I am."

"What an unbelievable deal finding Toby's Charger, huh? I never could understand why he'd run away, and it turns out he didn't after all."

"No. Ron, I'd like to ask you a few questions about Homecoming week."

"What do you want to know?"

"Toby thought he'd get crowned at the Coronation but didn't. How did he react?"

"I didn't really notice. There were three guys that got picked and three guys that didn't. I'm sure he was disappointed, but he didn't say anything about it, to me anyway."

"I've heard Toby was out of sorts the whole week before the game."

"Oh. I guess I didn't notice that either. He seemed tense, edgy, before the big game, but he was pretty doggone happy when he scored the winning touchdown, I can tell you that." His voice took on a happy note.

"I imagine. Did you see him after the game or know where he and Wendy were headed?"

"I didn't, and I have no idea what their plans were."

"I read that you were at the Homecoming dance. Did you go to one of the parties after the dance?"

"Nah, a bunch of us went over to Perkins and ate too much, I remember that."

"Did Toby tell you about anyone he was having trouble with, someone who was threatening him?"

"Threatening him? Why no. What are you getting at?"

"The victims in Toby's car were killed before they went into the lake."

Ron was silent for a time. "Someone killed them? Who could have done *that*? None of us had any real enemies. We got along pretty well."

That's what he thought, anyway. "Okay. Thanks for the information, Ron."

I checked Abe Greer next. He wasn't on the reunion list since he'd graduated the year before. I located an Abraham

Greer in Hopkins, a suburb of Minneapolis. A woman politely answered, "The Greer residence."

"Hello? Missus Greer?"

"It is. And who am I speaking with?"

"Sergeant Aleckson with the Winnebago County Sheriff's Department."

"Oh. Sergeant Aleckson, your county has been on the news every time I've tuned in this week."

"Yes." I had not tuned in myself.

"My husband lived there as a teenager, and he knew the boy who owned that car and the kids who were found in it. I have to say he was pretty shaken."

Oh? "Is he home?"

"No, he's at work. He's usually home by six, though," she said.

"All right. If you'd have him call me, I'd appreciate it."

"I'll do that. On the same number you called from?"

"Yes, thanks."

I hung up thinking about Abe and his wife discussing Toby Fryor's Charger, recovered from a local lake with the remains of two people in it. How many people had known the teenagers back then and were having similar conversations with their own families and friends?

I looked at my notes. I was waiting for calls from Ben at the regional crime lab, from Marge at Highland Park Senior High, from Keith Brady, and now Abe Greer. I stood and stretched, debating whether to check in with Smoke or keep digging through files.

Smoke phoned me instead while I was doing some toe touches. "Well, posting the sheriff's gas station photo has generated some activity, anyway. I've gotten, let me count . . .

nine phone calls from people saying they saw him there on Tuesday."

"Really, and did anyone say where he went after that?"

"One of them saw him turn southbound on Highway Fifty-five, but he didn't go that way himself. Whether the sheriff stayed on the highway, or turned due south on one of the county roads is anybody's guess. That's about it."

"Okay, so we know—or can be pretty sure—he had a full tank of gas when he left Rockwell. How far could he go before refilling?" I said.

"With that Buick of his? I'm thinking it might push thirty miles to the gallon on the highway. The tank size likely holds around eighteen gallons. I'm driving, so I need some help with the math."

I did a quick calculation and verbalized it as I went along. "Thirty times eighteen is five hundred and forty."

"Damn, he could get to Chicago, and then some, on a tank," he said.

"But the whole point is why would he go there—or anywhere else—without a good reason?"

"That is the point. The last report we have is that he was driving southeast so I think it's safe to say it was not to points north, or west."

"If he hadn't been so happy, especially since he got engaged to my mother, I'd wonder if he had some sort of a breakdown and decided to get away from it all."

"Yeah, he wouldn't be the first to do that."

I gave him a briefing of where I was at with the Fryor-Everton case.

"Something's bound to shake loose one of these days," he said.

I went back to the sergeants' office and had another look at the video from the gas station. Sheriff Twardy always stood ramrod straight, perhaps from having it drummed into him in the military, perhaps because he carried his title with pride and wanted people to know it. As I studied him on camera, I noticed his shoulders were hunched more than normal, giving him a more casual appearance. But it was the blank look on his face that kept grabbing my attention. The sheriff was one of the best at putting on a poker face when he needed to. But I'd never seen him looking like a zombie before. A zombie who pumped gas into his car, asked for a package of cigarettes, and then paid for his purchases.

When my phone rang, I hoped it was one of the return calls. Instead it was my mother, out of breath, like she'd run a mile. "Corinne, the pharmacist from Butler's Drug called . . ."

"Mom?" I heard her breathing, so I knew we were still connected.

"It's bad."

"What's bad, what is it?" I turned off the computer and gathered my things, ready to head out the door.

"They were looking through their prescriptions . . . and Denny . . ."

I did my best to calm my voice, hoping it would help. "Denny what, Mom?"

"He was supposed to pick up his medications on *Monday.* And they're still there. *Monday.*" The sheriff had gone missing on Tuesday.

"All right. I'll go to Butler's and talk to them, and then I'll stop by your shop."

"Thank you."

Jean was juggling customers and their needs at the pharmacy counter. When she spotted me, she used her fingers in a "come here" gesture. She stepped around the end of the counter, away from the people who were waiting, and I joined her there.

"How can I help you, Sergeant?"

I lowered my voice to a near-whisper. "I'm looking for some information on Sheriff Twardy's medication. Is there a pharmacist available?"

She glanced over her shoulder and signaled Leroy, the man with the most impressive eyebrows I'd ever seen. The first time I met him I wondered if he worked with the longer strands to make them curl up the way they did. "Sergeant Aleckson has a question," Jean said.

He studied me a second, no doubt shifting his thoughts from the medications he was counting to me. "Yes, sure." He finished his task and put a cover on the bottle. "We'll use the office."

I took the path around the opposite end of the counter from where I was and followed Leroy into the room in the back. "So what can I help you with?"

"My mother got a call from here saying that Dennis Twardy has meds he was supposed to pick up Monday, but didn't. As you know, he's been missing since Tuesday, and with today being Friday, Mom is pretty upset. Can you check to see when his last prescription would have run out?"

"I'll look it up." He sat down at the desk. The computer was on, and he typed in the sheriff's name. "According to our records, his refill should have started Tuesday. And he got the reminder call Monday."

"So you called, but he didn't pick them up?"

"That's correct."

"Is it possible he had meds left over from the last month?"

"Sure, people forget a dose once in a while. Since he didn't pick them up, that might have been the case."

"Actually, I wondered if he had taken an extra dose on Tuesday." I explained the sheriff's behavior at the gas station.

Leroy concurred with Dr. Dahlgren. "It's possible Dennis doubled up on his dosage, from the sounds of it."

15

When I walked into my mother's shop, the last thing I expected was to see her and David Fryor wrapped in each other's arms. They didn't even hear the bell on the door ring when I came through it. I stood there for an awkward moment, knowing it was innocent, but still. Some seconds later, when they finally pulled away, Mother noticed me. "Corinne! Did you come in the back way?"

They both looked burdened, so why embarrass them by telling the truth? Instead I said, "Hello, David, Mom."

"Hi Sergeant. I was just telling Kristen about the DNA genetic test."

"We both have a lot going on in our lives," Mother said.

"My dad told me he feels like he's in an episode of *The Twilight Zone*." Mr. Fryor had said the same thing to Smoke and me.

"That's a good way to describe it. If we could just make it all go away by turning to a different channel," Mother said.

The corners of David's lips lifted. Normally I wouldn't have discussed a case with anyone in front of my mother, but since David had filled her in, I told him, "We should have the results of the genetic test back this afternoon. Things went smoothly for the lab techs and they made it a priority."

"We appreciate that. Well, I should get back to Dad's."

"He's had a rough few days," I said.

"I'll keep you in my prayers," Mom told David.

He nodded and waved on his way out the door. "I'll do the same."

"David was a nice kid who matured into an even nicer man," Mother said. She was an astute judge of character.

"And he looks like he's a good hugger, too."

Mom's face colored. "Corinne. Well, as a matter of fact he is. He can relate to what I'm going through with Denny missing. His wife had a bad drug problem, and there were times she'd disappear for a day or two. She died of an overdose six years ago. David and his family have had more than their share of sorrows, including that his mother just died."

I nodded. "I didn't know about his wife."

She moved in close to me and took my hands in hers. "What did you find out at Butler's?"

"Nothing very conclusive. I talked to Leroy there, and he said Denny had gotten a reminder call on Monday to pick up his meds which were due to run out Tuesday."

Mother released my hands, folded her own, and brought them to her chest. "So you're saying he was out of them?"

"Leroy didn't know. He said people forget to take a dose here and there and that might have been what happened. Denny must have taken his meds with him, right? The bottles were missing."

"I would hope so. Did Leroy think Denny might have accidentally taken an extra dose?" She said.

"He said it was possible."

"Like Doctor Dahlgren said."

"Yes."

"But even so, the doctor said he should be back to normal when the meds were out of his system." Mother cast her eyes downward then lifted them to mine. "Where would he have gone, taking all that money with him and not telling me? Or anyone?"

I wondered how many times she, and I, and everyone else who knew the sheriff had asked that question.

I was at the Taco John's drive-thru window, picking up my order, when Marge from St. Paul's Highland Park Senior High School phoned me. I threw my bag of food on the passenger seat and pulled over to the side of the driveway to talk to her.

"Sergeant Aleckson, I have some information for you, but it's not very complete."

"I'll take anything you've got."

"Sheldon Viets was a student here his junior year and the first month of his senior year. He was in a foster home and ran away, according to his foster parents. They contacted the school to report he'd left them a note saying he was leaving. They didn't know where he went or if he'd be back. According to the records, he was eighteen and technically an adult who apparently took himself out of the foster care system."

"When was that? When did Sheldon run away?"

"Let me see here. October fourth, thirty-three years ago."

Oak Lea's Homecoming week. One day before the big Homecoming football game, and one day before Toby's Charger went into Whitetail Lake. Was Sheldon involved in the fateful altercation that ended in the murder of two teenagers? Pulses in my head pushed against my temples. "Marge, can you give me the names of Sheldon's foster parents and any contact information you had from back then?"

"Yes, their names are Mitchell and Linda Bedner." Marge spelled the last name and provided me with their address and phone number.

"How about his biological parents?"

"It says here they were both deceased," she relayed.

"All right. I understand that Sheldon was not a student there for long, but were there any behavior issues listed during that time?"

"Yes, as a matter of fact. Sheldon was suspended for three days for getting into a fight not long after he started school here. He suffered a black eye. The other boy wasn't injured, and he was suspended for a week."

"Did the other boy's name happen to be Rudy Medlin?"

"No it wasn't. But now that you brought up Rudy, I looked in his file, like you asked. Not much in there, really. He wasn't in school activities, including any sports. He had three separate suspensions for skipping school."

That never made sense to me. A kid is purposely absent from school, and he's punished by being kicked out of school for a time. I thought it'd be better for them to show up for some sort of work program instead.

Marge went on, "Rudy Medlin was an average student, and graduated from high school."

So he'd proved his father wrong by amounting to half a hill of beans anyway. "Thank you, Marge. One more thing, are there class photos available of Rudy and Sheldon?"

"Yes, such as they are."

"If you would scan them and send them to me, I'd appreciate it. You can send them to my phone number."

"Will do."

I added Sheldon Viets' name to the list of people who had known Rudy and Wendy and maybe Toby. He'd gone missing the same week as the murders. The catch was Sheldon had run away prior to Oak Lea's Homecoming night. I was counting on his foster parents to provide the reason he'd given for running away back then. And more importantly: did they know where he was now?

When I arrived at the sheriff's office, I carried in my lunch and briefcase, found a bottle of water from my supply in the break room refrigerator, and headed to the squad room. There was more room to spread out than in the cramped sergeants' office. I crunched away on a taco salad while reviewing my notes. The more people we talked to, the more the list of potentials to talk to multiplied. Rudy, Sheldon and his foster parents, Abe, and Keith. My gut told me at least one of them knew who had killed our two victims, and why.

I took the copies of the photos I had of Wendy Everton and Toby Fryor from my briefcase and set them on the table. Two smiling faces of kids with the world at their feet. Toby looked a lot like David Fryor, and it appeared they favored their mother's side of the family because neither bore much resemblance to Darwin Fryor. We knew Darwin was not the victim's father. The looming question was, was David the victim's brother?

That reminded me, Ben from the regional crime lab had indicated the reviewer would complete her work in short order, and that was hours ago. At the risk of irritating him, I dialed Ben's number at the lab for an update. "Oh Sergeant, I'm sorry. Joy said she was going to call you. She's the reviewer. Anyway, she got a call from her son's school saying he was sick before she even started working on your case. Joy had to go pick him up. Of course, that means she can't finish her work until Monday. She was a little frazzled and obviously forgot to call you."

I silently counted to three. "Things happen, so we'll just have to wait until Monday. I hope all is well with Joy's son."

"I hope so. Have a good weekend, Sergeant."

"You too." I got up and took a few laps around the big center table, trying to get control of my impatience. Some people waited weeks or months for DNA testing, and in the scheme of things, for all the years Toby and Wendy had been missing, a few more days was not much to ask. But a father and brother were in limbo, waiting for the results. The Evertons had closure, the Fryors did not.

I picked up my phone to call Darwin Fryor but thought better of it. After I wrapped things up at the office, I'd drop by and update the Fryors in person. It seemed kinder. I wolfed down my food then took a seat in front of a computer. I logged onto my favorite search engine to find what I could on Sheldon Viets.

Unfortunately, Sheldon Viets seemed to have done as good a job disappearing as his old friend Rudy Medlin had. It turned out Sheldon was not an uncommon name. But Sheldon Viets was not only rare; it didn't exist. There was not a single reference on the web.

The pictures of Rudy and Sheldon showed up from Marge in my phone messages, and I sent them to my email address. I accessed my account, opened the attachments of the photos, and printed them. I sat for a minute staring at each image. Rudy had blonde hair and a crooked smile that gave him a cocky look. Sheldon was dark-haired and had eyes the size of swimming pools. Both were nice-looking. I shook my head. *So where are you guys now?*

I set the pictures aside then located and dialed the phone number for Sheldon Viets' foster folks that I'd gotten from Marge. A young-sounding female answered with a chirpy voice, "Good afternoon." She lost her enthusiasm when I gave her my name and department. "Oh, well why are you calling?" When I explained, she said, "I don't know who Mitchell and Linda Bedner are. We've had this number for eight or so years now."

"All right, thank you."

But I had better luck searching for Mitchell and Linda Bedner than their foster son. The first thing that popped up on Mitchell Bedner was his obituary. It said he was survived by his wife Linda of Florida, and their three children—one who also lived in Florida—eight grandchildren, and three great-grandchildren. A sentence highlighted the twenty-seven foster children that had been part of their family through the years. I printed the page in case I needed the childrens' names.

Smoke walked in as I was picking the sheet off the printer. He glanced at the copy of the obituary I was holding. "Who's that?"

"He was Sheldon Viets' foster father."

"Ah, so you've uncovered the mysterious Sheldon's last name."

"Yes, but that's about it. No Sheldon Viets uncovered in my search so far. I'll see if I can locate his foster mother. Maybe she knows where he is." I crossed my fingers.

"Sounds like you're making progress."

"Some, but mostly it's been a hurry up and wait kind of day." I ran through the names and the information I'd gathered, the dashed hope on getting the DNA results that day, the visit to the pharmacy, and then to my mother's shop. "And when I walked in, David Fryor was there with her, and they were holding onto each other like there was no tomorrow."

Smoke's forehead creased into three lines when his eyebrows lifted. "Hmm, well I wouldn't be surprised if David hasn't wanted to do that for over thirty years now. And he finally had a good reason."

That came out of left-field. "What?"

"He was one of the many who had their eyes on your mother when she and your dad had that falling out junior year."

"What falling out?" I said.

"I didn't mean to speak out of turn here. I figured you knew about it."

"No."

"Then that'd be something for your mother, and not me, to tell you about. If she's so inclined."

"I hate it when you do that."

He raised a hand then dropped it on his chest. "I wouldn't have opened my big mouth had I known your mother hadn't ever mentioned it."

I had to ignore my burning curiosity. "You know I can't ask her about it now. Not with Denny missing."

"Yeah, I'd advise waiting. Besides, you know things were resolved and they got back together, so that's what's important," he said.

"I guess."

"Back to the sheriff; I am about to launch into a deeper search of his papers and his work and home computers. This is day four, and we're all about at wit's end trying to come up with something. I wish my mind would quit coming up with different scenarios. Like did he go somewhere to help a friend and something went wrong? We've heard from the medical community he might have had a drug overdose. Would that have made him vulnerable, and some thugs took advantage of him?"

"Smoke—"

"I know."

I nodded because neither of us had a good answer and when we tried to find one, more times than not it led to a bad ending. "If you're still at it when I get through my list of duties, I'll help you search."

"Sounds like a plan."

Finding Linda Bedner was a piece of cake compared to some others I'd tried to locate lately. It turned out she lived with her daughter in Naples, Florida. The daughter answered the phone then put her mother on. Mrs. Bedner was a bit confused about who I was and what I needed, but after I repeated myself and gave her Sheldon Viets' name, her mind cleared. "Sheldon, yes, of course. I thought of him so often in the early days, but not as much these last years. I hoped he'd let us know how he was doing, but we didn't get so much as a Christmas card."

"Missus Bedner, I understand Sheldon left you a note at the time telling you he was leaving."

"Yes, that's right. In fact I saved it, along with some photos we took of him. I have them somewhere in my things." At last, a ray of hope, if we needed copies of his photos.

"Did Sheldon say why he was leaving, what he planned to do?" I said.

"Not in so many words. And not in the note he wrote, either."

"What did it say?"

"When I find it, I can tell you exactly. But it was something like he'd made a decision, and if he told us about it we'd try to talk him out of it. That he was eighteen and knew what he was doing. He thanked us and said not to worry, that he'd be fine. That's about it in a nutshell," she said.

"Any idea what that decision was?"

"The summer before he started his senior year, he talked about going into the service, having a career in the military. And my husband and I thought that was a fine plan. But after he graduated, of course. Things were better at school, but we knew he wasn't very happy. Anyway, Sheldon turned eighteen in September, and we think he decided not to wait and joined one of the service branches."

"You said things were better at school. In what way?"

"Sheldon had a rough time of it, like so many children in the foster care system. His parents and sister died in a boating accident three years before he came to live with us. He didn't have any family who could take him. Sheldon was a caring boy who longed to be part of a family and to fit in at school. But there were problems at first."

"At home, at school?"

"Mostly at school, yes. He was picked on by some of the—what would you call them?—tough guys. They bullied him until one of them punched him in the hallway at school. Sheldon got suspended for that because he finally decided he had to defend himself and lifted his fists. A teacher broke up the fight before he hit the other boy," she said.

"Things changed after that?"

"They did, and the main reason was that a boy by the name of Rudy took Sheldon under his wing. The others left him alone after that."

"Rudy Medlin?" I said.

"Yes, that was his name." Maybe Rudy wasn't all bad after all, like his aunt had said.

"Did you talk to Rudy after Sheldon left, ask him if he knew where he went?"

"Yes, we did. We invited him over to talk. He said Sheldon hadn't told him he was planning to run away. He asked us if he could read the note, which he did. He looked quite upset and just shook his head."

"Did Sheldon ever go with Rudy to his grandfather's farm in Oak Lea?"

"Yes he did. Two, or maybe it was three, times."

"Did he talk about any parties at the farm, other kids he knew from Oak Lea?"

"Parties? Why no, he didn't. Or other kids, either. Sheldon said Rudy's grandfather was old and appreciated the company."

"Rudy had a cousin who spent time there also. His name is Harry Gimler."

"Now that name sounds familiar."

"Did Sheldon talk about him?"

There was a pause. "I just don't remember; it was so long ago."

"If you think of anything more, will you let me know?"

"I will do that, Sergeant."

Something else to run by Harry Gimler. He said he'd met Sheldon, but didn't remember much about him. Surely Rudy would have mentioned that his friend, who had been at their grandfather's farm two or three times, had run off, possibly to join the military. That would only be natural.

It was after two o'clock when I drove to the Fryor home. A white Chevy SUV pulled away from the curb just over a block away, and we met a couple of houses before Fryors'. I caught a glimpse of a bearded, gray-haired man behind the wheel before he pulled his sun visor down. He kept his arm raised, effectively blocking his face as he passed by. But there was no doubt in my mind it was the same man I'd seen at Whitetail Lake that morning. Did he live in the area, the neighborhood?

I parked in front of Darwin's home, walked up the driveway, and rang the doorbell. David answered seconds later and invited me in. "You're here with the DNA results?"

"Unfortunately, no."

When I explained the reason for the delay, he shrugged. "All in good time, right?"

"Right." I glanced around the living room.

"Is your dad home?"

"No, he went out to get some groceries. I offered to do it, but he said he wanted to. I think keeping busy and going places helps relieve some of his stress. Plus it gives him an excuse not to dig into my mother's things."

"Your mother's things?"

He nodded. "After she passed, it was up to Wade and me to decide what to do with her furniture and the rest of her possessions. At least she had downsized from a house to a condo. Neither of us wanted any of the furniture, so we had an auction house pick it all up. We donated her clothes and such.

"But she still had a lot of other things, personal papers, photos, some jewelry. I imagine our baby books are in the boxes the movers helped us pack up. That's what I want Dad to help me sort through. There are a lot of them over at her place. If we do a couple of boxes a day, hopefully it won't be too hard on him," he said.

"How long are you planning on staying?"

"Very good question, and I don't have the answer yet." He chuckled. "Good thing I can basically run my business from here, at least for a while. I'll fly to Texas for a day if I need to. The thing is, my dad needs me. I don't know how much longer he can stay here and maintain this house. I've had a woman come in to clean for the last few years. But I think Dad would appreciate having his meals prepared for him, and to not have to worry about all the upkeep here."

"You mean assisted-living?"

"Yes. When the time comes."

"Gramps has assisted-living, but it's my mother who provides it," I said.

David smiled. "He's lucky to have her so close and so willing to do that."

"Very true. Getting back to your brother's case, I wanted to ask you about a couple of people."

"Sure."

"Does the name Sheldon, or Shelly, Viets ring a bell?"

"No, why? Who is he?"

"He was a friend of Rudy Medlin, Mister Williams' grandson. I understand that Wendy Everton was pretty cozy with Sheldon at Butler's soda fountain the Saturday before Homecoming night."

"Wendy, really? I guess I'm surprised I didn't hear about it. Toby would not have liked that at all."

"I'm sure not."

"Who told you that, if I can ask?" he said.

"Dana English, now Smyth."

"Dana. Now that's a name I haven't heard in years. She had a major crush on Toby back in high school. And they had a thing for a while, until he started dating Wendy. Come to think of it, I think he was juggling the two of them for a week or more. But that's another story."

"I heard that Dana may have been jealous of Wendy because of Toby; that they had a little rivalry going on."

"Could be. Those are some hard years, aren't they? I've never talked to one person who'd like to go to back to being a teenager again."

"There were some fun times, but you're right. I know I wouldn't want to."

"Was there someone else you wanted to ask me about?" David said.

"Yes, the other one is more of a curiosity on my part. Is there a man in this neighborhood who's maybe fifty-five to sixty with a gray beard and ponytail? He drives a white SUV, a midsize Chevy."

David thought a moment and shook his head. "Not that I know of, but my dad would probably know. What about him?"

"I saw him sitting by Whitetail Lake early this morning, and then parked across the street from your house when I got here today. No biggie. Like I said, it just made me curious."

"Because you're a cop. I'll ask my dad and keep an eye out for him," he said.

16

I left the Fryors' and drove to Whitetail Lake. I parked by the lake and debated whether to pay Harry Gimler a visit now or wait until I'd gathered more information. There was a hint of a breeze in the spring air, and I rolled down my window to breathe it in. I was staring at the gentle ripples the surfacing fish were creating when my ringing phone pulled me out of my musing.

"Sergeant Aleckson."

"Hello, this is Keith Brady. My daughter got your message when she got home. She called me here at work to tell me because she thought it might be important."

"Thanks for calling, Mister Brady. It's about the investigation we're working on, about the victims found in the vehicle we pulled out of Whitetail Lake."

"Isn't that just a helluva deal? All those years nobody knew what happened, and come to find out they drove into a lake, of all things."

"That's not quite the way it happened. And in the course of trying to get the real facts of the case, we're talking to people who may provide us with some insights."

"Are you saying they didn't drive into the lake?" he said.

"It appears they had been killed prior to that."

"You're saying somebody killed them?"

People often had trouble processing tragic news. "Sadly, yes."

"Like some *madman*?" he said.

"We don't know who did it yet, and that's why we're gathering as much information as we can from people like you," I explained.

"What kind of information?"

"We have no idea where the two victims were killed, but we know the Dodge Charger had to have entered Whitetail Lake from the old Williams' farm."

"The Williams' farm? There was no road down to the lake from there."

"That's true. I understand you were friends with Mister Williams' grandson, Rudy Medlin."

"Yeah, we got to be pretty good friends for a couple of years. My family farmed the next place over. But let me tell you, Rudy was way more worldly than I was. I think it eventually got him into some kind of deep trouble," he said.

"Why do you say that?"

"He called me out of the blue, maybe five, six years after we graduated from high school. Anyway, he said was going to lay low for a while. He said a guy going by the name of Chet was after him."

"He said a guy *going* by the name of Chet?"

"That's the way he put it. Rudy said he'd been a friend, but he wasn't anymore."

"So you didn't know Chet?"

"Never met him. I thought it might have been one of his St. Paul buddies. But Rudy wouldn't say."

"Did he say why Chet was after him?"

"No, and I thought it might have been drugs, but I don't really know. I got the feeling that whatever they were involved with was against the law. Don't you think?" Brady said.

There were a number of other things, like a partnership gone sour, a fight over a woman, all kinds of disputes. "You have a point, Mister Brady. And when was the last time you saw Rudy, or talked to him?"

"That was it. That was the last time. It was, let me think now, twenty-seven years ago, or thereabouts." About the same time he cut ties with his family.

"No postcards, emails?"

"Not a word. And that was the other thing. He wouldn't tell me where he was calling from."

"Hmm." I paused a moment. "Rudy had a friend that he brought to the farm a few times, a boy named Sheldon. Did you ever meet him?"

"Sheldon? Yeah, at the Williams' place, the summer before senior year," he said.

"What was your impression of him?"

"Nice enough kid, personable, pretty quiet. Nothing else about him really stands out in my memory."

"Did Rudy tell you Sheldon had run away from his foster home shortly after that, in October?"

"No. I didn't even know he lived in a foster home."

"Okay, well I have one more person to run by you: Rudy's cousin, Harry Gimler."

"Harry, sure, he was at the farm once in a while. I can tell you he struck me as an odd kid. He mostly kept to himself. I think it was because he didn't much care for Rudy," he said.

"Why do you say that?"

"He didn't hang around him, you know, the way you do when you like somebody. He more or less avoided Rudy."

"Did you know Harry lives where the old homestead was?" I said.

"No kidding? There are some nice houses sitting there now. He must be doing pretty well for himself."

Maybe yes, maybe no. "Mister Brady, thinking back to those days, is there anyone you knew of that Toby Fryor or Wendy Everton was having any trouble with?"

"No, but then I didn't know either one of them very well, especially not Wendy."

"They went to Rudy's parties at the Williams' farm."

"I was more of his daytime friend. I had to get up early for chores. Probably like your folks did. You're Carl and Kristen's daughter, right?"

"I am."

All the conversations I'd had with people who knew my parents the last few days made me feel like half of the world's population knew who I was.

Harry Gimler would no doubt appreciate having the weekend off from seeing me and answering more of my questions. And they could wait. I drove back to the office to check on Smoke and see if he was uncovering anything valuable in his search.

Deputy Vince Weber was sitting at the sheriff's desk hitting keys on his computer keyboard. Detective Elton Dawes was standing in front of the open drawer of a file cabinet. They looked up when I knocked on the door.

"You didn't happen to bring food, did you?" Weber said.

"No, but there are places that deliver if you're in danger of passing out," I said with a smile.

"I'll probably survive," he said.

"IT ran a list of all the calls that have come to the sheriff's phone for the last month, and I got Ortiz and Mason checking them out. Chances are slim to none that somebody phoned him from their personal phone and made some sort of threat," Smoke said.

"But we wouldn't be doing our job if we didn't check. What about the numbers you got from the sheriff's home phone?" I said.

"One was his cleaning lady's cell phone. One was his closest neighbor hoping he was home and would answer. The third was a wrong number."

"Glad they all checked out."

Smoke nodded and pointed at the cabinet. "Of all the peoples' files I've had to look through in my career, this has been the hardest."

"Yeah, show her the folder full of hate letters," Weber said.

Smoke lifted the folder and handed it to me. I sat down, both drawn to it and repelled by it. I looked over each one, most from many years prior. "I wonder why he kept copies of all these notes and letters. Whenever I got one, I turned it over to whatever detective was on-call at the time, and haven't looked at any of them since," I said.

"If I kept every note I got from that Leopold character who was writing all that crazy stuff a few years ago, I'd have a folder thicker than the sheriff's," Smoke said.

"Yeah well, I've had my share too. And I could probably tell you from memory what most of them said. I sure as heck don't need to read them again. I'll tell you the ones I do keep are the ones where a person takes the time to say thank you. We do our job, and some people hate us for it, but more people appreciate what we do helping them," Weber said.

Smoke nodded. "Chief Deputy Kenner went through all the personnel files of deputies and other staff who were involuntarily discharged. There were a few he wondered about, but tracked them down and had no concerns."

I read some of the more hostile letters in the stack then turned to Smoke. "You read all these and no red flags went up for you?"

"No red flags. Most of those people are either in prison, or mental hospitals, or made their way off to greener pastures. Or they're dead. Thankfully, the sheriff hasn't seemed to trigger anyone's anger for quite some time."

I put the notes and letters back in the folder and closed it.

Weber folded his beefy hands then stretched his arms out. A few of his knuckles cracked. "I've laid my eyes on every single email, including the ones in the deleted folder, and I find nothin' I'd call suspicious. No 'Let's meet in Chicago for a reunion of army buddies.' Or, 'Leave the office, go home, clean out your safe, and drive to Minneapolis.' Nothing."

"Any reason to do a thorough forensics' check of the computer, Vince?" Smoke asked.

"Nah."

Smoke lifted a folder out of the drawer. "Looks like some of his wife's papers." He set it on the desk. "Think we should have a look-see?"

I nodded.

"Ya never know, there might be some clue tucked away in there," Weber said.

Smoke pulled the top bundle of papers out. "It's a deed to a house, in Dennis Twardy's name."

"Where?" Vince said.

"Iowa. In a town called Lyndale. Why do I know that name?" Smoke said.

"Lyndale Avenue in Minneapolis maybe?" Vince said.

"That's where Denny's wife was from," I said.

Smoke nodded. "Sure, that's right. I know when his wife was alive they went down there a few times a year. But I don't recall him ever saying he owned a house there."

I moved next to Smoke and he passed the papers to me. "Nothing in that file showing he sold the property?" I said, and looked at the deed.

"Not that I've come across," Smoke said.

"The address is Two-ten Oak Avenue. How big is Lyndale, I wonder?" I said.

"I'll give you the answer, pronto," Weber said, and launched into a search.

"While you're at it, check to see if they have a police department," Smoke said.

"Okay, Lyndale, population three hundred and sixty-four. That'd be negative on a PD. The Worth County Sheriff provides patrol for the city."

I stepped in behind Weber and he shrugged his shoulders like, even without turning around, he felt me crowding his space. So I moved to his side and leaned against the desk. "How about a city hall?"

"Yeah, with a clerk and everything, plus a mayor, and city council."

I pulled out my memo pad. "What's the phone number?"

Weber read it to me then Smoke said, "Good idea, Corky. Check to see if they know if Dennis Twardy rents the house out, or if they've seen him in their fair city."

The problem was—I discovered as I listened to city hall's message—they were closed on Fridays. I held up the phone, shook my head then hung up.

Smoke continued through the file folder. "I'm not finding anything about any renters."

"In a small town like that, you'd think somebody'd notice if all of the sudden there was activity at Two-ten Oak Avenue," Weber said.

"Especially if they see it's the man who's been on the news all week," I said.

"That's the thing. Let's keep looking for more clues," Smoke said.

I wrote down the Worth County Sheriff's number then replaced Twardy's papers in the file. We worked for another hour, but nothing else popped out for us.

"Smoke, it wouldn't hurt to have Worth County do a house check," I said.

"I'm thinking the same thing," he said.

"Sheriff could've had some sort of breakdown, and he headed down to Iowa to decompress, or something," Weber added.

It made about as much sense as anything else.

Smoke made the call, requesting a welfare check and a call back. The dispatcher said she'd send someone over, and the area deputy would let Smoke know what he found out. Weber headed home, and I stayed behind to tell Smoke about my conversations with David Fryor and Keith Brady, and to tell him about the man in the Chevy SUV.

"There is something about him that seems off," I said.

"Maybe one too many times getting *off* on drugs."

"Smoke—"

"At least that's true of the old stoners I know, who are still around. What's his plate number?"

"I didn't get it. The second time I saw him, when I realized it was the same guy, I would've had to whip my squad car around on a dime to get it."

"And you didn't want him to wonder why you are so interested in him."

"Exactly, especially since I don't really know myself."

"Very likely someone who either knew the kids—maybe he's a classmate—or he's following the story on the news and wanted to check things out for himself."

"An ambulance-chaser-groupie kind of guy?"

Smoke laughed in his deep baritone, a sound that had the power to both tickle and charm me.

My phone rang. I looked at the dial and recognized the number I'd called earlier. "I believe this is the call I've been waiting for." I pushed the talk button. "Sergeant Aleckson."

"Hello, this is Abe Greer."

"Thanks for calling back, Mister Greer."

"My wife said you're working on the case of the kids who were trapped in that car and drowned in Whitetail Lake way back."

When people didn't have the facts they came up with their own versions. I gave Abe the same basic information I'd given Keith about the crime we were investigating.

"I'm having trouble wrapping my mind around all this," he said.

"You and just about everyone else. We believe Toby and Wendy must have been at one of Rudy Medlin's parties at his grandfather's farm that night. But we haven't been able to locate anyone else who was there."

"Oh," he said.

"You were there?" I said.

"Homecoming night? No. I came home from college for the weekend to catch the football game and to see some old friends. Anyway, Rudy was at the game too with a guy I didn't know."

"Do you remember the guy's name?"

"We didn't get to introductions. The two of them walked by the bleachers where I was sitting so I yelled out Rudy's name. He looked up and waved and said something like, 'stop over later,' and then Toby Fryor ran over thirty yards for the winning touchdown and everyone went wild. I lost Rudy in the crowd," he said.

"You said you didn't go to the farm later that night?"

"No, I'd gotten my act together that first month away at college, and I figured if I went over to Rudy's I'd drink 'til I was drunk, and I didn't want to waste the whole next day. I thought I'd drive out to Mister Williams' farm on Saturday instead. It'd been a while since we'd connected, and Rudy and I were pretty tight for a year or so, back in my party-hardy days."

"That was smart. So where'd you go after the game?" I said.

"Home. After you're out of high school, things change. At least they did for me. My mom lived alone in an apartment so I went there to spend some time with her. I think we watched a movie."

"Can you describe the boy who was with Rudy at the game?"

"No, I only got a quick look. All I remember about him is that I didn't know who he was."

"Tall, short?"

"I'm trying to picture him . . . wait, when you put it that way, my impression is that he was a little shorter than Rudy, maybe around six feet."

"Anything else?"

"No."

"Were you in contact with Rudy after that? Did you go to his house like you'd planned?"

"I did, the next morning, toward noon. And when I saw him I was especially happy I hadn't been there the night before," he said.

"Why's that?"

"Rudy looked awful, like he'd barely slept. His eyes were bloodshot red. He needed a shower and a good night's sleep. And he was not himself, at all."

"Why do you say that?"

"It was like he was afraid of something. He was edgy, paranoid. I'd never seen Rudy act like that from drinking beer, so I thought he'd taken some drugs. I wondered about the guy who'd been with him at the game, and asked Rudy about him.

I told him if that friend of his was into drugs, he should steer clear of him," he said.

"What'd he say?"

"He stammered, and he wasn't very clear about it. He wouldn't go into details, but he said the kid hadn't hung around long after the game. He said there hadn't been a party there after all. And then his cousin came out of the house and just stood there staring, more like glaring, at us. He was upset about something, no doubt about that. Everything about that morning at the Williams' place felt wrong. I left a few minutes later," he said.

"What was his cousin's name?"

"Harry."

"Did Harry look like he'd been partying with Rudy?"

"No, Harry hung out with his grandfather most of the time, or was off doing something on his own. He never partied with us, and I think he hated when Rudy had his friends over."

"Hated? That's pretty strong," I said.

"Well, it seemed like it to me," he said.

"Did you and Rudy remain friends, keep in contact?"

"No, we didn't. I haven't seen him since that Saturday morning, and we lost touch after that. He left a message on my answering machine a few years later saying he had to disappear for a while. No reason, no explanation of any kind. I didn't have Caller ID back then, and he didn't leave a number so I couldn't call him back."

"What did you think he meant about disappearing for a while?" I said.

"I was optimistic that he'd straightened himself out, gotten clean. I thought he needed to get away from the bad influence of his friends who weren't clean. I figured he'd surface one day and look me up," he said.

"Word has it that his family hasn't heard from him for twenty-seven years."

"His family either? That doesn't sound good."

"No, it doesn't. Mister Greer, you remember Elton Dawes?" I said.

"Sure, and I hear he's a detective with your department. I imagine he feels terrible about Toby and Wendy, too."

"Yes, he does. He's here with me, if you'd like to say 'hi.'"

"Okay."

Smoke raised one eyebrow in question, but I handed him the phone. "Hi, Abe, quite the deal, huh? . . . Yeah, she's Carl Aleckson and Kristen Brandt's daughter . . . No, by the time I came back to Winnebago County it had been torn down and there were new houses there. . . . Harry Gimler . . . Yup . . . Well, if you think of anything that might help us, give us a call. . . .Thanks."

After he'd hung up, Smoke said, "And you wanted me to talk to him, why?"

"To get your impression of him, see if he seems sincere, honest, to you."

"He does. You don't think so?"

"Actually, I do. When I talked to Keith Brady, he said he wasn't a partier. Yet Harry named them as the two regulars at Rudy's parties. Both Keith and Abe said they weren't at the Williams' farm for an after-Homecoming party. And according to Abe, when he saw Rudy the next morning, Rudy told him there hadn't been a party there after all."

"Huh."

"Again, according to Abe, Rudy looked and acted like he had taken drugs that made him fearful. So, did Rudy shoot the kids when he was under the influence of a chemical, and then when he was more rational, realized what he'd done and decided to cover it up?" I said.

"You got me. And if we could find the guy, we would ask him," Smoke said.

"We know somebody killed our two victims, and I think that person had help getting the bodies in the car and pushing it down the hill into the lake."

"I'm with you there, little lady. If we're talking about Harry Gimler, we know damn well he's hiding something. We'll have to keep prodding him until we find out what it is."

"Abe said when he was talking to Rudy that morning Harry came out of the house and glared at them. And that Harry *hated* Rudy having parties there."

"Now we know why he sits at home and drinks alone. He hates parties," Smoke said.

I shook my head. "Maybe so much so that he lost it one night, and killed a couple of Rudy's party friends."

"Hmm."

"Abe said Rudy left him a final message around the same time he had his last contact with his aunt and Keith Brady. His aunt told me Rudy seemed afraid when he visited her. He told everyone he was going to lay low for a while. Twenty-seven years is a very long while."

"You got that right," Smoke said.

17

When I picked Queenie up from Gramps' house that night, she was not nearly as happy to see me as when I rescued her from the confines of her kennel at home. She was sitting by Gramps' chair when I stepped into his living room. Mother came in from the kitchen with a dish towel in her hand and a hopeful look on her face.

I smiled, trying to radiate some encouragement. "Smoke has been leading the effort to find out everything he possibly can about Denny. When he was going through his files at work, Smoke found a deed to a house Denny owns in Lyndale, Iowa."

Her head jerked back like she was dodging a punch. "That's where his wife was from, but I don't know anything about Denny having a house there."

"Maybe it was her family home. After she died, it would have gone to Denny."

"He's never said a word about it. And we've had a lot of deep conversations—about our future together, about your father, and his wife." Her face softened. "He told me they met at a dance at the Surf Ballroom in Clear Lake when they were still in high school. With Denny being from Mason City, Clear Lake was about halfway between their towns."

I wasn't familiar with the area. "Maybe he thought he told you about it?" I said.

"Denny is a very private man in many ways. He was so broken after his wife died. I think there are still things he's not ready to talk to me about."

We didn't know it at the time, but Mother had likely hit the nail on the head.

I was soaking in a hot bath, willing the eucalyptus oil I'd added to the water to do its stress-relieving magic, when my cell phone rang. I groaned loud enough to alert Queenie who was resting on the rug. I picked the phone off the ledge and looked at its face. "What's up, Smoke?"

"They found the sheriff and it's not good." I stood up so fast, water splashed over the side of the tub, and my foot slid a foot or so on the slippery floor. Queenie barked. "Where are you, what's that noise?" he said.

"I was in the tub. Tell me." Between my pounding heart and loud breathing, I had trouble hearing what he said. "Say again."

"I just got off the phone with the Worth County deputy. He went to Two-ten Oak Avenue and didn't get an answer at the door. He did a walk around the house, looking in the windows. He discovered the back door was unlocked. He knocked on the door, but got no response. Since he had a check-the-welfare call, he took it upon himself to go in, and thank God he did. Denny was lying on the kitchen floor. He'd apparently fallen and hit his head on the table, or a chair."

"Dear Lord, he's not dead?" I was only semi-aware that I was patting my body dry with a towel.

"No, but he's not exactly coherent. He had his wallet on him so they know it's Dennis Twardy. The paramedics are with him now, and they're advising air lifting him to the trauma center at Mayo. I said to go ahead." The Mayo Clinic in Rochester, Minnesota.

"Okay. My mother will want to get down there right away, no matter what."

"Get dressed. I'll be over shortly. We can make it there in about two hours."

We. "Okay, I'll call Mom."

My mother was at home. I gave her the lowdown, but didn't give her a chance to ask questions. "Mom, we'll talk on the way. Grab your overnight bag, and we'll be there soon." She wanted more details, but I cut her off. "I'm standing here naked and Smoke is on his way." Then I disconnected as she was saying "Corinne—"

I heard Smoke's car horn short blast in my driveway about six minutes later. I phoned him to say I'd be out shortly. I grabbed my large leather purse that doubled as a travel bag, threw in some essentials, and a sweater to dress up the jeans and knit top I'd put on. I slipped on a sweatshirt, attached my pancake holster to my jeans, holstered my Glock, grabbed my ID and wallet, and ran down the stairs with Queenie at my heels.

I opened the door to the garage then went in, and opened the door to Queenie's kennel. "Okay, girl, you have a nice warm bed to sleep in, and plenty of food and water. I won't be home tonight, but I'll have somebody take you to Gramps' house in the morning."

Her forlorn-looking face pulled at my heartstrings, even though I knew she'd sleep all night and wouldn't miss me until the next day. I ran back into the house then headed out the front door and hopped into Smoke's Ford Expedition.

"You are filling my vehicle full of the best fragrance. What is it, pine?"

"Eucalyptus, from a different evergreen tree."

"I may have to add that to my Christmas list." As if he had one.

"Mother should be ready by the time we get there. She keeps an overnight bag packed in case she needs to stay at Gramps'."

"I splashed water on my face and brushed my teeth but didn't think past that," he said.

"I grabbed a few things, thinking we'd be there all night."

"I'll hit the gift shop in the morning, if need be."

Mother was waiting on her front step in the dark, holding her bag in one hand and her lined raincoat and purse in the other. Smoke and I both got out. He grabbed Mother's bag, and I opened the back door to climb in there.

"When it comes to getting ready, you two are the fastest women of any I've ever known," Smoke said, probably to ease the tension.

"With something this important, there is no time to waste," Mother said, calmly and matter-of-factly. "Corinne, I'll sit in the back seat. You help Elton navigate."

"Okay."

The thing I found most strange about my mother was in the face of a real and known emergency, she turned into the queen of level-headed calm. She said she felt like God was holding her in His arms. I believed her, but also wondered why she didn't let Him hold her when she dealt with all the other things that caused her to stress out.

"What exactly did that deputy tell you, Elton?" Mother said.

"Our conversation was on the brief side, and he had the paramedics there before he called me. He said Denny was lying on the floor next to the table and had a goose egg on the front side of his head. He was conscious, a good thing. But when the deputy asked him questions, Denny looked at him like he didn't understand what he was being asked. And when he tried to talk, his words were too garbled to understand. The paramedics are the ones who recommended Mayo's trauma center over a closer facility."

"The deputy thought he fell, meaning there were no signs of a struggle?" I said.

"Correct, I forgot to add that. No signs of a struggle."

Smoke called ahead to let the hospital know we were coming and to give them our contact information in case they needed to reach us before we got there. The medical staff had found the sheriff's medical card in his wallet, but they asked Smoke other questions, such as the name of his primary care physician, his known medical conditions and allergies. Smoke handed his phone to Mother. She had more accurate information than he did.

Smoke and I made a number of phone calls: to Chief Deputy Mike Kenner, my Grandma and Grandpa Aleckson, my brother John Carl, my friend Sara, and a few other sheriff's personnel so they could get the word out that the sheriff had been found. The chief deputy said he'd handle the media announcements. My mother called one of her employees and asked her to run the shop the next day. We decided there was no reason to disturb Gramps. If he wasn't sleeping, he was close to it.

The Mayo Clinic Hospital, St. Mary's Campus in downtown Rochester where the Division of Trauma, Critical Care, and General Surgery department was housed, was fairly easy to find and access, even at night. I'd been to Rochester, but not to any of the Mayo Clinic facilities.

"I'll drop you off at the entrance and go park in the ramp," Smoke said.

When the vehicle stopped, I told Mother, "Leave your overnight bag in the car for now."

Mother and I went into the lobby and were directed to the emergency department. We told the admissions receptionist who we were looking for. She asked for our names and our relationship to Dennis Twardy, then checked to see if we were allowed to see him. After a bit, she got the okay to let us in. "Let's wait for Smoke," I said.

Mom's anxiety was building, and so was mine. I knew she wanted to get to Denny's side as fast as possible, but I needed Smoke by my side, to lend whatever support we might need. I sent him a text message, *Waiting for you at emergency admin*. He responded with, *OK*. And he was there in short order. The receptionist buzzed the three of us through the door that led to the emergency rooms. "Dennis Twardy is in room thirty-six," she said.

"A little bigger than Oak Lea's hospital," I quietly said as we stepped into the corridor.

The door to 36 was closed, so Mother knocked then opened it and stepped in. A sharp intake of air escaped her lips and made my body tense in response.

Denny was hooked up to machines that monitored his vital signs and had an IV dripping fluids into him. I thought at first we'd been sent to the wrong room, but after studying his face, I saw it was him after all. The area around his eye was varying shades of purple and green, and there was a good-sized bump on his head that stuck out just above his temple.

A nurse was bent over him, holding a touch thermometer to his temple. She pulled it out and looked at us, the group that had crowded into the small room. My mother put her hand over her mouth, and tears exploded out of her ducts and down her cheeks.

Smoke reached up and rested a hand on the top of her shoulder for a few seconds when she said, "Denny, it's Kristen," and then she moved to the bottom of the bed. The sheriff turned toward the sound of her voice, but there was no indication he recognized her. His face was void of any expression, and my heart went out to him, then to my mother when she turned to Smoke and me with her eyebrows raised and her lips pursed. I gently pulled her back as Smoke stepped in closer to the sheriff.

"Sheriff?" he said.

Denny looked at him and closed his eyes slightly, crinkling up the crow's feet beside them, like he was trying to remember something, anything.

The nurse said to us, "He had a computed tomography—CT—scan shortly after he arrived. It's much faster than an MRI, and it uses X-rays to get clear and detailed pictures. We use the scan in trauma cases, and it should tell the docs what they need to know, like if he needs surgery."

"Surgery?" I said.

She focused on me. "We should have the CT results momentarily. They'll likely need to relieve the pressure that hematoma is causing. We have a fine group of doctors who perform thousands of surgeries here every year. Our trauma surgeons are the best of the best, so Dennis is at the right place. The surgeon will talk to you about it."

Smoke inched toward the head of the bed. He put on his reading glasses and moved his face in for a closer look at the bump on the sheriff's head. In the center of it was a line, like whatever he struck, or was struck with, had a sharp edge. Smoke pulled out his phone and snapped pictures of it from several angles.

When he finished, I traded places with him and captured some shots of my own, in the event that something happened to Smoke's phone. Mother closed her hands over Denny's hand—the one without the IV needle—offering him some comfort.

The nurse left and returned a few minutes later. "They're advising surgery, so we'll begin prepping Dennis. You can go to the waiting area, and the surgeon will meet you there."

The neurosurgeon assigned to the sheriff was Dr. Charles Heath, and it didn't take me a minute to decide if I needed brain surgery, he'd be the one I'd want to perform it. He was confident, sharp, and relaxed. Most of all, he knew what needed to be done and was up for the challenge.

"I'm going to get right down to brass tacks. Are you all okay with that?" he said.

We nodded, and I hoped my mother truly was.

Dr. Heath brushed at his elbow. "Dennis has a couple of things going on. First he had a stroke, and then he suffered a head trauma that gave him that tennis-ball-size lump on his head. We need to get in and take care of that so we'll have an idea what damage the stroke may have caused."

"You're saying he had a stroke first?" I said.

"Yes, that's my opinion."

"Is that why he fell?" Smoke said.

"It may have been a factor, but with this type of stroke, and the area it's in, I would say not directly. A stroke occurs when the blood flow to the brain is interrupted or blocked, and causes damage to the brain cells. There are three types, but I'll tell you about Dennis's.

"He had what appears to be lacunar, a type of ischemic stroke that's caused by blood clots. A lacunar stroke happens when the small arterial vessels deep inside the brain get blocked. The most common cause is chronic high blood pressure."

"He has that," Smoke said.

The doctor nodded. "Lacunar strokes account for about twenty percent of all strokes."

"Denny acts like he doesn't even know us," Mother said.

"That hematoma is putting a lot of pressure on his brain. But he's being prepped for surgery now, so we can take care of it ASAP. I'll be using a computer to help guide me during the procedure. It's very cutting-edge technology." He smiled and so did I. He knew we were tense, and I appreciated the levity.

The doctor went on, "I don't anticipate this to be a very lengthy procedure, but there'll be plenty of time for you to go to the cafeteria, get something to eat and drink. Be sure to pick up a pager at the front desk so we can let you know when Dennis is out of surgery and in recovery. I'll touch base with you then and let you know how it went."

Dr. Heath excused himself, and Mother, Smoke, and I looked at each other. "I don't think I had supper," Smoke said.

"I don't even think I had lunch," I said then remembered it was Taco John's. "Never mind."

"Let's get the pager then you two need something to eat," Mother said.

Smoke and I picked at our sandwiches while Mother sipped on an apple juice. "I have to trust that the doctors will get Denny back to normal," she said

The lump in my throat made it tough to swallow the bite of chicken salad I was chewing on. "One step at a time, Mom."

"I've seen a lot of people recover very well after a stroke, Kristen. Let's keep the faith," Smoke said.

She nodded, sniffed, and got up. "I need to use the restroom."

After she was out of earshot Smoke crossed his arms, put them on the table then leaned in. "This is a helluva deal, all the way around. I'm not completely convinced the sheriff wasn't assaulted."

"I know. What made him go down to Lyndale, Iowa in the first place, and why didn't anyone notice that he was there? Where did he park his car? And where are the thousands of dollars of cash he took from his safe?"

Smoke blew out a breath "We're not going to get good answers to those questions unless he recovers enough to tell us. And now that you brought up his car, I didn't think to ask the Worth County deputy if it was there. We were talking in the middle of a medical emergency, and I wasn't thinking straight. And if I had been, I would've had him snap some photos of the kitchen and the sheriff and send them to me."

"The deputy didn't suspect foul play."

"No, and that's why I want to see what he saw, see if I have the same assurance," he said.

"How far is Lyndale from here?" I pulled out my phone and found the Internet icon then typed in the question. "Okay, from the Mayo Clinic, it's ninety miles. An hour and a half. Or if you drive, just over an hour."

Smoke chuckled. "Maybe after I've had some sleep."

"Hopefully the sheriff had his keys on him. We'll have to ask the staff."

We were in the waiting room when a series of lights on the pager flashed and then it buzzed. Mother jumped to her feet, and I realized she had better reflexes than either Smoke or me. Or she was the jumpiest. We skedaddled to the reception desk where the young woman told us Dennis Twardy would be in a recovery room for about an hour and would then be moved to the intensive care unit. Dr. Heath would be out to talk to us shortly.

The doctor's optimism encouraged us. "The surgery went well. I'm very pleased. We relieved the pressure from Dennis's brain, and we'll give him the best care possible in his recovery. He was dehydrated, so we'll continue to get fluids into him. Tomorrow—oh, I guess it's later today by now—we'll increase the nutrients. I understand he was alone for a while before he was found."

Smoke gave Heath a synopsis of what we knew, from the time the sheriff walked out of his office Tuesday morning, until we got the call from the Worth County deputy Friday evening. The doctor listened with one hand across his stomach and the opposite elbow resting on it. He pinched at his chin as he listened.

"Would you like to see the video of the sheriff at the gas station? I have it in my email," I said when Smoke finished.

"Yes, I would," Dr. Heath said.

I accessed the account on my phone, and clicked on the attachment. "It's small, so enlarge it if you need a better view."

The doctor took the phone from me, expanded it then held it close to his face. He nodded and said, "Ah, I wouldn't doubt that Dennis suffered the stroke prior to that, and it caused both his behavior and that flat affect. A fair number of lacunars are silent, and that means people don't have classic stroke symptoms. But the stroke can affect a person's mood, his personality, his cognitive functioning, memory, and reasoning."

"Memory and reasoning?" Smoke said.

"Yes, it's possible Dennis lost his more recent memories, and went back to what he remembered from some time ago. Or his memories could be jumbled together somehow." Dr. Heath shook his head. "The fact that he went to his house, emptied his safe, and then drove to a home he owns in Iowa but doesn't live in, indicates impaired reasoning. He must have had an army of angels with him on that long drive."

We couldn't argue with that.

The doctor gave me back my phone then said, "We've taken some blood and are running tests to check Dennis's medication levels, but from what you've said my guess is that he ran out of them, and that's what caused the stroke in the first place." He'd said high blood pressure was a common cause.

"How long will he need to stay in the hospital, Doctor?" Mother said.

"The average stay is around three days, but we may keep him another day or two, depending on his physical condition. Then he'll likely be moved to a nursing care facility for rehabilitation."

"A nursing home?" Mother had done her darnedest to keep Gramps out of one for several years, and now it appeared she had no choice with her fiancé.

Dr. Heath gave her a warm smile. "We'll know more when the anesthesia is out of Dennis's system, and we can start the evaluation process. But he'll be on pain meds for a while, so we have to factor that in too, since they can skew the results."

"When can we see him?" Mother said.

"We discourage visitors in the intensive care unit. I'd advise waiting until after Dennis is moved into a regular patient room. You should get some rest yourselves in the meantime," he said.

I had been winding down, ready to call it a night hours ago when I climbed into a hot bath. But things changed drastically with a phone call. The doctor said his goodbyes and left. Smoke guided Mother and me to a corner. "We should follow doctor's orders and get some sleep. There are a lot of hotels around. Kristen, you packed a bag; Corky did too. I can buy a toothbrush at a corner store. How about we get checked into some rooms for the night and figure out tomorrow's plans in the morning?"

Mother started to protest, but I cut her off. "Smoke's right. As much as we want to maintain a vigil with Denny, we all need sleep. Knowing that Denny's here, being cared for in this wonderful hospital, should make us feel a little better."

Mother sighed then nodded.

The Kahler Hotel was a short walk away, and we had two rooms secured there in short order. I would have picked Smoke over my mother to room with, but I knew neither one of them would have gone for that idea, so I didn't bring it up. Mother and I had a choice of a king-size bed or two doubles, and we went with the doubles.

Smoke's room was on the same floor, and after he walked us to ours, he said goodnight and headed down the hall to his own. It didn't take long for Mother and me to get situated. We got ready for bed, and then I climbed under the covers of what felt like the most comfortable bed in the world. I stretched my tired muscles and was lying there thinking of all the things that had happened the long day before, and of all the people I'd talked to, looking for information in the Toby Fryor-Wendy Everton investigation.

The day had started with an early morning run and was ending almost twenty hours later in a hotel room in Rochester, a short distance from the sheriff's recovery room bed at the Mayo Clinic, St. Mary's Hospital. *Sheriff Twardy*. The blank look on his face, the lack of recognition from him, was haunting. I prayed the surgery had relieved the pressure on his brain, and he'd be back to the way he was.

I found out Gramps was right about my mother's snoring when the sounds woke me up in the middle of the night. She had tossed and turned for a long time after we'd gone to bed. But despite her restlessness and my own contemplations, I'd fallen fast asleep. I blinked at the alarm clock and when I saw it was 4:36, I smiled for two reasons: it wasn't yet time to get up, and my mother was sleeping deeply and soundly. I turned toward the wall, pulled a pillow over my ear to block out the snoring, and was dead to the world within seconds.

18

Mother, Smoke, and I ate breakfast at the hotel and tried to map out our day. Smoke talked to Chief Deputy Kenner. He, along with a number of others, wanted to visit the sheriff so Smoke said he'd find out what the hospital advised and let him know. Mother called Gramps, but couldn't choke out the words, so I talked to him instead.

"Thank the Good Lord you found him. Tell your mother I'm holding good thoughts," Gramps said.

"I will. And Gramps, is it all right if Queenie spends the day with you again?"

"You know she's always welcome."

"Thank you. I'll have one of my friends bring her over in a little while."

When I hung up, Smoke said, "Thanks for reminding me. I talked to my neighbor about Rex before I left, knowing we'd likely be gone overnight. He and his son are good about looking after my boy when I'm away."

Smoke phoned his neighbor, and I phoned my friend Sara. I gave her the latest on the sheriff and then asked if she could deliver Queenie to Gramps' house. We'd barely had a chance to talk all week, and when it looked like it would turn into a lengthy conversation, I told her I had to go but promised we'd sit down for a long chat very soon.

When the server delivered our food, Smoke and I dug into our plates of eggs, hash browns, bacon, and toast like teenage boys in a school lunchroom. In contrast, Mother daintily picked away at her omelet and fruit cup. At least she got some nutrition into her body.

We were still eating when Grandma Aleckson phoned me. They were in Oklahoma, upset because the transmission had gone out in their Chevy Equinox, and it would be at least Monday before they could get it fixed. "We're stranded here," she said.

I assured her we'd be fine, and told her not to worry about something they had no control over. *Something to keep in mind yourself, Corky.*

When I relayed Grandma's news, Mother pushed her plate aside. "If it's not one thing, it's another. I don't know how you two feel about it, but I'd like to spend at least one more night here, close to Denny."

"Sure, we'll make that work," Smoke said.

My phone dinged alerting me I had a text message. *Where are you?* It was from John Carl.

I'd sent him a late night message about Denny's surgery and how it had gone, and that we'd checked into the Kahler Hotel for the night. I thought it was a funny question, but I wrote back saying we were having breakfast in the hotel, and we'd be heading to the hospital soon. When John Carl walked up to our table a minute later, I closed my eyes and opened them again to see if I was imagining things.

It was him all right. I jumped up and threw my arms around him then Mother uttered, "John Carl!" She wasn't the only one with tears in her eyes. When Mom was out of her chair, I moved aside so she could hold her son, something she couldn't do as often as she liked. After a while, she stepped back, moved her hands to his, and studied him. "What are you doing here? How did you know where to find us?"

John Carl turned his head in my direction. "Corky. After she sent me a message last night, I booked an early morning flight to Minneapolis." One thing about John Carl: even though he had moved to Colorado mainly to escape our mother's over-involvement in his life, when the chips were down and he was needed, he faithfully showed up.

"It means the world to me to have both of you here," Mother said.

Smoke had been waiting in the wings, and when Mom let go of John Carl's hands, he tapped him on the shoulder, and then gave him a hearty hug. "Always good to see you, John Carl." Smoke had told me when he saw John Carl he felt like my father was there for a second. They looked that much alike. Smoke pulled out a chair for him and we all sat down.

"John Carl, you better eat some breakfast," Mother said.

"I don't want to hold you up," he said.

"Don't be silly. The hospital has our phone numbers and said they'll call when they move Denny to a regular room," she said.

Smoke waved the server over. John Carl glanced at my half-eaten food and said he'd have what I was having. The server poured coffee all around then left to place his order. We brought John Carl up to speed on what we knew about the sheriff's stroke, head injury, and late-night surgery results. And Grandpa and Grandma's car problems.

Then we headed over to St. Mary's Hospital to wait.

It was 11:48 a.m. when Dennis Twardy was declared medically stable and moved to a private room on the third floor of the Francis Building. Mother, John Carl, Smoke, and I entered quietly when we saw him lying in his bed with his eyes closed. The IV drip delivered nutrient-filled fluids and medications to aid him in his healing. The nurse had told us he would be drifting in and out of awareness. We'd been in the room for some minutes before Denny slowly opened his eyes and looked at us. But he displayed not a single sign that he knew who we were. I put my arm around my mother's waist to offer my support.

Within seconds, before we had a chance to greet him, he floated back into seeming unconsciousness. We waited for a time then Smoke signaled the rest of us out of the room, into the hallway. "Kristen, now might be the best time for Corinne and I to go to Denny's house in Iowa. We can check things out there, make sure the doors and windows are secure. And then pick up his car and drive it back."

"Oh."

"The nurse said Denny's going to be sleeping a lot this first day, especially. I wouldn't be suggesting it if you didn't have John Carl here with you," he explained.

She mulled that over a minute. Then she reached over, rested her hand on John Carl's, and looked at Smoke. "How long do you think it will take?"

He lifted his palms. "It's ninety miles one way. I'm thinking it'll be five hours, give or take, depending on whether or not we encounter any unforeseen events."

Mother nodded. "Maybe it is a good time to go."

"We should find out where they put Denny's things. I'm hoping his keys are with the rest of his stuff," Smoke said.

"Let's go ask the staff," I said.

Smoke and I went to the nurse's station and spoke to the supervisor. When she learned Smoke was a detective in Sheriff Dennis Twardy's office, he had no problem getting the bag of items. We carried it back to the sheriff's room where Mother was sitting on a chair close to the head of the bed. Smoke handed her the bag and asked if she'd check the pockets of his pants for his keys. She pulled them out and handed them over.

"Thanks, Kristen."

Two hours later Smoke and I were sitting in his vehicle outside a modest, one and a half story home at 210 Oak Avenue in Lyndale, Iowa. Three cement steps with a black iron railing led to the front door. There was a picture window on one side and a smaller window on the other. The scene was surreal. It was like that dream where you discover a secret room in your house you didn't know was there. But this was an entire house and one the sheriff had kept from everyone, including my mother.

"Why would he keep his ownership of this place to himself?" I said.

Smoke opened his door. "I have no idea. I don't see his car, so I hope it's in the garage." He used his thumb to point at the detached structure.

We got out of the Expedition and stood there for a minute, assessing, then we walked over to the garage. Smoke tried the knob on the service door, and when it turned without resistance, he pushed it open. "There it is," he said and pointed at the sheriff's car. It was the only thing in the otherwise empty garage. A damp, dank odor surrounded us when we went inside.

"Now that we know where it is, let's go make sure everything's locked up in the house, and if we happen to see anything out of place, we'll take a closer look," he said.

"Okay."

Smoke followed the cement walk to the side door. He found the right key on the second try, and we stepped inside onto the landing. The basement entrance was straight ahead and there were two steps to the right that led to the kitchen. The house was circa 1940s. The kitchen was small, with the original cupboards, from the looks of it.

A table and four chairs sat in the center of the room. Smoke and I stopped and perused what would have been the area where the sheriff had fallen. "He had a closed wound so I wouldn't expect to see blood anywhere. And I don't."

"No, I think the deputy was right. Denny must have either caught the side of the table or the chair when he fell," I said.

"The edges are squared off, not rounded, and I can see how he might have stumbled and caught it like this." Smoke did a partial demonstration.

I pulled out my phone and found the photos I'd taken of the sheriff's hematoma. "Yeah, that's the way it looks." I handed him my phone. "If someone had hit him on the head, he would have had to use an object with a sharp edge, like one of these chairs."

Smoke nodded. "Let's take a walk through the house, see if anything's disturbed. Otherwise I'm fairly confident it was an accident."

"Possibly caused by the stroke, or not having his medications," I said.

"Yup."

We wound our way through the rest of the house. There were two small bedrooms and a half-bath on the upper level. A larger, furnished bedroom, bathroom, living room, and dining room made up the main level, and the basement was a big open space. A furnace, water heater, washer and dryer were the only things down there.

"Do you suppose he hid his cash in here somewhere?" I said.

He lifted his shoulders. "We'll probably have to wait until he gives us the answer to that."

We went back out the side door, making certain the door was locked behind us, and headed to the garage.

"Man, I hope the smell hasn't penetrated inside the car," I said.

"This garage needs a healthy dose of fresh air and sunshine, to be sure. If it's too bad, you can take my Ford and I'll drive his car. Bad odors don't bother me like they used to."

"A part of me feels like we're committing a crime, motor vehicle theft."

"We could wait until Denny is better and get his permission, but we're here now. If it were me, I'd be happier knowing my car is safe and sound in my own garage."

I thought of my GTO. "You're right." I held out my hand for the keys.

Smoke passed them over then looked at the garage door. "It's got an old latch that you have to slide over after you close it. I'll do that after you back out." He slid the heavy door up, and I climbed into the driver's seat. When I glanced over at the passenger seat, I saw the empty pill bottles lying there. I picked them up, opened the door, and held them up for Smoke to see.

"Ah, so maybe Denny had them in his car as a reminder to pick up his prescriptions," Smoke said.

"Maybe," I said, dropped them back on the seat, and closed the door. I adjusted the seat, started the engine, and backed the car onto the driveway. It didn't feel as strange as I'd thought it would. The garage smell was there, but would clear with the windows open. I rolled all four of them down then got out of the car and waited for Smoke to finish up.

"All set," he said when he'd shut the service door behind him. He nodded at the sheriff's Buick. "You good with that?"

"I'm good. We talked about checking with the neighbors to see if any of them saw Denny here the last few days. Someone must have seen the emergency vehicles here last night and wondered."

He gave his head a mild bop. "You're right." He scanned the area with his eyes. "How about I go north and you go south for a few houses, then we'll cross the street and head back."

"Okay." I turned off the sheriff's car, but left the windows open to let the air and sun work their magic.

The first house I checked to the immediate south was obviously vacant. There was a thick hedge of bushes between that one and the next where I knocked on the front door. When there was no answer, I left a note asking the owners to call me if they'd noticed any activity at 210 Oak Avenue since Tuesday. I stuck the note and my business card in the door.

An older man answered the door at the next house, but said he hadn't seen anyone at the house recently. He had gone to bed early the night before and hadn't seen a squad car or ambulance on the scene. "I see a car in the driveway every once in a while. I think it's someone who checks things out, since nobody's lived there for some years now."

"Do you know who that house-checker is?" I said.

"No, sorry to say, I don't. And I forget the name of the couple who owns it. It was the lady's folks who had it before they died."

I nodded. "Thanks for your time."

I crossed the street and a younger couple opened the door of the house that sat directly across from Denny's.

"Minnesota?" the man said when I introduced myself and told him where I was from and why I was there.

I learned they had lived there just over two years and had never met Dennis Twardy. They said a light went on in his kitchen every evening about dusk and stayed on for a few hours, like it was on an automatic timer. They didn't pay much attention to it anymore, not like when they'd first moved in. They'd seen a man around sixty years old stop at the house now and again. He'd go in for a few minutes then leave. They had never talked to him. They'd been out the evening before and had missed the activity there.

"The next time you see the house-checker, I'd be grateful if you'd go over and give him my card. Ask him to call me. Tell him it's about Dennis Twardy and it's very important." I wrote Dennis Twardy on the back of two cards and handed them over. They both looked at the cards then nodded.

"Thank you for your help," I said and turned around. Smoke was making his way back to the sheriff's house. I crossed the street and met him in the driveway.

"Any luck?" he said. When I gave him my brief report, he said, "It's unbelievable nobody we talked to saw the deputy or heard the sirens of the ambulance last night. Granted, the folks I talked to were elderly and retired early."

"Yeah."

"It seems Denny kept a very low profile down here. I found out about the same thing from the three people I talked to. One knew Denny's in-laws when they were alive and spoke to his wife a couple of times when she and Denny made the occasional trip here. That same man said there's a caretaker of sorts, and a lawn service that takes care of the yard in the summer, and a company that gets rid of the snow in the winter."

"Does he know the caretaker's name?" I said.

"No, he mostly watches the world from his living room and has never talked to the guy."

"The sheriff must have the caretaker, et cetera, in his phone contacts."

"If we only knew where his phone is."

At the edge of Lyndale, Smoke's missing phone question was answered when I slammed on the brakes to avoid hitting a squirrel that ran across the road in front of me. When I heard something bounce on the floor mat, I almost hit the critter anyway. I pulled to the side of the road and stopped. Smoke pulled over behind me, got out, and jogged to my door.

"What's up? You didn't hit him," he said.

"No." I pointed at the floor. "Look what was hiding under the seat."

Smoke stuck his head partway in my open window for a better look and smiled. "Ah, the prodigal phone returns." He went around the car, opened the door, snatched up the phone, and pushed the on button. "Dead as a doornail. Now for a charger."

I took the phone from him and looked at the connection port. "It's a different size than mine. Why don't you check the glove box?"

Smoke slid onto the car seat and popped the latch on the box. When the door fell open, he said, "Holy shit."

I leaned over as a stack of bills started sliding out. "Whoa."

He held out his hands. "Looks like we hit the jackpot twice in two minutes, missing phone, missing money. There's a whole lot more than ten big ones like your mom had guesstimated."

"We need something to put them in, like a bank bag," I said.

"No doubt." He gathered the bills into a pile then handed it to me, and I needed to stretch both hands to hold them all together.

Smoke pushed his seat back for a better vantage point. He pulled out the unopened pack of cigarettes and the phone charger. "Just about everything we were wondering about in this one little box."

"I'll plug in the phone, and it should be charged by the time we get back to Mayo," I said.

"Good plan. Sheriff's probably got a million missed phone calls by now."

"Let's hope he'll realize how much he's been missed very, very soon."

Smoke nodded. "I got evidence bags and a blanket in my vehicle. I'll feel better if we put the money in a bag, put it in Denny's trunk, and cover it up. The sooner we can get it all securely back in his safe, the better."

"Yes."

Smoke went to his vehicle, and I pushed the button to open the sheriff's trunk. When we met at the back of the car, Smoke pushed the trunk door open wide and said, "Another revelation."

I looked inside and laying there was the sheriff's duty belt and Glock, along with his uniform shirt with all of the brass attached. "It seems crazy that he'd put it in his trunk, but I guess it makes about as much sense as anything else."

"I guess."

We put the bag of the money next to the other items and covered them with the blanket. When we got back on the road, I phoned my brother and told him our status. He said Denny had been mostly sleeping since we'd left. He'd open his eyes for a minute then fall back asleep again. The medical experts said it was helping him heal.

We made it safely back to St. Mary's, and Smoke followed me into the parking garage. We found side-by-side spots on the top level. I unplugged the sheriff's phone and stuck it, along with his keys, in a side pocket of my bag. Smoke was waiting by his vehicle when I joined him.

"Let's spend some time with the sheriff and give your mother and John Carl a break. And then I'd like to head home and get those items back in place." He blinked at the sheriff's car.

"I agree. I talked to Gramps on the way here, and he's fine with Queenie staying there as long as necessary. Or forever." I smiled.

Smoke looked at his watch. "It's coming up on five o'clock. Let's see how everyone's doing, and then we'll figure out what our next course of action should be."

When we stepped into Room 316, I first took in the overall scene then zeroed in on my mother's profile, and her hand on Denny's, her fingers capturing his. John Carl was sitting in the corner, working on his laptop. He saw us before Mother did, nodded, and stood up then set his computer on the chair behind him. Mom turned her face to mine and her lips curled up in a slight smile that didn't erase the sadness in her eyes.

Looking at the man in the bed, I still found it difficult to believe it was Sheriff Dennis Twardy. Illness and injury had him at the mercy of a medical miracle. He'd always had a strong presence. A number of times he put the fear of God into me when I'd messed up, and he'd called me to his office to advise me on the errors of my ways.

But when he was with my mother, he was a kinder and gentler soul, and I was genuinely happy for both of them. I'd accepted he would one day be my stepfather, but didn't think I'd ever be able to let go of the fact that he was the sheriff, my boss.

I blinked away tears before they spilled out of my eyes then moved behind my mother and put my hands on her shoulders. John Carl came and stood beside me. Smoke hung near the end of the bed.

"Denny's about the same," Mother said.

"What do the doctors and nurses have to say?" I asked.

"Doctor Heath was by a while ago to check on him and said it's early yet. In some patients, once the pressure of the hematoma is relieved, they can get back to normal pretty fast. But with the stroke, well . . ."

"He doesn't seem to recognize us yet," John Carl said.

"Corky, why don't you take your mother and brother out for a bite to eat? I'll hold down the fort here," Smoke said.

I saw the relief on John Carl's face. "Good idea," I said.

Mother nodded and slowly pulled her hand away from Denny's. She slid out of the chair and stood up. I mouthed, "Thank you," to Smoke as my family and I headed out the door. We didn't say much while we waited for the elevator, or on the ride down, or until after we'd settled at a table in the visitors' cafeteria with our trays of food.

I quietly told them about our trip to Lyndale, the house, what the neighbors had said about the caretaker and others who helped maintain the property. My mother and John Carl listened without asking any questions. When I told them Smoke and I felt we needed to return the "items" to the safe, my mother said, "Yes, I'd feel better if you did."

"Mom, what do you want to do?" John Carl asked.

"I'm going to stay here at least one more night."

"Okay then." He looked at me. "I'll stay with Mom."

Mother grinned from ear to ear. "Thank you. But when do you have to fly home?"

John Carl scrunched his face together, the way he did when he had news most of us would have blurted out long before. "I don't."

"You don't what?" I said.

"I don't have to get back anytime soon. Emily is getting married." Emily was his ex-wife.

Mother's fork fell out of her hand and clinked on her plate.

I swallowed wrong and started choking. When I stopped enough to take a sip of water, I managed to say, "What? Why didn't you tell us?"

"I am telling you," he said.

My mother pulled out her calming voice from somewhere. She touched John Carl's hand with her own. "I'm so sad for you, dear. I know you were hoping she'd have a change of heart."

John Carl looked down. "I did until a few months ago, and then I finally realized it wasn't going to happen."

"I can't believe she's getting married," I said.

He shrugged. "We're selling the house."

Mother's face brightened a bit. "Are you still thinking of moving home?" As much as she wanted their marriage to work, that would be the big bonus for her if it didn't.

John Carl, a man who didn't smile much, smiled. Big. "Grandma and Grandpa offered me a deal if I want to buy their house."

"Their house in Oak Lea by *us*?" I was stunned for two reasons. John Carl had moved to Colorado to get away, not only from our mother's hovering, but also because both sets of grandparents and I were all close by. We all knew what he was up to, whether we wanted to know it or not.

The second reason was my grandparents had been encouraging me the past couple of years to move from the home I'd built to their older farmhouse. And I was strongly considering it. But no matter; if John Carl got it instead, that was fine with me.

Mother smiled. "John Carl, my prayers have been answered. Those prayers anyway." Her smile faded when she uttered the last sentence.

I took a last drink of water and grabbed my bag from the back of the chair, pulled out the sheriff's phone and car charger, and passed them to my mother. "His phone is nearly fully charged. Whether or not you want to leave it on until Denny's able to take calls is up to you."

Mother put the items in her purse. "Okay."

"Smoke and I should get on the road before long. But you know I'm just a phone call away if you need me." I looked at John Carl. "Will you make sure Mother gets to her hotel room at a decent hour tonight?"

He nodded and Mother raised her eyebrows.

19

Smoke and I made the trip back to Oak Lea in the two vehicles. The sun had been down over an hour when we pulled into Sheriff Dennis Twardy's driveway. The automatic garage door opener was clamped to the sun visor, and when I pushed the button the door went up, and I drove in.

I depressed the trunk button and it popped open, and then I got out of the car, taking the sheriff's keys and my bag with me. Smoke went straight to the trunk and pulled out the duty belt, uniform shirt, bag of money, and blanket. "I'll put this in my car." He held up the blanket then jogged over, opened his back door and tossed it on the seat.

I followed with my own bag and put it on his front passenger side floor.

We walked to the house entrance door inside the garage. "Let's go out the front door when we're done," he said as he pressed the button mounted on the wall. The garage door closed as we stepped into Denny's kitchen.

I flipped on the lights. "I'll leave his keys here." I dropped them on the counter then lifted my arm, palm up. "After you."

Smoke raised his eyebrows and took in a breath. We headed down the hallway that led to the sheriff's bedroom. Smoke found the light switch inside and turned it on. We walked to the closet, and he handed me the shirt. I slipped it onto a hanger and hung it on the pole.

"I'm going to put his side arm in the safe." He pulled it out of its holster and set it on the top shelf. "I feel silly even saying this, but neither one of us was ever alone with the money, if it ever comes to question."

"You never know," I said.

"I think we should keep the money in the bag rather than messing around with it." He set it in the safe and then took a picture of it before closing the door. "There. As far as we know, Denny is the only one who knows the combination. Ready to get out of here?"

"More than. It feels creepy in his house tonight."

"That's because Denny is supposed to be here, and he's lying in a damn hospital bed instead. It feels downright empty in here."

We turned off the lights then made our way in the dark to the front door. I punched in the alarm code Mother had provided to disarm it, opened the door, and then I reset the alarm. "Okay, we have twenty seconds to get the heck out of here." I took off in a sprint.

Smoke shut the door. "Very funny, little lady." He joined me at his vehicle, and as we climbed in, we discussed our next stop. "When I talked to Gramps about an hour ago he told me he'd rather have Queenie spend the night there."

"That's just as well. She's good company for your gramps."

When Smoke pulled into my driveway, I said, "It's Saturday night, and since neither one of us has a hot date, do you want to come in and wind down with a beer? I think I even have some of Mother's pasta leftovers in my fridge."

"Food you say? And beer?" He turned off the ignition. "Sounds like unwinding here is way better than with a bowl of peanuts and yogurt raisins at my house."

"Yogurt raisins?"

"They aren't bad. I'm trying some more healthy options."

I laughed out loud. "Whatever."

We entered through the front door then I did a quick house check, and Smoke headed to the kitchen. When I joined him, he had two bottles of beer sitting on the counter. He popped off the tops and handed one to me.

"Thanks." I took a long sip then set it down and opened the refrigerator. I found the bowl of chicken and broccoli with penne pasta in a parmesan Alfredo sauce. Smoke stepped in beside me, and I knocked into him when I turned around. He reached out to prevent the bowl from falling from my grip.

"I thought for a second it was going to be peanuts and yogurt raisins after all," he said. I gave him a little shove with the bowl then set it on the counter. When I lifted the lid, he leaned over. "It even smells good cold."

"If I heat the whole bowl, we should be able to finish it," I said.

"With no problem."

I put the dish in the microwave then gathered the eating utensils we needed. "Would you like to sit at the kitchen counter or eat in the dining room?"

"What the heck? Let's be civilized and sit in the dining room."

He helped me set the table then I looked in the refrigerator for something to go with the pasta. I found a bag of Caesar salad I'd bought and forgotten about. A look at the expiration date told me it was still good for two more days. I opened it and mixed it in a bowl then handed it to Smoke. He carried it to the table while I found hot pads to lift the bowl out of the microwave. I took it into the dining room then we sat down. When I bowed my head for a silent prayer, Smoke interrupted, "Say it out loud."

"Lord, thank you for this food and for friends. And please heal Denny. Amen."

Smoke was smiling when I raised my head. "Amen."

We dished up and made appreciative sounds as we ate, enjoying my mother's fine cooking. We needed a little break, some time to decompress. But with so many unknowns surrounding the sheriff's condition and the Fryor-Everton case, it was impossible to completely relax.

Smoke stood and picked up his empty plate. "You want another beer?"

"I do, but I better not. Mother and John Carl will call if something happens, and I might need to head down there. It could be at midnight or four in the morning. Who knows?"

Smoke disappeared into the kitchen for a minute, returned with a beer, and sat back down to wait for me to finish eating. "I'm still trying to make myself believe your brother is moving back to Oak Lea."

"You and me both. And Mother too, I'm sure."

"I still do a double take when I see him. He could be Carl's twin, and I'm looking forward to getting to know him better."

I nodded. "John Carl is not the easiest guy in the world to get to know. He's naturally shy, more of a loner. But once you break through all that, you'll find a topnotch guy. And smart. Ask him just about any question, and he usually has the answer. He's one you want on your team."

"I've been looking for a good Trivial Pursuit partner."

I smiled. "It'll be great having him back, but weird with him living in our grandparents' house."

"That will be a change, all right. I'm sure your mother's over the moon." Smoke took a sip of beer. "And that raises the question; will her fiancé be back to normal anytime soon, or ever?"

"I'm trying to stay positive. He wasn't kidnapped, and he's being treated at the Mayo Clinic." I put my fork on my plate, stood up, gathered what dishes I could hold, and carried them to the kitchen. Smoke followed behind with the rest. He set them on the counter by the sink.

"Hey, thanks for helping me finish up that pasta," I said

"Any time at all. It really hit the spot." He picked up a dish towel. "I'll dry."

I turned on the water, added detergent then set the dishes in the sink. "Thanks, but I'll just let them soak overnight."

"Yeah, well what if you get that phone call and have to leave? It might be Monday before you get back, and I can tell you from past experience that dishwater gets pretty stinky, even by the next morning."

"Okay." We dug into the chore. "Smoke, with those couple of things bubbling to the surface on the Toby and Wendy case, I'm torn between getting back at it on Monday or being with my mother and giving John Carl a breather."

"I'll tell you what, how about we make the trip down to Rochester tomorrow, and then you can decide?"

I nodded. "If I don't hear from Mom during the night, that'll work for me."

"Hard to believe Denny went into surgery just about twenty-four hours ago. It seems way longer than that. What time should we leave tomorrow?" he said.

I considered for a second. "Let's plan on nine."

I stared at the dark ceiling from my bed for a long time that night trying to fall asleep, but I couldn't quiet my mind. Sheriff Dennis Twardy was dealing with illness, injury, and surgery. The question was, why had he headed down to Iowa with a big wad of cash in the first place?

My thoughts drifted to John Carl. So my ex-sister-in-law was getting married. The woman who didn't want to be married had apparently changed her mind. And he was moving back to Oak Lea and buying my grandparents' house, no less.

And then there were all the upsets with the Toby-Wendy case. The DNA genetic test results comparing David Fryor's sample with that of the male victim was set to be completed by Monday. That would settle things, one way or the other, for their family.

The most frustrating part of the investigation was finding at least one person who knew what had really happened that night. Like Harry Gimler, perhaps? We were not ready to rule him out yet.

My ringing phone woke me up at 8:12 the next morning. It was my mother. "Good morning, dear."

"Hi, Mom, how's Denny doing?" I sat up realizing Smoke would be picking me up in less than an hour.

"He's still sleeping a lot." When she paused, I heard her sniffle. "I don't know if he'll ever remember who I am, Corinne."

"Hey, it hasn't even been thirty-six hours since his surgery. His brain has to heal and that takes time," I said.

"I know, but it's so difficult seeing him like that, not looking like himself at all. They're talking about moving him to a nursing home, maybe the day after tomorrow. Either Tuesday or Wednesday."

"Are they making recommendations of a place?"

"I told them I'd like him to be in Oak Lea. So they're going to see if Parkwood Nursing and Rehabilitation Center has an opening. They have a wonderful rehab program, from what I've been told."

"That's good to know. Smoke and I are planning to drive down there this morning. Can I bring you and John Carl anything?"

"Oh. Well, thanks, but I'd rather you stay there to be near Gramps. It'd be nice if you'd take him to church."

"I can do that, if you're sure."

"I am. John Carl is here."

When we disconnected, I called Gramps first. We talked a bit then I told him I'd be over to get Queenie shortly, and would pick him up for church at 10:10.

"That'd be just fine, Corky," he said.

I phoned Smoke and brought him up to speed

"Okay then, I'll play catch-up here at home, and if we're needed we can get there lickety-split," he said.

"Thanks, Smoke."

Sitting in church, with Gramps by my side, gave me more comfort than I had thought to hope for. When he reached over and took my hand, like he had when I was a little girl, it made me long for the days when life was more carefree. Toward the end of the service, Pastor Hobart read through the list of special prayers, and I wondered if he added the one, "For those who put their lives on the line to defend us, including members of the military and peace officers," because he'd noticed I was there.

As it turned out, I was very grateful he'd sent up that prayer because, as it turned out, someone close to me in the sheriff's department, and maybe me along with him, might not have survived a critical incident without the divine protection he'd asked for.

Gramps and I had lunch at The Sandwich Shoppe where their beef sandwiches were made from meat they roasted themselves, not from deli meat. My personal favorite, however, was their chicken salad; I'd never had better anywhere else.

It was good for Gramps to get out, for both his physical strength and emotional well-being. After lunch, I talked him into coming to my house for a while. We were on County Road 35 waiting to take a left on Brandt Avenue when I noticed the long-haired, bearded man in his white Chevy SUV in the line of oncoming traffic. He gave me a quick glance as he passed. I had to wait for five more cars before I could turn around and follow him. And no one seemed to be in a particular hurry—in keeping with what my Grandpa Aleckson called them: Sunday drivers.

"Gramps, I need to catch the license plate of a vehicle that just went by, so hang on." Gramps didn't say a word when I did a quick U-turn and headed east. But when the line of cars went around a big curve, I noticed the vehicle in question was no longer among them. *Damn.* There were a number of cross streets and driveways between Brandt and that curve, so the chances of picking the one he'd taken would be a crap shoot.

"I lost him."

"Just who is it you're after?" Gramps said.

"I'm not after him, exactly. There's something about him that's off, and I want to find out who he is."

He leaned in toward me. "Your gram had that sixth sense, too."

"Gram did for sure. Me? I think mine comes from my experience dealing with all the people I do, more of a keen sense. And this guy is sending off bad vibes as far I'm concerned. I haven't had a face-to-face with him yet, but I've seen him a few times in his vehicle. The first was by Whitetail Lake, then he was in Mister Fryor's neighborhood, and now he's back on County Thirty-five. Maybe he was at Whitetail again."

"He could be a fisherman, or maybe he lives out that way."

"You are absolutely right." There was no reason to pound on the subject with Gramps. If the man lived in the area, I was bound to see him again.

Spending a few hours together was therapeutic for both Gramps and me. We talked for a while about my mother and how the sheriff's healing might progress. About John Carl moving back and buying the Alecksons' house. About my grandparents getting stranded and delayed when their car broke down.

After a time, Gramps drifted off to sleep in an overstuffed chair with his legs extended, his feet resting on a hassock, and Queenie close beside. I brought the afghan Gram, his wife, had made for me and smiled as I spread it across him. He stirred slightly then seemed to fall into an even more peaceful sleep. He was an easy guy to have around.

John Carl and I sent text messages back and forth a few times. Sheriff had a number of visits but slept off and on throughout them. If he'd recognized anyone, he hadn't given any indication of it.

Chief Deputy Kenner phoned mid-afternoon. "Sergeant, I just left St. Mary's Hospital, and I wanted to tell you I think your mother is being a real trooper through all this. But it sure is tough seeing the sheriff laid up like that."

"I'm glad you went to see him. He might be more aware than he's able to communicate."

"I think so too."

"Mike, I've been wondering about something. Detective Dawes didn't look through the sheriff's cell phone after we found it. He didn't want to without permission. We were counting on Denny being able to tell us what happened, but it looks like that might take a while. He must have the number for the caretaker of his Iowa house in his contacts. We should find out if Denny talked to him, or anyone else in that area code, in the days before he left."

"Under the circumstances, I have to agree with you. If your mother wants to take a look, I'd be okay with that. I'll take responsibility, and if the sheriff calls me on the carpet down the road, I'll deal with it."

"Thanks, I'll talk to Mom."

Twenty minutes later my brother called with three Iowa phone numbers that were in the sheriff's contacts. And my mother learned, in her search of his calls, that one of them— Bob Leffew—had phoned Denny about an hour before he went missing that Tuesday morning. When I passed the information on to the chief deputy, he said since Smoke was the lead investigator in the case, he'd be the best one to handle the follow-up.

"I'll give Bob Leffew a jingle, see if we can shake something loose," Smoke said when I relayed Kenner's directive.

"I'm anxious to hear what he says."

"What are you up to now?" he said.

"Now? Not much, sort of cleaning. Why?"

"I thought we could do a three-way call between Leffew, you, and me. That way, if you have any questions you could ask them while he's on the phone."

"Sure, call when you're ready."

Within minutes, I got the call. Smoke covered the introductions then told Mr. Leffew that Dennis Twardy was having some medical problems, and we were talking to people in his contact list.

"I appreciate that 'cause I've been a little worried about him," Leffew said.

"Why's that?" Smoke said

"I called him the other day, wondering if he had any special instructions for the lawn, now that spring is here."

"And what'd he say?"

"To treat the lawn with weed and feed, like usual, and use my judgment if there's anything else I should do. My wife always helps me put a couple of plants by the doors to make it look like someone lives there.

"But here's the deal . . . my wife's been suffering through what Denny's wife did some years back, fighting a bad cancer. The good folks down here are even having a big benefit for her in a couple of weeks."

"We're sorry to hear about your wife, Bob," I said.

"Thanks. It's been rough, that's for darn sure. But we're trying to stay as upbeat as we can. Sorry, I didn't mean to get off-track. Anyhow, the reason I mentioned being worried about Denny is, he got real upset when we talked about it, then he got quiet and couldn't seem to talk anymore. He just hung up. I figured it was because he knew what I was going through and didn't know what to say."

"Bob, did you know Denny was at his place in Lyndale for a few days this past week? Probably from Tuesday, maybe Wednesday until Friday night."

"What? Well no, I had no idea. Why in the dickens wouldn't he have let me know that? Mind you, it's not that we're close friends or anything, but I know my wife would have appreciated if he'd stopped by. She and Denny's wife were best friends from first grade on. That's how we got connected."

"I can't speak for Denny of course, or get into any real details, but he took a fall and is at the Mayo Clinic recuperating," Smoke said.

"That's a real shame. Tell him we're pulling for him, and we'll touch base when we can."

"We'll pass that along," I said.

"Thanks for talking with us." Smoke gave his contact information then Bob hung up.

"Are you still there, Corky?" Smoke said.

"Still here."

"He seems like an up-and-up guy."

"He does, and I'm putting a possible scenario together here," I said.

"You mean the one where Denny gets news from Bob that is so upsetting he suffers a mild stroke?"

"That's the one. And with Bob mentioning the benefit, it might have triggered the sheriff to empty his safe so he could give the money to Bob's wife. Of course I'm speculating."

"But it makes sense."

"Yes it does, Detective."

"I'll give Kenner a call."

20

The next morning I was eager to get back to the Fryor-Everton case, but thought a short run might help jump-start my body. I dressed then clipped my S&W and cell phone on the waistband of my pants.

Queenie was disappointed that she wasn't going. "Sorry girl, this is going to be a quick one."

I slipped out the front door and walked to the end of the driveway then gradually worked up to about a seven-minute-mile pace on Brandt Avenue. I passed Gramps' house and continued to County 35 then decided to go as far as Whitetail Lake before I turned around. That was my 1.5 mile marker. As I got closer, I saw the white Chevy SUV sitting by the lake. A few seconds later, the turn signal started flashing and the vehicle pulled away from the shoulder onto the roadway.

My heart pounded harder as it came nearer and my elbow pushed against the S&W, making sure it was there even though I had no concrete reason to believe I was in danger. Who was that man? The opportunity I'd been waiting for was now, and I didn't want to blow it. As the SUV drove past me, I read the license plate, and repeated it over and over in my mind. When I was sure I was out of the driver's sight, I stopped and sent myself a text message with the plate number.

I couldn't get home fast enough, and I was panting noisily when I punched in the code to open my garage door. I jumped in the unmarked squad car the chief deputy had assigned me while I worked on the Fryor-Everton case, and started the engine. I hit the on button of the mobile laptop then backed out of the garage. The laptop seemed to take forever to fire up, and when it was finally ready, I typed in the white SUV's plate number. A few seconds later, I had the name, address, and birth date of the owner: Chester Thorne, age 51, and a resident of Minneapolis. It wasn't a name I recognized. If he lived in Minneapolis, why was he hanging around Oak Lea, and more importantly, by Whitetail Lake?

I shut off the engine and phoned Smoke as I headed into the house to get ready for work.

"Chester Thorne, you say? I can't remember ever hearing that name before."

"No, me either. He's clean and clear." Meaning he had a clean driving record and was clear of outstanding warrants. "I'm going to run a criminal history on him when I get to the office and then ask Harry Gimler and Rudy Medlin's other two friends if they know who he is."

"Wait a minute. Didn't Keith Brady tell you that Rudy Medlin said a guy named Chet was after him?"

"A guy *going* by the name of Chet. Ah, I didn't think it through that far, that Chet is a nickname for Chester. Good thing I have you to hold my hand."

"Yeah, well, you've had a thing or two going on the last few days. I'll tag along when you meet with Gimler. I'm interested in what he has to say and watching him while he says it. Now that we've got the sheriff back, I'll be able to spend more time on Toby and Wendy's case."

"Good. I'll be at the office in about thirty minutes."

"See you there."

On my drive into town my mother phoned me with the latest report.

"The surgeon was just by on his morning rounds and said the team of doctors and nurses decided Denny is stable enough to move to a nursing home tomorrow. But when the staff checked with Parkwood, they found out there wouldn't be a bed available until Wednesday. Doctor Heath said that was fine."

"I'm glad he'll be close. How is he doing, overall?" I said.

"His vital signs are good. No fever. He can walk, but only with assistance for now. Denny seems to understand basic things, like he's not supposed to get out of bed unless someone is there to help him. He's learned to push the nurses' call button when he needs to use the bathroom.

"But he's not talking much except to ask where he is, at least a dozen times. I don't think he fully understands he's at the Mayo Clinic. The medical staff believes he'll keep healing and improving. The worst part is that he doesn't know who people are. Not me, not even Mike Kenner. And he's known him many, many years," she said.

"It'll come. Have you decided if you'll be staying until Wednesday then too?"

"I will, and John Carl's fine with that."

"We all appreciate him being here. And I'd be happy to run down after work today or tomorrow, if you'd like."

"Spend the time with Gramps instead. He told me he had the best time with you yesterday," she said.

"Hey, I had the best time with him." I pulled into the sheriff's parking lot. "I'm at the office so we'll talk later."

"I love you, dear."

"You too, Mom."

I grabbed my briefcase, headed into the building, and found Smoke in his cubicle. He was reading a criminal complaint and slipped off his glasses when I said, "Hello."

"Hello, yourself. I can run that criminal history, if you've got Chester Thorne's info."

I fished the paper I'd written it on out of the side pocket of my briefcase and handed it to him. "I'll run to the squad room and print out his vehicle registration, so you can see what he looks like."

I took care of that, and when I returned to Smoke's desk he shook his head. "Nothing shows up in the criminal records on him."

"Figures. I got my hopes up that Chet is the Chester I've been seeing and that he'd have a record. But nothing, not even a traffic violation." I gave Smoke the sheet with Thorne's information and driver's license photo.

He studied it a moment. "He looks like a cross between a mountain man and an old hippie, all right. And he seems vaguely familiar. But with his eyes half-closed, and most of his face covered with hair, it's hard to say why that would be."

"I thought the same thing the first time I saw him, when he looked at me. Maybe it's that similar-looking scowl we get from a lot of the people we arrest."

Smoke chuckled. "That could be it."

My phone rang and I said, "Yes!" when I recognized the number on the display. "It's the regional crime lab." I pushed the on button. "Sergeant Aleckson."

"Sergeant, it's Ben over here at the lab."

"Hey, Ben."

"I know that you and the Fryor family have all been on pins and needles wondering about the test results. I think Joy, our reviewer, got here at the crack of dawn to finish up. You ready?"

"You know it."

"There is no way that David Fryor and the male victim found in the Charger are related, much less brothers." My heart dropped into my stomach. The good news was that Mrs. Fryor had not gotten pregnant with Toby by a man who was not her husband. But then, what happened to Toby Fryor all those years ago, the night Wendy and another young man had been killed?

"Will you repeat that for Detective Dawes? I'm handing him my phone."

Smoke took the phone from my hand. "Hello. . . . No kidding. That opens up a whole other can of worms. . . . We appreciate the ramped-up efforts by you and your staff. . . . Yup, you too." He hit the end button and handed the phone back to me.

"A can of worms is right. I'll give Mister Fryor a call to see when it'd be a good time to stop by," I said.

"I'd just head over there, if I were you. I'd go with you, but I should finish reviewing these complaints first."

"All righty." I picked up my things. "When do you want to go to Harry Gimler's place?"

Smoke gave his desk a tap. "That's right. I got to thinking about the Fryors and put old Harry out of my mind." He pushed his chair back and stood up. "I'll finish these up later. Let's go visit those folks."

We drove to the Fryors', but no one was home. I thought about trying to reach David on his cell phone, but decided against it. "Let's try back later," I told Smoke.

Smoke headed to Harry Gimler's house next. I wondered what condition he'd be in and was relieved when he opened the door and appeared sober. Nor did he smell like a perfumed Christmas tree. "Deputies," he said without a smile.

It seemed Smoke was waiting for me to go first, so I piped up with, "Good morning, Harry. Mind if we come in for a few minutes? We have a name and a picture to run by you."

"All right, but just so you know, I'm working." He reluctantly led the way to his living room. The den door was open. I snuck a glance inside and was drawn to the striking appearance of the paneling made from his grandfather's barn. I was pleased he'd repurposed some of it.

Harry offered us seats and I sat next to him on the couch. "We're wondering if you know a man by the name of Chester Thorne," I said.

Harry didn't have time to consider the question before he answered, "No, I don't. Why do you ask?"

"Think back to the party days at the farm. Anybody named Chester ever show up?"

"Not that I know of. I gave you the names of the ones I remembered," he said.

"How about Chet?"

"Chet?" The way his head turned slightly made me think he did. "No," he said.

I'd folded the sheet of paper with Chester Thorne's driver's license information so that only his photo was visible. I handed it to Harry. "Here's a fairly recent picture of him."

Harry's shoulders twitched, like maybe he did know him after all. He shook his head. "And I don't think I'd want to know him."

"He doesn't have the friendliest face in the world, I'll give you that," Smoke said.

I stood up, took the paper back, and stuck it in my back pocket. "Anything else you've thought of from back then? Things that didn't seem right, other people Rudy hung around with?"

He shook his head. "No."

I stood up. "We'll let you get back to work then."

Smoke and Harry got up and we all started toward the front entry. I stopped at the den's open door. "Do you mind if I take a look at the inside of your room? I love old barn wood."

Harry hesitated then said, "If you can stand the mess."

"Looks pretty tidy, if you ask me," Smoke said.

We stepped in the room, and I admired the weathered wood and the craftsmanship of the installation, and wondered about the cost. And then I spotted something curious on one of the boards and pointed to it. "Harry, did your grandfather have beef cattle that he shot in his barn?"

Harry's chin pulled into his neck. "What are you talking about?"

Smoke walked over for a closer look. "Yup, I'd be willing to bet a thousand dollars that it's blood. Look at the spray pattern."

Harry squinted his eyes then opened them wide. "You think those little dots are blood?"

Smoke and I both said, "Yes."

"My grandfather owned a shotgun, but I never saw him use it. I remember him telling me about shooting a fox that was killing his chickens. Maybe it was in the barn. And to answer your question, no, he didn't have beef cows. Just dairy."

The height of the blood drops on the panel was consistent with something much taller than a fox. "Where did he keep the gun?"

Harry processed the question a moment. "In the barn, standing in a corner."

Smoke honed in on that. "He kept a loaded gun where kids could get a hold of it?"

"No, he never kept it loaded. He stored the shells on a shelf, too high for kids to reach. And we weren't allowed to go near it, anyway."

But not everyone followed the rules. I willed my voice to be calm. "Harry, any idea what happened to your grandfather's gun?"

He gave a small nod. "It's in a shadow-box frame in my family room."

Smoke turned to him, and in an even voice said, "May we see it?"

"What's going on here?" Harry said.

"You really don't know?" Smoke said.

"Know what?"

"Homecoming night, thirty-three years ago, two teenage kids were shot in your grandfather's barn. And then their bodies were stuffed into Toby Fryor's Dodge Charger, and the car was pushed into Whitetail Lake."

It's a good thing Harry hadn't been drinking because watching him stumble to his desk, and plop down hard on a layer of papers, made me think he wouldn't have made it if he'd been drunk. "The two people in the car were *shot and killed*?"

"Yes, that's what happened. Tragically. But we didn't know where it'd happened. I think we've just gotten our answer. Sergeant?" Smoke looked at me.

I nodded. "It looks like it was in Mister Williams' barn."

Harry's face grew paler by the minute. "I didn't know, I swear I didn't know." Harry shook his head back and forth a few times. "That must have been what my cousin Rudy meant when he told me he'd helped his friend do something really bad. I suppose it was around that time. He was afraid something would happen to him if he said what it was."

"And he gave you no indication what it was?" Smoke said.

"No, and I would never have guessed anything like that." Harry put both hands on the back of his neck and looked at his knees. "Rudy said it was best if I didn't know."

"What was his friend's name?" I said.

"He wouldn't tell me that either."

"Who did you think it might have been?" Smoke said.

"I have no idea. Every once in a while guys would show up here that struck me as troublemakers, but I stayed clear and never even heard half their names."

"Harry, why didn't you tell us all this in the first place?" I said.

"I didn't think there was any reason to. I figured those kids must have driven into Whitetail accidentally. No way did I connect it to the bad thing Rudy told me about."

"Then what 'really bad' thing did your teenage mind think Rudy was referring to?" Smoke said.

"I don't know; that they stole something or maybe beat a guy up. I didn't want to think about what it might be." Harry stood up, turned, and looked out his den window toward the lake. "I can't believe the couple in the car was shot and then pushed into Whitetail." Harry was visibly distressed. And probably about to fall off the wagon.

"Harry, show us that gun. Please," Smoke said.

Harry turned around slowly then lifted an arm in a "follow me" gesture. Smoke and I trailed after him to the steps off the front entry and then down to the lower level where an older model Remington pump-action shotgun was prominently displayed on the wall above a fieldstone fireplace hearth. And inside the deep glass front frame, next to the gun, was a box of shells. I doubted two pieces of evidence could have been more neatly or attractively packaged.

Smoke blinked a couple of times, like he didn't believe what he was seeing. "We'll need to take that into evidence. Either with your permission, or else we'll get a warrant."

Harry didn't utter a sound. He just stared and nodded. He had unwittingly openly displayed key pieces of evidence in a decades-old double homicide in his home. The man who supposedly had done his best to avoid trouble was now smack dab in the middle of the investigation of those murders.

Smoke phoned for Major Crimes to respond to our location then put a hand on Harry's shoulder. "Let's go back upstairs. Sorry to rock your world this way. Who would have guessed that the sergeant asking to have a look-see at your paneling would lead to this?"

Brian Carlson and Todd Mason, assigned to the Major Crimes Unit for the week, responded to Harry Gimler's house in short order with a bag of equipment. Mason closed the blinds in the den to shut out the light, and Carlson applied luminol to the area on the plank of paneling in question. The spatters lit up, as we'd expected. "So it looks like we need to take this board with us," Mason said.

Smoke delivered the bad news to Harry who was sitting in the living room, staring out the window. He didn't even flinch. "I understand. I've got more wood in my shed, so I can have it replaced."

That perked Smoke up. "Mind if we have a look at that? There may be more with blood evidence on 'em."

Harry nodded.

"Is that a yes?"

"Yes."

"Can you show us where they are?" Smoke said.

Harry slowly got out of his chair and walked to the front door. He then led the way to a two-story shed I estimated was eighteen feet wide by twenty-four feet deep. There were double doors on the front, secured with a keyless entry system. He opened the doors and needlessly pointed at the stacks of barn wood. The piles started by the back wall and took up about one fourth of the space. There were a number of old tools hanging on the front walls, but the floor was otherwise clear of items.

"We'll have a look then restack them as best we can," Smoke told Harry.

"I'll wait in the house then," Harry said.

I felt sorry for him. I couldn't help it. He was no doubt grappling with the magnitude of it all. He seemed to have limited coping skills, and things might get worse for him before they got better, especially without professional help.

Smoke apparently felt a little bad for Harry, too. "All right then, the sergeant will go with you."

Harry's eyebrows went together in a frown.

Thanks, Smoke. "It's not that we think you're going to compromise the evidence, Harry. It's a chain of custody issue," I said.

"Oh."

Harry and I went back inside his house and sat in the living room for a very long twenty-three minutes while Smoke, Mason, and Carlson examined pieces of barn wood.

Smoke returned to the house ahead of the deputies. "Harry, we removed three more boards from your collection, and will need to take them into evidence to run tests on them. Deputy Mason is getting a release form for you to sign."

Harry nodded. "Okay."

Smoke headed into the den. Carlson and Mason came in, and Mason handed me a clipboard and pen. Then they joined Smoke in Harry's den. I read over the release form listing the items that we were taking from Harry's residence then gave it to him. "Do you have any questions?" I said.

"No." He signed the form then gave it back to me.

It took another eleven minutes for the team to photograph and remove the blood-stained plank. Not that I was counting. But standing guard, instead of being part of the action, was not easy for me. Especially since Harry could not be coaxed into any kind of conversation.

Todd Mason carried the piece of paneling out of the den and Brian Carlson opened the front door for him. "Catch you later," Brian said.

Smoke went to the lower level and returned with the framed Remington shotgun and box of shells. "This is it then. Thank you for your cooperation and assisting the Winnebago County Sheriff's Department."

I got up, went over to Harry and offered my hand. He looked at me for a second then reached out his own hand and shook it. "It's strange the way things happen sometimes. Give me a call if you find you need to talk to someone. I've got some contact with professionals who are really good at listening."

"Thanks, maybe I will."

That gave me some hope for Harry Gimler.

21

I was working on reports in the squad room when my phone rang. When I saw it was David Fryor's number, I switched mental gears from the pay dirt we'd hit at Harry Gimler's to the DNA results the Fryors were waiting for. "Hello, David."

"Sergeant, my dad and I were sorting through the boxes at my mother's house, and we found some letters you need to see. Old letters from Toby." There was urgency in his voice.

"Where are you now?"

"At Dad's house."

"I'll be there in about ten minutes."

"Thanks."

I saved the report I was writing on a flash drive and stuck it in my briefcase. Smoke was in a meeting with the chief deputy, and there was no reason to interrupt them. I left the office and drove to Darwin Fryor's house. When I pulled into the driveway, David was waiting for me by the garage. He was squeezing a balled-up hand with the other one, and wearing a grim expression. I got out of my car in a heartbeat and joined him.

"I stopped by earlier today, but you weren't home," I said, in case that was a reason he was upset.

"You got the DNA results?" he said.

"I did."

"As it turns out, we know the boy in the car was not my brother. It couldn't have been Toby."

No wonder he looked about ready to crawl out of his skin. The old letters had already given him the answer. "Let's go inside," I said.

"My dad is trying to come to grips with it all, and I'm trying not to feel *this* angry. I don't want Dad to feel any worse than he already does."

I put my hand on his arm. "Let's go inside," I said again.

He looked at me for a second. "Okay. Come in, and join our family drama."

Mr. Fryor was sitting in a La-Z-boy with his feet up. He pushed the lever to sit upright when he saw me. "My wife deceived us all these years. How could she have picked one son over me and her other two boys?" It was a major family drama, and a question from the patriarch I couldn't answer.

"David said you found some old letters," I said.

Mr. Fryor nodded. "Starting back thirty-two years ago, a year after Toby ran away. Why would he do that anyway? The only thing we could come up with is he was running away from whoever it was that killed Wendy and the boy with her in the car. But Toby should have known the police would have protected him. *We* would have protected him."

Or he ran away because he was the killer. "Since Toby's car ended up in Whitetail Lake, we know he didn't take it with him when he left. Did he say who he ran off with, who he rode with?" I said.

"No, we haven't found any mention of that. Yet anyway," David said.

"Where did he go after he left Oak Lea?" I said.

David sank onto the couch and reached for the box sitting on the coffee table. He patted a spot next to him, so I sat down. "Not sure where he went to first, but he traveled around. He asked Mom for money, and she sent it to him. A pretty good chunk of it, too."

"I had David read me some of the letters, but there's still a lot we didn't get to yet." Mr. Fryor took out a handkerchief and rubbed his eyes with it. "Toby had the world at his doorstep then he takes off, leaves it all behind, and has us all wondering why. Almost all of us, that is."

I nodded. "You said the first letter came thirty-two years ago. There were no letters from the first year?"

"No, not that we've found," David said.

"And that's about the time my wife, Adela, left. Just about a year after he disappeared," Mr. Fryor said.

"He must have contacted Mom sometime during that first year, though," David said.

"I figure that's the reason she left, so she could keep Toby's secret," Mr. Fryor added.

People did illogical things for what they thought was a logical reason.

David handed me a stack of letters that had once been held together by a rubber band, evidenced by a few pieces still clinging to the envelopes. "This is the first batch."

I fingered through them, noting the postmarks. "He traveled a lot. Missouri, Kentucky, Tennessee, Illinois. From the dates on this pile, it looks like he sent a letter about once a month or so."

"And then the letters stopped fifteen years ago," David said.

"Really? Did you check for possible emails, phone records after that?"

"Not yet. This box of letters sort of stopped us in our tracks."

Understandably. "So what did Toby write about?" I said.

"One thing that struck us in one of the letters, he said something like, 'After what happened to Wendy, it's not safe for me come home again.' It sounds like he might have been in danger, that he was being threatened. And given the fact that he stopped writing, something might have happened to him after all," David said.

"It makes you wonder," I said.

"Take the box, see if there's anything in there that might help find him," he said.

"Why would Adela keep this from me, from all of us?" Darwin Fryor said. He was struggling, and it would take time and a lot of healing for him to come to terms with his ex-wife's decisions and actions.

I noticed there were no return addresses on any of the envelopes. I pulled a letter out of one and saw it was signed "Boo."

"Boo?" I said to the Fryors.

David answered. "That's what Mom called Toby when he was little."

"It's on account of Toby being on the rambunctious side, and getting lots of cuts and scrapes. He'd go find Adela with a pout on his face and say, 'Boo,' meaning he got hurt and needed a Band-Aid. So she called him Boo," Mr. Fryor said.

"Ah." I scanned through the letter and found nothing of import, at least not relative to our investigation. Toby was likely smart enough not to have put anything incriminating in writing, in the event his mother came clean or his letters were ever found.

That reminded me of something Darwin Fryor had said on our first visit.

"Mister Fryor, you mentioned that you hired private detectives when Toby went missing. And that your wife abruptly, in your opinion, called them off after what was it, six weeks?"

"Yes, right in there."

"So it's possible that was the first time Toby contacted Adela," I said.

Darwin and David looked at me with blank faces.

"I don't suppose you have phone records from back then?" I said.

"I don't suppose so. My wife took care of the household bills, and after all these years I just don't know," Mr. Fryor said.

"We've still got boxes over at Mom's to get through. We're planning to have another shot at them tomorrow. Hopefully," David said.

"You've had a lot to contend with in the last week," I said.

"It's been an emotional roller coaster, that's for sure." David tipped his head toward me and frowned. "Now that you know Toby wasn't the boy in the Charger, do you folks in the sheriff's department have any idea who it is?"

"No. Our biggest unanswered questions are: who is the male victim, and who killed the two victims? We did catch a break today. We found evidence that narrows down where the shooting took place."

"Where was it?" David said.

"The chief deputy—who's the acting sheriff for the time being—asked that we keep those details quiet for now, while we continue to investigate."

David nodded. "I understand. Thank you, Sergeant. You have a tough job."

"Sometimes it is that." I stood and picked up the box. "You have my number. And I know Detective Dawes will want to have a look at these letters, too."

"Sure. If you need to keep them for any reason, maybe we can get copies. My brother Wade might want to read them."

"Of course."

Smoke phoned me about an hour later. I was in the squad room finishing my report from the morning. "Hi, Smoke, are you sitting down?" I said.

"Yeah, if sitting in my car on my way to pick up some lunch counts."

"I guess it does. Anyway, the Fryors had a rather interesting find at David's mother's house."

"You make it sound like an archeological dig."

"Given the age of the find, that's not far off. It's a box of letters written by Toby to his mother, starting a year after he disappeared, and stopping about fifteen years ago."

"I'm pulling over." A moment later he was back. "What in the hell?"

"It seems Adela Fryor was helping Toby keep his life and times under very deep wraps. She didn't tell anyone else in the family about it."

"That is unadulterated craziness."

"I agree. And besides wondering why Adela did what she did—from a legal standpoint that is—the poor Fryor family is devastated."

"Yeah, I'm trying to imagine what it's like having a bombshell like that dropped in your lap. So can we have a look at the letters?"

"Yes, I have a box full of them in my trunk and wondered if the letters would be considered evidence."

"Not unless Toby committed some offense and put it in writing. It's not a crime to run away. In his case though, it's more than a little suspicious that he disappeared the night Wendy and an unknown male were killed and pushed into Whitetail Lake. Maybe there's something in those letters that gives some answers."

"That would be a godsend. The Fryors didn't read them all, but David told me Toby made a comment that it wasn't safe for him to come home after what happened to Wendy."

"Not safe, huh? I know kids can get intimidated by gang members and hoodlums, but those same kids grow up and eventually contact the authorities."

"Sometimes those kids dig holes so deep they don't know how to get out again," I said.

"That's true enough. Now that I think about it, I'm not so sure Toby would have been all that intimidated in the first place. Then again, we don't know what was going on with those characters he may have fallen in with at the Williams' farm. The ones Harry Gimler talked about."

"I was hoping when Harry saw that picture of Chester Thorne he'd say, 'I remember him.'"

"Same here. You're going to show Thorne's picture to Keith and Abe?"

"I think the easiest thing is to email them the photo itself with the information removed. And to Rudy Medlin's old high school in St. Paul for them to check on it too."

"Keep in mind that Chester Thorne may have had nothing to do with Wendy, or Toby, or Rudy," Smoke said.

"I am. I just need to find out for sure so I can get him out of my head."

"I understand. Where are you now?"

"At the office."

"I'll meet you back there shortly. Do you want anything from Burger King?"

I looked at the time: 3:10. "Sure, a double burger and fries would be good." That'd take care of lunch and supper.

I finished my report and was able to reach both Keith and Abe on their cell phones and got their email addresses. I'd decided to wait to contact St. Paul's Highland Park Senior High for the time being. Smoke came into the squad room as I was preparing to send the photo file.

"Here's your food. Do you want to eat in the break room?" he said.

"Sure, you go on ahead. I'll be there as soon as I'm done here."

Smoke glanced at the computer screen. "No wonder so many people hate their driver's license photo. Chester's looks more like a mug shot."

"He doesn't look any friendlier in person," I said.

"I feel like I've seen him somewhere, but I just can't place him. He sure looks older than fifty-one, more like he's seventy."

"He has not aged well, that's for sure."

Smoke shook his head. "No. Well, carry on and I'll see you in a few." He headed out the door.

Smoke and I were the only ones in the break room, and we theorized about the possible series of events that had taken place after the football game on Homecoming night all those years before.

"Toby had to have been at the Williams' farm that night. At least we know his car was there," I said.

"He was involved somehow. There's no doubt in my mind about that. The fact that he ran away tells us one of two things. Either he was in on the murders, or he did what he did to protect his own life," Smoke said.

"David Fryor told me Toby had been crabbier than usual that week. I know you've probably gone over it a thousand times in your mind, but knowing what you do now, did you notice anything negative going on between Toby and Wendy that night?"

Smoke shrugged. "Toby was on the moody side, and there was the extra pressure of wanting to win the big game. Add to that he didn't get crowned Homecoming King. When I look back, one thing that stands out in my mind is Toby and I barely talked that night. After he and Wendy disappeared, I figured he'd been avoiding people so he wouldn't give away their plans of running away. As it turns out, there was a whole lot more going on than that."

"His letters might give us some insights."

"Yeah, let's have a look at them."

I got the box of letters from my car and met Smoke in an interview room—a good place to go through them. The letters had likely been organized by the year, but some piles were more intact than others. The Fryors had been through the box enough to know the years the letters had been written. Smoke and I sorted them into stacks, in chronological order.

"I didn't know Toby's mother very well, but one thing I did catch was how she doted on him," Smoke said as we worked.

"And then she kept his very big secret and took it with her to her grave," I said.

"What have we got, seventeen years of letters? And it looks like he wrote close to one a month. Only a couple hundred, give or take. How about we read for an hour or so and call it a day?" he said.

"Sounds good to me. I need to pick something up for Gramps' supper tonight."

"I meant to ask how things are going with your family. They're moving the sheriff to Parkwood in the next day or two, huh?"

"Yes. This is all so unreal."

"It is that."

"Mother and John Carl will stay in Rochester until they move Denny back. My grandparents should be there any time now. They're planning to hang out at the hospital, at least until tomorrow."

"Good to know."

"I'll be relieved to have them back home again. They help my mom with Gramps and help keep things sane."

Smoke sniggered. "I'll have to hang out with them more often."

"It might help." I grinned and picked up a letter. "I guess the best place to start is at the beginning."

After we'd read a while without finding anything noteworthy Smoke said, "I have a theory."

"Yeah?"

"There are no letters the first year, yet Missus Fryor called off the private detectives after six weeks. Toby must have contacted her in some fashion."

"That's what David thought, too," I said.

"I think Missus Fryor would have destroyed anything that might've incriminated Toby, had he been party to the murders. And saved the ones with general information of where he was or what he was doing."

"That's a good theory, especially since the first letter reads like the second chapter of the book. The beginning is missing."

"We'll keep at it. Who knows what we'll find out?"

What we were about to find out was not in any of the letters.

22

I brought Gramps a chicken dinner with mashed potatoes and gravy from the deli and sat with him while he ate it. We talked again about what my mother's future with Denny Twardy might look like, and how wonderful it would be to have John Carl nearby again.

Sara phoned shortly after I got home. She'd gotten back from a conference Friday night, delivered Queenie to Gramps' house Saturday morning, and then spent the rest of the weekend with her parents. We'd sent a few text messages throughout and knew we were due for a marathon gab session soon.

"I can't stop thinking about Sheriff Twardy. It's such a shock," she said.

"That's for sure."

"Your Mom's still doing okay?"

"Within reason. Thank God John Carl is with her."

"He's a good guy, no matter what you say," she said.

"Yeah, yeah, yeah." I chuckled. "So how are you doing?"

"You know how it is when you're gone from work for a week. I've been playing catch-up and actually just got home from the office. I suppose it'll be hard for us to plan an evening of pizza and conversation until things settle down."

"We could shoot for Friday."

"Friday it is then. Back to that brother of yours, how's he doing?"

"I wanted to tell you this in person so I could see the look on your face when I did. But here goes, John Carl is moving back to Oak Lea and buying my grandparents' house."

"No way!"

"Way. Emily is getting married."

"No way!"

"Way. So that took care of John Carl's last ray of hope for reconciliation."

"It's time for him to move on. Way past it, in fact," she said.

"I agree, but he's super loyal, and it isn't easy for him."

"Oops, one of my probationers is returning my call. Gotta go, 'bye."

I said, "'Bye," but she was already off the line.

I heard back from both Keith Brady and Abe Greer, and neither one had recognized Chester Thorne from his photo or had ever heard his name before. It was possible he may be the Chet that Rudy Medlin had referred to, but how could we verify that?

Queenie and I went outside to burn off some energy. We played fetch the ball in the backyard until the sun went down, and I was all played out. Queenie was close to it. We headed back inside, and after we each had a long drink of cold water, I went into the sanctuary of my den office, plopped on the couch, put my feet up on the coffee table, and stared for a long time.

I tried to steer my thinking away from the sheriff's condition, all that the Fryors were trying to come to terms with, and wondering how my mother was coping. John Carl sent me a text message saying my grandparents were staying overnight with them in Rochester. One less concern.

"Well, Queenie, I'm going to try to finish that soak in the bathtub I started a few nights ago." I checked to be sure the doors were locked then I checked again, a reflection of how uneasy I felt with all the unsettled issues and distraught people in my life.

As I got undressed for my bath, Chester Thorne's driver's license printout fell out of my pants pocket. I picked it up and stared at what could easily be called his ugly mug. It wasn't because of his features either; it was what seemed to be lurking beneath his outward appearance.

I hadn't thought to ask the Fryors if Toby had ever mentioned hanging out with Chester. Then again, David told me Toby hadn't kept him in the loop, as far as his social activities were concerned. As it turned out, it appeared his mother was Toby's confidant. In any case, it was worth running Chester's name by them. I put the paper on the dresser next to my wallet and climbed into a hot, bubbly bath.

I was at my desk in the sergeants' office early the next day, going over deputies' reports, when Chief Deputy Kenner stopped by.

"So Dawes told me his old friend Toby made himself known in the form of some old letters to his mom."

I pulled a copy of his old high school photo out of my briefcase and threw it on the desk. "For nearly a week he had us going, thinking that he was one of the victims in the

Charger. But worse than that, look what he put his family through all these years."

"It's a crying shame, if nothing else."

"I've run both an Internet and a criminal history search on Toby Fryor, but nothing has shown up. His letters stopped fifteen years ago, at least according to what was in the box his mother kept. If he's still out there, he's got to be going by a different name."

"Who's this other character you've been checking on?" Kenner said.

"His name is Chester Thorne. And the only other guy by that name I found in my Internet search was from New York. He was born in the late eighteen hundreds, and died in the fifties. Chester apparently keeps a very low profile, and the three people I asked to look at his DL photo, besides Smoke, don't recognize him."

"Probably some guy who got caught up in the story of the recovered vehicle."

"It's possible, but I think he's got some kind of connection to the case. Whether he knew the kids or partied at the farm, I don't know. But I feel like it's something."

"You got his DL printout with you?"

I retrieved it from my briefcase. "Here you go."

"He looks like an old hermit, and not exactly someone you'd want to meet in a dark alley."

"Not exactly. And I shouldn't tell you this, but if I see him again, I am going to look very hard for any kind of reason to pull him over."

Kenner covered his ears and smiled. "I don't think I heard that."

"He could have been one of Rudy Medlin's friends. I'll ask Rudy's old high school in St. Paul to check their records. I'd pay Chester a visit at his home, but we have nothing to connect him to the case."

"Cold cases are never easy, and when you can't locate anyone who was at the Williams' farm that night, anybody who knows what really happened, it's about impossible. And on top of it all, we have no idea who the male victim in the car is."

"That's one of the worst parts for me, not knowing who he was. Could he have been a street kid his family didn't report missing? Rudy hung out with a rough crowd in St. Paul, and some of them made their way to his grandfather's farm from time to time. We're going to need a miracle to figure who killed those two, and why."

The way we got the answers to those questions, however, was not what I'd classify as a miracle. Then again, sometimes the devil is in the details.

Chester Thorne had never been a student at Highland Park Senior High School, according to Marge, the administrative assistant who checked the records for me. I contacted nineteen high schools in the Minneapolis and St. Paul areas over the next hours. Not one had a record of Chester Thorne ever attending their school.

It was early afternoon when I phoned Darwin Fryor to ask about Chester. I got the answering machine and decided to try David's cell phone instead of leaving a message. David's phone went straight to voicemail. I asked him to call me when it was convenient.

I picked my share of Toby's letters out of my briefcase, and read through most of them. There were references about times he'd spent with his mother and how great that was. But he never named the places where they'd met. Adela may have gone to wherever he was living at the time. It would have been chancy for him to return to Winnebago County, no matter what kind of a risk-taker he was.

I phoned Smoke and filled him in on what I knew. Then he said, "I'm tying up some loose ends on that burglary over in Little Mountain from two weeks ago. It got put on hold with all of our other stuff going on. And then I'll be heading home. I want to read through some more of Toby's letters."

"Yeah, I have maybe fifteen more of them myself. I'm going to finish them before I leave the office. In case he happens to mention a name, I'll be able to run a criminal history on it. And when David calls back, I'll be interested to find out if he and his dad found any more correspondence between Toby and their mother."

"Don't work too hard."

The day had raced by, even though I hadn't gotten as much new information as I'd hoped for. And there was nothing earth-shaking in the rest of the letters. I packed them, along with some papers in my briefcase, and drove home. After attending to Queenie, I changed into my running clothes then clipped my phone and the pancake holster holding my Smith and Wesson on my pants.

"Okay, Queenie, I'm going on a run. And when I get back, we'll go visit Gramps. Okay?"

She moved her head back and forth and barked, letting me know I couldn't get on the road fast enough.

I stopped to check in with Gramps on my way by his house. He was sitting in his usual spot in the living room, but the television was off and he was reading instead. It was peaceful without voices blasting out of that box for a change.

"Hey, Gramps, how was your day?"

"Just fine. Your grandma called and said she and your grandpa will be home around supper time. They're going to pick up some food and bring it over here to eat. They're hoping you'll be able to make it too."

"You bet. I can't wait to see them. And I can bring something too, like maybe a bottle of wine."

Gramps smiled. "I'm sure we'll drink it if you do."

"See you later then." I got back on my run.

I mentally reviewed the events of the previous day. We'd learned that Toby was without a doubt *not* the boy in the Dodge Charger. We'd suspected as much when the victim's DNA didn't match Darwin Fryor's, but when it didn't match David's either, that cinched it.

Then the Fryors found proof that Toby had been alive and hiding in some manner since that Homecoming night. At least until fifteen years ago. The question was, had he been at the Williams' farm when Wendy and the unknown male were killed? If so, was he a witness, or did he have an active role in their murders? Unless we found a witness from that infamous night, the case would remain as cold as ice.

My phone rang as I was running past Whitetail Lake. I pulled it out of its holder and slowed to a walk. "Sergeant Aleckson."

"Hi, it's David. Sorry, but my phone was dead and I forgot the charger at Dad's house. We were over at my mom's going through more stuff."

"Not a problem. How did it go today? You didn't happen to find any more correspondence from Toby did you?"

"No, not yet anyway. I'll take a look at Mom's computer tomorrow. Finding the letters yesterday was really hard on Dad, especially. He just sat on Mom's couch and stared while I went through the boxes today."

"I feel so badly for him. For all of you, David. The reason I called earlier is I was wondering if you remember Toby ever talking about a boy named Chester Thorne."

"What did you say?" When I repeated myself, David made a muffled sound then said, "Chester Thorne? *Chester Thorne?* That was my grandfather's name. My mother's father. Is that the name Toby's been using?"

I didn't know what to think and stopped dead in my tracks. Smoke had seen Chester Thorne's photo and hadn't recognized him as Toby Fryor. Although he thought he looked familiar. "David, I have a copy of Chester Thorne's driver's license photo. It'll be a while, but I can bring it over later for you to have a look. If you'll be home."

"We'll be here all evening. Chester Thorne. I *cannot* believe it."

"No. I'll call before I come over."

At least at that point in time, I thought I would.

Smoke lived about a half mile away so it was as easy to stop by as to call him later. I picked up my pace then slowed again as I headed down his driveway. I spotted the white Chevy SUV I'd been seeing for days parked off to the side, next to the line of trees, out of sight from where the house sat. Dear God!

I darted into the wooded area. Whatever Chester Thorne—or Toby Fryor—was doing there was not good. I moved so I had the house in view, hoping Smoke was in the yard with him. I saw Smoke's dog Rex lying on his side on the ground next to the front step. It looked like he might be dead.

My heart pounded as I pulled out my phone and dialed 911. Officer Robin answered, "Nine—"

I cut her off. "Robin, it's Aleckson. I'm at Detective Dawes' house, and I need back-up. His dog is down, and there's a suspect's car—Chester Thorne's car—hidden in the trees by the driveway. I don't know where Dawes is, or what we got here, but something's wrong. And tell the deputies no sirens and to stay out of sight."

"Ten-four, Sergeant. Weber's just cleared a scene about seven or eight miles away. I'll get him rolling your way and see who else is close."

"I'll keep my phone on so you can monitor."

"Copy that."

I stuck the phone back in its holder and ran to the where the trees ended and the lawn began, maybe thirty feet from Smoke's house. I bent over and scooted as fast as possible to the front door. Rex was breathing, but something was definitely wrong with him. I gave him a quick pat on the head then tried the front door knob. It wasn't locked so I turned it, pushed the door open a crack, and listened. When I heard a man's voice coming from the kitchen, I drew the Smith and Wesson from its holster.

I planted my body next to the wall and crept along. As I got closer to the kitchen, I was able to make out what the low, growling voice was saying. "Wendy just didn't get it. We were meant to be together. I forgave her for getting knocked-up. But not two months after the baby was born, she finds someone new. I knew I had to get rid of him, but as it turned out, they died together. Fools."

Smoke didn't answer him.

"Wendy's baby, that's why I'm here. I knew it had to be either you or Aleckson who was responsible . . ." My brain went into another place, hearing the reference to my father, and I didn't hear anything else until he said, "So let's make this as clean as possible. We'll walk to the end of your dock and finish it."

None of his words made sense, but the last ones kicked me into gear. I stepped into the doorway and trained my Smith and Wesson on the back of the man who called himself Chester Thorne. The man I believed was Toby Fryor. He was waving a handgun back and forth.

Smoke was sitting in a chair some feet away from him. There was blood running down his face from a cut by his eyebrow. His hands were behind him, either tied or cuffed, and a piece of duct tape covered his mouth.

The scene was out of a nightmare but was actually happening.

My vision tunneled and I focused on the wicked man standing not eight feet away. He had stolen lives and was planning to take another, one I valued as much, or more, than my own. "Toby Fryor, drop your weapon and turn around." He turned around but held onto his gun. "Drop your weapon!"

He lowered his arm at his side, but the gun remained in his hand. He sneered at me, and his eyes were like the black of night, the time when evil ones did horrendous things under its cloak. "Ah, Sergeant Aleckson, you should have left well enough alone, stirring things up with your fancy tests. I figured somebody would find my Charger in Whitetail Lake with two skeletons in it a long time ago. My wallet and jacket were in the car, and I've been waiting years to be declared legally dead."

"Funny thing, Toby, but even after all that time on the bottom of that lake in the cold water, the victims were not skeletons. They were pretty well-preserved, in fact."

His eyebrows shot up in surprise.

"And you didn't think we'd check the DNA to identify the victims?"

"Nobody'd even heard of DNA identification back then."

"So who was it, Toby? The male that was with Wendy in your car?"

"Some kid I thought was my friend, but he stole my girl. Who cares?"

"What's his name?"

"Sheldon. Wendy decided she was in love with him, and thought she'd run away with him. Away from *me*. She left with him after the game, and I followed them over to Rudy's grandfather's house. Neither one would listen to reason."

"So you killed them, shot them with Mister Williams' gun. And what about Rudy Medlin, where is he?" I tried for as much information as I could get.

"He was eaten by fish years ago."

"Twenty-seven years ago?"

"Maybe."

"Where'd you put his body? A lake, river, what? In Minnesota? Somewhere else?"

He didn't answer my question. "He was going to the police, and I couldn't let that happen. I got two things from him at least: his ID to use for a while, and his car to take me far away from Oak Lea."

His hand lifted that instant. But before his gun was in the firing position, my finger was on the trigger of the Smith and Wesson. I zeroed in on his chest like it was one of the practice targets I'd shot at hundreds and hundreds of times and emptied my gun into him.

As Toby Fryor collapsed to the floor, I saw the bewildered, then pained, then blank, then unseeing set of looks dance across his face.

23

"Sergeant." I heard Vince Weber's voice behind me, but I couldn't move. My eyes were fixed on the man crumpled on the floor. I was watching intently to be certain he was dead. "Sergeant," Weber said again. "He's down, and he's not getting up again. Ever again, Sergeant."

"It's Toby Fryor." I dropped my arm, but couldn't loosen the grip on my gun. Nor could I turn my back on the body. That is, not until Smoke made a moaning sound. That broke the spell and effectively changed my focus.

"Vince, take my gun. My fingers are frozen and we need to help the detective."

He holstered his Glock then moved in by my side and gently pried my fingers loose. "I got it. I'll call for medical help and for the ME."

"And Chief Deputy Kenner," I reminded him.

"Right."

I made a wide loop around Toby Fryor's body, knowing he was dead but not completely trusting that knowledge. Smoke squeezed his eyes together like his head hurt. I touched his shoulder. "Can you turn, and I'll free your hands first? It's better if you're the one to pull that tape off your mouth." He gave a slight nod and slid his body a quarter of the way around in the chair. He was wearing handcuffs. "Vince, I need your cuff key."

Weber hurried over. "Communications will get 'em all coming and notify Kenner." He pulled his key out of his breast pocket and was about to give it to me but changed his mind and unlocked the cuffs himself. "Your hands are shaking bad, Corky."

So they were, along with everything else in my body. When Smoke's hands were freed, he lifted and stretched his shoulders and arms, then shook the feeling back into his hands. He reached up and ripped the tape from his face in one quick motion. It made his face flinch. "Damn." He started to stand but wobbled left then right. Weber and I each put a hand on his shoulders to hold him down.

"Let's wait for the paramedics," I said.

"You probably got a concussion," Weber added.

Smoke leaned against the back of the chair then reached over and took my hand. "I owe you, big time."

Before I could respond, Smoke's house turned into pandemonium. Deputy Amanda Zubinski came in, followed by Deputies Holman, Levasseur, and Ortiz in what seemed like seconds. They were all careful to keep a wide berth around the body, and each one did a visual check of Smoke. The paramedics rushed in with their bags and attended to Smoke who refused to go to the hospital. But he said he'd see a doctor.

When the chief deputy arrived, he looked at the size of the crowd. "No wonder I had to park in Timbuktu." He studied Toby Fryor's body and the gun lying in his open hand. He shook his head then walked over next to Smoke and me, and put an arm around my shoulder. "Thank God you two are okay. You know the drill, Sergeant. You'll go on administrative leave of absence while we conduct the investigation. But it should be straightforward and go pretty quick. In any event, I want you to think of it as a well-deserved vacation."

"Yes, sir." An officer involved shooting required administrative leave, and I was fine with that, especially knowing Smoke would likely need some nursing help for a while.

"Chief Deputy?" Weber said.

"Yeah, Weber?"

"I witnessed the shooting, sir. And Sergeant Aleckson turned over her revolver to me. I checked, and it's empty. No bullets," Weber said and patted his left pants pocket.

"That'll expedite things. And good thinking, Sergeant, leaving your phone on. Communications has the recording. Whether it's high quality or not, we can work with it. Each of you needs to write out your statements, and the interviews will be more of a formality than anything else." Kenner turned to Weber. "And when the Major Crimes team gets here, you can turn the firearm over to them."

Weber nodded.

Kenner took a step closer to Smoke. A paramedic was applying a butterfly bandage to the cut above his left eyebrow. She then pulled a cold pack from her bag, wrapped a cloth around it, and applied it to the lump that surrounded the cut. "Hold it there for a few minutes. It'll help take the swelling down," she said.

"That's frigid," Smoke said.

"Do you need something for the pain?" the other paramedic asked.

"Nah, I got some ibuprofen here, but thanks."

The paramedics finished patching Smoke up then packed up to leave. "Be sure to get in to see a doctor," the first one said.

Smoke muttered something that sounded like both "yeah" and "nah." It could have been either one.

Kenner bent over for a closer look at Smoke's shiner. "Detective, it looks like you took a good one."

"I didn't hear a damn thing until he was in my kitchen with me. When I turned around he clobbered me, I'm guessing with his gun. What'd that bastard do to Rex? I know he would've alerted me if he could have."

"Don't worry, Rex is alive. He's sound asleep outside your door. I'm guessing Rex got shot with a tranquilizer gun because I pulled a dart out of his side," Kenner said.

I was so intent on seeing what was happening with Smoke's intruder, I hadn't even noticed the dart when I patted his head.

Kenner continued, "I called a veterinarian, and he's on his way to check him out, make sure he's okay."

"I should go out there, be with him when he wakes up," Smoke said.

"No, I'll put someone on doggie detail." Kenner turned to the roomful of deputies. "Okay, listen up. Weber, this is your service area, so you'll stay to help process the scene with the Major Crimes team. Zubinski, I'd like you to sit with Detective Dawes' dog Rex until the Vet gets here. And for the rest of you—thanks for responding so fast, but it's time to get back to your own service areas. We're covered here."

Deputies Brian Carlson and Todd Mason, on Major Crimes, came in as the other deputies, with the exception of Weber, were filing out.

Kenner spoke to Carlson and Mason. "It's none other than Toby Fryor," he said.

"Geez, just last week we'd thought it was his remains we pulled out of Whitetail," Carlson said.

"Yeah, that's what we thought, all right. For a while, anyway," Kenner said.

Mason turned to Kenner. "Doctor Bridey Patrick is on her way over from Ramsey. She'll be here shortly for the remains of the real Toby Fryor," Mason said then looked at me. "How are you doing, pal?"

I shook my head. "Still pretty numb."

The chief deputy and the deputies all nodded and assured me I'd be okay, each in their own words.

"Mason, I got the sergeant's firearm. We'll need to get it into evidence," Weber said.

Mason nodded then walked over to Weber, pulled an evidence bag from his pocket, and opened it. Weber dropped my gun inside, and Mason sealed the bag.

"Sergeant, Detective, are you up to writing, or at least dictating your statements today?" Kenner said.

"I think I can write mine," I said. After the adrenaline dump, I felt drained.

"I'm gonna have to dictate mine to somebody," Smoke said.

Chief Deputy nodded. "Okay, I'll get that taken care of. And I'll let you know if the BCA needs to interview any of you, like I mentioned. Sergeant, I don't see any blood spatter on you, but a fine mist isn't always easy to spot. We'll collect your clothes, in case the BCA needs them."

I looked down at my light blue shirt, black pants, and black running shoes. "Okay."

"Dawes, I'll check on Rex, see if the vet's here yet," Kenner said.

I looked at Smoke. "First, you need to see a doctor. Then you'll need a place to stay while they process your house and clean it up."

"Nix on the doctor, this old noggin of mine is as hard as a rock. Fryor got me where it hurt, but he would've done a lot more damage about another inch over."

"Then how about a compromise? Let Doctor Patrick have a look at it, see if your eyes are focusing right. If she says you don't have to go in, we won't make you," I said.

"She doesn't work on live people."

"Then it'll be a treat for her."

"To treat me?"

I shook my head instead of answering and smiled.

Kenner came back in and reported the veterinarian was with Rex, and Rex was waking up. "Vet says your dog might be a little sleepy, but should be back to his old self tomorrow."

"Thank God," Smoke said.

"I'll tell you what, we can either put you and Rex up in a hotel room for the night or—"

"No, I'll—" Smoke started.

"He'll stay at my house. I've got a guest room and a den office that works, too. And Rex is always welcome," I said.

Kenner nodded. "Okay. Let's get you out of here."

"Chief Deputy, before we go, I think Doctor Patrick should take a look at Smoke's head, see if she thinks he needs to go to the hospital."

"Good idea."

Smoke answered Doctor Patrick's questions and told her he'd lost consciousness for only a moment. He promised he would go to the hospital immediately if he experienced any confusion, drowsiness, double or blurred vision, nausea, vomiting, dizziness, or showed signs of memory problems. And then I promised her I would watch him for the same signs.

Weber helped Smoke get some things together for himself and Rex, and then Zubinski gave Smoke, Rex, and me a ride to my house. She came in to assist Smoke with his report. Rex was able to walk the short distance from the car into my den office with some help but collapsed on the rug and fell back asleep a second later. I hoped the veterinarian was right when he said Rex should be back to normal by tomorrow.

Smoke settled in on the couch in the den office, mainly to keep an eye on Rex. Mandy sat on the armchair with her clipboard, blank report form, and pen. "All right, Detective, you dictate and I'll record."

I heard Queenie barking like crazy in her kennel.

"Mandy, I'm going to shower and change and put these clothes in the bag for you. Then I'll rescue my dog so she'll settle down."

"That's fine," Mandy said.

I hurried upstairs and completed my tasks then carried the paper bag with my clothes and shoes downstairs and set them on the kitchen counter. I went into the garage where

Queenie was jumping around and gave me her "get me out of here" whine when she saw me.

"Queenie, some very bad things happened, and now we've got guests. It's Deputy Mandy, and Smoke, and Rex, and you need to be on your best behavior. Smoke has a bad headache and Rex needs to sleep."

She didn't understand all of that of course, but she knew something was wrong. Our den office had been converted into both a deputy's office and a hospital. Mandy was in an official capacity, recording what Smoke was saying. Smoke didn't greet Queenie with his usual friendly petting. Instead he dangled a hand by his knee. Queenie gave it a lick then went over to Mandy who scratched her head until Queenie left to check on Rex. He was snoring away, and Queenie stretched out beside him. I looked at Smoke and shrugged.

"It looks like my watchdog has his very own bodyguard," he said.

"If I didn't live in an apartment, I'd get a dog like that," Mandy said.

I smiled with pride. "I'll be in the kitchen writing my report."

The next hour went by in a blur. After Smoke and I finished our reports, Mandy Zubinski left to file them at the office. I crept quietly back into the den office. Queenie was still keeping tabs on both Rex and Smoke and wagged her tail when she thought I was joining her in the watch. Smoke was stretched out on the couch and appeared to be dozing. I pulled the afghan my Gram Brandt had crocheted for me from the shelf in my den office closet.

When I covered Smoke, he opened his eyes. "Hi."

"Hi. Can I get you anything to eat or drink?"

"Maybe later. Thinking about Toby kind of takes away my appetite." He pushed himself into a half-sitting, lounging position.

"For me, too. How are his father and brothers going to react to all of this? David is a nice, nice man, very genuine. So is his dad. I was supposed to go over there later, to show them Chester Thorne's DL photo."

"I'm sure the chief deputy is delivering the news in the best way possible. He's good at that."

I nodded. "Before we left, Kenner told me he's arranging a debriefing for us. We need one, and so does Vince."

Smoke closed his eyes and pulled the afghan in tighter against him. "It's just a hell of a deal."

I phoned John Carl, told him all that had happened and asked him to break the news to Mother—as gently as possible. I said I'd talk to Grandma Aleckson myself. "I was invited to have supper with them at Gramps' house tonight."

"Corky, no wonder Mom freaks out about your job. I worry about you, too."

"I don't know what to say except I know, and I'm sorry. But being a cop is all I've wanted to do for as long as I can remember."

"I guess it has. I'll fill Mom in."

"Thanks, and one more favor. Will you call Sara and tell her too, and let her know I'll talk to her tomorrow." The news would be around the county departments in no time.

"I can do that for you. You know Mom will be calling you as soon as I tell her."

"Yes, and I want to talk to her—after you soften the blow."

"Hang in there," he said and disconnected.

I stared at the phone for a minute before dialing my grandmother's number. Grandma Aleckson was the one person in the world who'd always understood me better than anyone else. It seemed like we had been cut from the same cloth, forty years apart. When she answered her phone, hearing her voice shook my pent-up emotions and unshed tears loose, and I broke down crying.

"What's the matter, My Heart?" Her pet name for me.

"It's bad . . . like last year . . . when I had to shoot . . ." My voice cracked.

"Langley Parker." When I remained silent, she said, "Where are you, dear?"

I managed to say, "Home."

"We'll be there in a few minutes."

I wanted to tell her it was all right, that I was all right, but that was a lie. "O-k-kay."

I was barely off the phone when Mother called. I sniffed and made myself stop crying. "Hi, Mom."

"Corinne. Tell me you're all right, that you weren't injured."

"I wasn't hurt, and Grandma and Grandpa are coming over."

"I wish I wasn't so far away."

"You'll be back tomorrow, and that's when I'll need you."

"I love you so very much, and I never want anything to happen to you."

"That'd be good. And I love you too, very much."

When we hung up, I peeked in the den office to check on Smoke and our dogs. Queenie was the only one who opened her eyes when she heard me. I eased the door shut then headed out the front door to wait for my grandparents. Their car came from the opposite direction of where they lived, so I figured they'd been at Gramps' house preparing for dinner. They pulled in the driveway and stopped then got out of the car. Even in their seventies, they were both active, and fit, and strong.

I met them halfway and we stood on the sidewalk in a three-way embrace for a good minute. I was finally able to get some words out. "Smoke's sleeping in my den office. He got hit on the head. And his dog got drugged, and I stopped there on my run, and Toby Fryor was there with a gun, and I shot him."

My grandparents stepped back an arm's length and stared at me. "Toby Fryor? Wasn't his body just recovered from Whitetail Lake?" Grandma said.

I shook my head. "It wasn't him."

"No? I think we better go inside so you can tell us the whole story," she said.

My grandpa, a man of very few words, gave me an encouraging nod.

We went into the house quietly enough, but Queenie whined at the den office door seconds later. I let her out, and she lapped up as much attention from my grandparents as she could get in a minute then headed back to her station by Rex.

The three of us followed her, looked in the room, and then I closed the door. "That's something to behold in a dog so young," said the man of few words.

We made ourselves comfortable in the living room, with Grandma next to me on the couch and Grandpa in an armchair not two feet away. The whole story of the past week, every detail I could think of, spilled out my mouth. With the exception of what Toby Fryor had said about Wendy, Smoke, and my father. And then I confessed, "I have to come to terms with the sheer terror I feel knowing how close Smoke came to dying. If I hadn't gotten to his house when I did, Toby Fryor would have killed him."

Grandma took my hand in hers and massaged it. "God put you in that place, at that time, for that reason." She didn't have to spell out what that reason was. "And you have to concentrate on that—the good outcome, not the bad set of circumstances."

I heard the den office door open and jumped up. Smoke leaned against the jamb. My grandparents came up behind me. The corners of Smoke's lips lifted when he saw them. "So I must be in heaven after all."

Grandma moved in front of me and put her arms around him. "Elton, you're a sweet talker. My, you've got a nasty bump. Let's get you back to bed."

"I'd rather sit for a while, if I can join you."

"Sorry if we woke you," I said.

"Nah, I come close to falling asleep, and then my mind shifts into high gear, and I can't shut it off."

Grandma slipped her arm behind his back to support him, and Grandpa reached out and shook Smoke's hand. "Sorry you're hurt, but we're glad it wasn't worse," he said.

"Thanks."

Smoke managed the short distance with Grandma's help and sat down on the couch. "Do you want more ibuprofen?" I said.

"Good idea, sure."

I went to the kitchen for water and the pills, and when I returned Grandma and Grandpa were sitting in the armchairs on either end of the couch. I handed Smoke the bottle of ibuprofen. He shook out a few then took the glass of water and washed them down. He gave the glass and bottle back to me. I set them on the coffee table then sat on the opposite end of the couch.

24

"Corky saved the day," Smoke said. "I didn't figure out it was Toby until I came to and he opened his big mouth. I recognized his voice, even from all those years ago. Older-sounding, obviously, but it was Toby's voice."

"What a shock that must have been," Grandma said.

"Yes and no. Yes that he was in my house. But I was starting to wonder if this Chester Thorne character Corky kept seeing was Toby after all. He must have had some facial surgery done, because his nose was a lot smaller, and his cheek bones were more prominent."

"That makes sense, why he looked familiar, but you didn't recognize him," I said.

"I'm sorry I ever thought of him as a friend. He killed three innocent people that we know of, all because he was a narcissistic bastard. Sorry." His eyes moved from Grandma to Grandpa.

The corners of both my grandparents' lips lifted like they thought he could use that word if he damn well pleased.

We talked for a time, mostly about Dennis Twardy and his future and how that affected Mother and her future. And then about John Carl and his future. After we'd exchanged opinions, Grandma brought the discussion back to the Fryors and the Evertons.

"I can't imagine how Clifford and Verna Everton will ever forgive Toby for what he did."

"No," I said and paused before I moved to another topic. "Grandma, what did you think of Wendy Everton?"

Smoke shifted and cleared his throat. Grandpa looked straight ahead, and Grandma's eyebrows drew together like she had been asked to solve a complex mathematical problem. "Why do you ask?"

"Because right before he died Toby said something about Wendy and Carl being together during their junior year."

The air in the room got very, very heavy after I asked that question.

"Grandma?"

"Well, it's true that they did go out a few times."

"Why? I mean Carl and Kristen had been two peas in a pod since they were kids. That's what Mother always said."

"And she'd be the one to talk to about it," Grandma said.

"I feel like there's some kind of a cover-up going on here. Smoke told me the same thing. But now is not the time to talk to her, not with everything on her plate."

Grandma shrugged. "Then it can wait. It's something that happened over thirty years ago. They had a little spat then got over it. And thank heavens they did, otherwise we wouldn't have you and John Carl. Not to mention that Kristen has always been the daughter we never had ourselves."

Looking in Grandma's eyes, I was certain she knew nothing about what Toby had accused their son of, that Carl was one of two boys who had likely fathered Wendy's baby. If there really was a baby, that is.

"You're absolutely right, Grandma."

I'd find a quiet way to get my questions answered so my mother and grandparents wouldn't be troubled by them. It seemed it was a touchy subject even after all these years.

Grandma got up. "We left your gramps in the lurch, Corky. Arnold, let's get back there, and then I'll bring some soup back for these kids."

"I like the sound of that. Being called a kid," Smoke said.

Grandma smiled at Smoke then turned to me. "Your mother told me she had some of her hearty chicken dumpling and vegetable soup in the freezer. So that's what we were warming up on your gramps' stove when you called."

"Having a bowl of Kristen's soup sounds even better than being called a kid," Smoke said. And the prospect of a comforting meal sounded good to me, too.

As Grandma and Grandpa were on their way out the door, I got a text message from Sara: *What can I do?* I replied with, *Thanks, nothing tonight. See you soon.* She sent me a smiley face back.

When Grandma was getting our supper ready in the kitchen, Chief Deputy Kenner stopped by to check on Smoke and me. He pulled me aside. "I wanted you to know I was over at Fryor's place and had a lengthy discussion with Darwin and David."

My body tensed, and I braced myself while I waited for the details. "How are they doing?"

"You know, surprisingly well. I didn't try to sugarcoat anything. We have Toby's confession recorded via your cell phone. Not that I went into detail about that, but I told them he admitted to killing Wendy, a boy named Sheldon, and Rudy Medlin. And that he planned to kill Detective Dawes. And he would have shot you too, but you stopped him before he did."

I shook my head. "They must be in total shock. They thought Toby was the boy in the Charger. Then the DNA said he couldn't be Darwin's son. Then they found the letters Toby wrote to his mother which proved he'd been alive after all, and now this."

Kenner reached over and put his hands on my shoulders. "I can assure you of one thing, they accept full well that he needed to be stopped, and they actually applaud your bravery. They know you had no choice."

There was not a smidgen of a doubt about that. Toby would have killed me and then Smoke if help hadn't gotten there in time. "Thanks, Mike."

Kenner left shortly after that, assured we were in my grandmother's capable hands. Smoke and I ate in silence after Grandma left then he took his spot on the couch in the den office. I coaxed Queenie from her position so she could eat. Then I brought in a bowl of water for Rex to drink when he woke up.

The calls and text messages from fellow deputies and friends were piling up on my phones, but I ignored them. Tomorrow would be soon enough to return them.

Smoke patted the area on the couch next to him. "Come and sit here for a bit." I sat down, facing him, with the side of my thigh touching his hip. He took my hands in his. "I've had some close calls in my life, especially on the job, but I wasn't sure if I was gonna get out of that one. Truth be told, I don't think I would have." His voice cracked, bringing tears to my eyes.

"Smoke—"

He put his finger over my mouth. "Turn around so I can hold you."

I moved so my head was in the crook between his chest and shoulder. I slid one hand under his shoulder blade. He took the other and rested it on his stomach.

"It's been a while since we slept together on this couch," I said to lighten the mood.

"Ah yes. That time we were in the dregs of that cult case, and the worst was yet to come. This time the worst is behind us. It's over. You saved my life." He grasped hold of my hand.

He'd done the same for me. "I owed you one."

"You're saying we're even?"

"Pretty close."

"Yes we are." He put his finger under my chin, lifted my head, and gave me a gentle kiss. My heart bounced around in my chest, and the rest of my body heated to what felt like well over one hundred degrees. But then he moved his head and the moment ended.

After resting in silence for a bit, I said, "Smoke, getting back to what Toby Fryor was saying about my father and Wendy—"

His body stiffened. "Corky, we covered this already. It's not my place to talk about it. Whatever happened was between the two of them, and they're both gone."

"So there was something. That's what you meant when you let it slip about my parents having a falling out junior year, and what my grandma confirmed. Did Carl break up with Mother to date Wendy back then?"

"I will tell you everything I know after you talk to your mother. I promise you that."

"All right, but I have a question for you, a personal one. If Wendy had really had a baby—"

"I could not have been the father. Things never went that far between us. It was close, and then that fire started in my fish house and saved the day."

"Smoke—"

He put his finger gently on my lips. "Sorry. I need to get a little shut eye." And a minute later his breathing had settled into a sleeping rhythm.

I was a long way from falling asleep and didn't want my restlessness to disturb Smoke, so I moved slightly, easing his hold on me. I looked at our dogs and smiled. Queenie was maintaining her watch on Rex, and I was awed by her commitment.

The evening shadows crept into the den office through the open door of the living room. Under different circumstances, I would have relished being in Smoke's arms, cuddled up on a couch. But I couldn't relax after the traumatic events of the day, and the raw emotions they'd stirred in me.

I relived each second, from the time I was halfway down Smoke's driveway and saw the vehicle I believed belonged to the long lost—in more ways than one—Toby Fryor. The more I focused on that moment, the more panicked I felt. And that made no sense because Toby Fryor was dead, and Smoke and Rex were recovering.

My distress wasn't logical, but it was real and it was because it took me back in time to the last time—the first time—I'd had to shoot a perpetrator, an evil psychopath named Langley Parker. The dreadful part was that Parker had killed the man I'd been dating before I had a chance to stop it. After that, I hadn't been able to work on patrol for months.

I'd lost Eric Stueman to a madman, and I'd come close to losing Smoke to another.

Toby Fryor's hateful words and audacious actions kept playing over and over in my mind, and I couldn't shut it off. I carefully slid the rest of the way out of Smoke's arms and rolled off the couch.

I was outraged that Toby had taken the lives, and hopes, and dreams, from so many. He used people. He took what he wanted, and when his selfish plans were thwarted, he killed. That's what he'd done to Wendy and Sheldon after they'd fallen in love and made plans to get away from Toby and his control.

Then when Rudy Medlin threatened to turn him into the police, he'd killed him too. Those were the crimes we knew about, but I doubted they were the only ones Toby had committed over the years. What had sent him down that path? Anger, hatred, narcissism, the obsessive need to control others, what?

In the end, Toby's final decision cost him his life. He chose suicide by cop over incarceration, dumping the burden on me. I needed the control it had over me, the intensity of it, to lighten. But I knew it wouldn't dissipate for some time to come. Therapy and support from my family and friends would help it along, thankfully.

I went back to the moment when Toby Fryor was talking to Smoke about Wendy having a baby. Was he really planning to kill Smoke because he thought Smoke might have been the father of the baby? That made no sense.

And why had he named my father, Carl, as another possibility?

I wanted to verify whether or not Wendy had given birth, but how could I ask Mr. and Mrs. Everton about it in light of everything they were dealing with?

I did a final check on the sleepers in the den office, turned off lights, and crept upstairs to bed.

The co-mingled smells of brewing coffee and bacon woke me up Wednesday. I threw back the covers wondering who was cooking up a storm in my kitchen. I pulled on a hooded sweatshirt, my favorite cover-up, over the tank top I slept in. And my pajama bottoms were decent enough to wear in public. At least some people thought so, I'd noticed from personal observation.

I went downstairs and was greeted by a welcome scene. My grandma was standing over the stove. Smoke, Grandpa, and Gramps were on stools at the counter island sipping coffee. Rex and Queenie were sitting at attention, sniffing the aromas floating around in the air.

"'Morning," I said and drew everyone's attention, making me feel a little self-conscious. I greeted Rex first. "Hey boy, you are looking as fit as a fiddle. Welcome back." I scratched behind his ears until Queenie stuck her nose in my hand to get a little consideration herself.

I gave each of my grandparents a hug and smiled at Smoke. "Aside from that bruise, you look much better than last night. How do you feel?"

"I think I might live after all."

"So how did I get so lucky to have four of my favorite people gathered here for breakfast?"

"Your grandma thought you needed to put a little meat on your bones," Gramps said.

My grandma waved the spatula she was using to turn a pan full of scrambled eggs. "That's not what I said. I thought you and Elton needed a hearty breakfast, is all. And you don't always have the ingredients to make one, Corky." That was an understatement and a nice way of not addressing my lack of cooking skills. "Looks like everything's ready," she declared.

Grandpa took that as his cue to get up and help Grandma get the food on the table. I tried to pitch in, but Grandpa put his arm around my waist and led me to the table in the dining room where Smoke pulled a chair out for me. There was a place setting for each of us, and I was puzzled how I'd slept through most of the preparations. Unless it was because I'd fallen asleep only a few hours before. In no time at all, the table was filled with pitchers of orange juice and milk, bacon, scrambled eggs with fresh tomatoes, onions and green peppers, toast, and fried potatoes. A regular big farm breakfast.

Grandpa and Grandma were the last to sit down then we all bowed our heads. "I'll say grace," Grandma said. "Thank you, Father, for watching over us, especially Corinne and Elton yesterday. Keep Kristen, and John Carl, and Denny, safe as they travel to Oak Lea today. Give us the strength we need in the days ahead, and bless this food to our bodies. Amen."

We each added our own "Amen." There was no question we'd need extra strength today, supporting Mother with Denny's long-term prognosis still up in the air.

What none of us knew at that moment was we were about to receive unexpected, life-changing news and our family would need great strength to work through it all.

25

We got word from John Carl that Dennis Twardy would be released from St. Mary's Hospital early afternoon. Parkwood Nursing and Rehabilitation Center was sending a van to pick him up and expected to be back with him by 4:00 p.m.

"Mom wants to make sure Denny gets settled in then I'll bring her home," John Carl said.

"Should we meet you there?" I said.

"I think we better play it by ear. I know Mom would appreciate that, but the doctors warned us that the move might make Denny anxious, and having fewer people around is probably better."

"I guess that makes sense. All right, John Carl, you know we're all here if you need us."

"Thanks. Corky, you're sounding a lot better today, not as tense," he added.

"Yeah, it'll take some effort for a while. I had a hard first part of the night because I couldn't shut off my brain. And then about four o'clock this morning it was like I'd taken a tranquilizer, and I fell into a deep, deep sleep."

"A good thing," he said.

By late morning, Smoke was ready to go home. His house had been processed, and Chief Deputy Kenner had given the okay. "As much as I appreciate the hospitality and all the great food, Rex will feel better in his own environment," Smoke said.

I looked at him, checking to see if all was well. "Are you sure you can manage on your own?"

He nodded. "If we need anything, I'll call. Half the department has offered to bring me food and what have you, so I'll be fine. Aside from a little headache and a lot of kicking myself in the behind for letting Toby Fryor get the best of me, that is."

"He didn't get the best of you. He played dirty, making sure Rex couldn't alert you, and then he attacked without warning."

"Yeah. When I woke up in the middle of the night, I thought about Wendy and that boy Sheldon, and wondered how everything happened that Homecoming night. Piecing together what the medical examiner said about Sheldon getting shot in the back and Wendy getting shot in the front, and then from what Toby said, it must have been a dreadful confrontation."

"And Toby must have gotten Rudy to help him. Probably threatened him," I said.

"Probably."

My briefcase was on the floor next to my computer, and I pulled out Wendy's and Sheldon's photos. I had a look then passed them to Smoke. "I wrestle with that in all the cases we've worked on, with all of our victims. Did they know what was going to happen to them, or not? We can't ask the ones who didn't survive. In Wendy's case, and with Sheldon too, I think they recognized Toby was a bad dude, and they believed they had to run away to escape from him."

"They should have gone to their parents, or the authorities."

"Sheldon lost his parents, and was in foster care. Wendy—if it's true—had just had a baby and maybe didn't feel she could go to her parents with more boy trouble. Who knows? They were young, with teenage brains, and not making the best decisions."

"You got a point."

After giving Smoke and Rex a ride home, I didn't quite know what to do with myself. Since I was on administrative leave, others in the sheriff's office were notifying Sheldon Viets' foster mother, Linda Bednar, Rudy Medlin's aunt, Annette Jenry, and his cousin, Harry Gimler. *Harry.* I'd pay him a visit in the next day or two, in an unofficial capacity, to see how he was doing. I'd also talk to Mrs. Bednar, Mrs. Jenry, and Marge at Highland Park Senior High School.

Even Queenie seemed out of sorts after losing her guard-duty position. I returned the dozens of phone calls, text messages, and emails then puttered around, waiting for my mother and brother to be home again.

Mr. Everton phoned me in the early afternoon. "My wife and I were wondering if we could stop by to see you sometime soon, to thank you for what you did, and to give you something."

"I appreciate that, but I can't take any gifts for doing my job."

"Well, we'd like to stop over, if we could," he said.

I'd gotten a lot of nice thank you notes and phone calls over the years. "Okay. I'm at home now, and should be here for the next couple of hours, if that works for you."

"We'll be over in a little while then."

"Do you know where I live?" I said.

"Over on Brandt Avenue?"

"Yes."

I hung up wondering if it'd be inappropriate to ask them if Toby was telling the truth about Wendy. Toby might have been trying to shock Smoke into some sort of confession that he'd been intimate with Wendy. And then he threw my father's name into the mix besides.

Mr. and Mrs. Everton arrived a short time later, and each gave me a warm hug. Tears ran down Mrs. Everton's cheeks, and she hugged me again. Queenie perked up, happy to have visitors and a little action.

"Come on in. Would you like something to drink?" I said.

"No, no, we won't be long," Mrs. Everton said.

We went into the living room and sat down.

"We knew Toby was too possessive of Wendy, but we'll never understand how it ever could have come to this," Mrs. Everton said.

"He wasn't right in the head, that's for damn sure. But he can't hurt anyone else, and that's thanks to you, Sergeant. We'll always be grateful for that," Mr. Everton said.

I managed half a smile.

Mrs. Everton leaned in closer. "And how is Elton Dawes doing? We heard he took quite a blow to the head." News traveled fast.

"He's recovering, fortunately." I thought about my looming question, and either I had to ask it or I'd explode. "I apologize if this is a bad time, but Toby said some things, and you may be the only ones who have the answers."

The way Mr. and Mrs. Everton looked at each other, I had the sinking suspicion they knew what I was going to ask.

I made myself continue, "Toby said Wendy had a baby the summer before her senior year."

Mrs. Everton sniffed then dabbed at her nose with a tissue. "I don't know why Wendy told him about it. We'd managed to keep it secret from everyone else in Oak Lea. We even took her to a doctor in another town. Wendy and I went to stay with my sister the first week in June, after school was out for the year. Even at going-on seven months along, she was able to hide it, due to the way she carried the baby."

"And the baby, was it born healthy?" I said.

"Oh yes, it was a little girl. She was small, but fine. Finding good parents to adopt the baby was Wendy's decision, and we supported her in that. It would have broken my heart to see the baby and then have to let her go, so I didn't," Mrs. Everton said.

"And the baby's father, did he have a say in it?" I said.

Mrs. Everton looked down at the tissue she was twisting in her hands. "No, he didn't know about it. Wendy refused to tell even us who it was. But we've had our suspicions for a while."

My heart started hammering in my chest when Mrs. Everton reached into the pocket of her sweater, pulled out a photo, and handed it to me. My vision blurred for a second and then focused on a face that was all too familiar. She could have been John Carl's twin. I was overcome by emotion, and tears welled in my own eyes.

"Her name is Taylor. She contacted us last year, looking for her birth parents. She had Wendy's name, but her father was listed as unknown," she said.

My face was coloring and there was no way to stop it. "Have you met her?"

Mrs. Everton kept her gaze downward and nodded. "She lives here in Minnesota, and we arranged to meet in a restaurant. She sent us a picture so we'd recognize her."

"When we saw the picture we figured out who her father must be. And when we saw her in person, there was no doubt," Mr. Everton said.

Mrs. Everton shook her head. "But we didn't say anything to her about that. It's been eating at us for months now, trying to decide if we should tell your family or not. Then when all this came out about Wendy, when it was all over the news, Taylor called us. She'd never known Wendy, but she still grieved, of course."

"We thought you should know. We tried to think of a way to tell your grandparents, but after we saw how well you handled the most difficult of things, we decided to tell you instead," Mr. Everton said.

Sometimes I was my own worst enemy, and I didn't want that particular ball in my court.

"Did Taylor say anything about her life growing up?" I managed.

Mrs. Everton nodded and smiled. "She was raised in a good home. And now she has a family of her own."

That threw me for another loop. "You mean she has children?"

"Three of them. Two girls and a boy."

Astounding. I was an aunt, John Carl was an uncle, and our grandparents had great-grandchildren. But my mother and Gramps were not part of that family at all.

"Taylor. What's her last name?"

"Franson. She's married. Her maiden name was Hall." I kept staring at the photo, trying to accept this new reality. "You keep the picture. Her phone number is on the back if you decide to contact her," Mrs. Everton said.

I turned it over and saw there were numbers there, but I didn't read them. "Okay."

The Evertons must have taken that as their cue to leave because they both stood up. "We know what a shock this must be for you. If you want to talk some more about it, be sure to ask. And the other thing, we told Taylor we're arranging a memorial service for Wendy. She said she'd like to come," Mrs. Everton said.

I started to ask when they were going to have the service, but I didn't want to know. "Okay, thanks."

With that, the Evertons left. I started pacing. *John Carl and I have an older sister. John Carl and I have an older sister.* But it didn't matter how many times I said it, I couldn't comprehend it. Then I looked at Taylor's photo again, and knew the chances that her father was any other than Carl Aleckson was very unlikely. Genetic testing could give us the answer, yes or no.

Mother wouldn't be home for a few hours, so I decided to go to her house and look through her high school yearbooks. She kept them, along with some photo albums, on a shelf in her living room. I told Queenie to hang tight and drove there with Taylor's photo in hand. I let myself in using the code to open the garage door then literally ran to the living room.

I grabbed the books from my parents' sophomore, junior, and senior years, and sat down on the floor. I opened the books one at a time, and perused the head shots of every male, taking a moment to admire Smoke's. There was not one other boy who was as close a match to Taylor as my father was. My cell phone rang, and a wave of guilt rolled over me when I saw it was my mother.

Deep breath. "Hi, Mom."

"Hello, dear. Well, we're about halfway home. We decided to follow the van, and then after they get Denny settled in at Parkwood, we'll come to your house so we can talk."

Maybe that was not the best idea, but what could I say? "Okay, see you then, and drive safe."

"We will."

We disconnected and my feeling of guilt was replaced by a sense of panic wondering how everyone would react if I told them about Taylor. Correction, *when* I told them. It wasn't my secret. The information belonged to the whole family.

My father had always been a larger-than-life figure whom my mother and grandparents, and even Smoke, idolized. I knew that often happened when a well-loved, and a good person besides, went long before his or her time. And in my father's case, he had also died a hero's death. But Carl had been a human being, with failings and weaknesses, like everyone else.

I closed the yearbooks and replaced them on the shelf. If Carl had known about Wendy's pregnancy and had been named as the father, his life may have taken a very different turn. My parents might not have married. In a strange way, I had Wendy to thank for that much. If she had revealed the name of the boy responsible for her pregnancy, John Carl and I would probably not have been born.

Even though Smoke was recuperating, I had to confide in someone, and he was the one outside my immediate family, besides Sara, I trusted most. But Sara hadn't known Wendy or Carl, and Smoke had. I drove to his house and was greeted by Rex who acted like his old self again. "Hey, boy." I knocked on the side door and called out, "Hello?" then let myself in, with Rex close behind.

"I'm in here." Smoke was lying on the couch in the living room reading a book. He sat up when he saw the look on my face. "What's wrong?" I sat down next to him and handed him the photo. After not much more than a glance he said, "I'm not so sure I'm ready to hear who this is."

"The Evertons gave it to me a little while ago. Her name is Taylor. She contacted them looking for her mother. They met her a few months ago."

"Corky, I swear I didn't know, and I'm positive Carl didn't either." He couldn't seem to take his eyes off Taylor's image.

"Wendy's parents didn't even know who the father was because Wendy wouldn't tell them. And then Taylor sent them her photo, and they suspected it was Carl. When they met her in person, they had no doubt."

Smoke finally looked up. "What are you going to do?"

"That's why I'm here, to get your advice."

"I wish the Evertons would have waited until things settled down somewhat."

"I know, but they didn't, and now we have to deal with it."

"We, huh?" He set the photo on his coffee table and reached for my hand. "Yeah, I guess I'm in on it too. Let me think. Okay, if I were you, I'd tell the Aleckson grandparents first, then John Carl, then your mother. She can decide about your gramps. That'd be my advice."

And that's what I did, the next day. After Sheriff Dennis Twardy was reasonably comfortable at Parkwood. After my mother and brother had a better night's sleep in their own beds. After my grandparents had a chance to settle in after being at their second home in Arizona for three months. After I had time to work up more courage.

I paid Grandma and Grandpa a visit.

My grandma appreciated when people got straight to the point, so I broke the news by handing Taylor's photo to her. It was the first time in my life I'd ever seen her fight for a breath. She stared at it a moment then passed it along to Grandpa without saying a word. He had a strained look, and made a strange gurgling noise.

I swallowed. "She's Wendy Everton's daughter, born the summer between her junior and senior year."

Grandma's eyes filled with tears. Neither one of my grandparents seemed able to talk as I relayed all that the Evertons had told me.

At the end of my story, Grandpa shook his head. "If that don't beat all."

"What are we going to tell Mother?" I said.

Grandma folded her hands and nodded. "Carl told Kristen . . . she knew about the . . . indiscretion with Wendy, and she forgave him. But this is going to take her breath away. There is no question about it."

"What about John Carl?"

After some discussion, Grandma called John Carl. Mother was at the nursing home visiting Denny, so that part was easy. Grandma asked John Carl to stop over, and he was there a few minutes later. When he walked into the kitchen, his eyebrows went up in a questioning look. We must have painted an unusual picture, the three of us sitting around the table looking uncomfortable, like our clothes were on too tight or something.

"What's going on?" he asked as he slid onto a chair.

"We have a sister. Our dad had a daughter that he never knew about," I blurted out.

"Not funny, Corky." John Carl looked at each of our faces for a sign that it wasn't true.

I handed him the photo. He took one look and said, "Wow." Then I told him the story, and that she'd be in town for Wendy's service, and that I didn't know what to do about it.

"Well, you can meet her if you want, but I don't think I can," he said.

I'd had a day to mull it all over. "Taylor reached out because she wanted to find her birth parents. They're both gone, but we're here, and we're the closest blood relatives she has. Think about it, about what's the right thing to do."

John Carl looked at Grandpa and Grandma. "Are you thinking of meeting her?"

Grandpa leaned over and put his hand on Grandma's arm. "Mother?"

"Come to find out we have another granddaughter, and three great-grandchildren. I look at that as four blessings we didn't know we had."

"There you have it," Grandpa said.

The burden of being the only one in the family who knew about Taylor lifted when I shared it with them. We decided to tell Mother that evening. She'd been through hell with all that had happened to Denny and then with me, but it wasn't fair to keep the truth from her, even for a few days. Taylor was planning to attend Wendy's memorial service the Evertons would soon hold.

Grandma invited Mother, John Carl, and me over for dinner. After we'd eaten, Grandma did me a big favor and gently broke the news to Mother. She was on emotional overload, and her reaction shouldn't have surprised us. She got up without uttering a word and left the house. The four of us looked at each other then we all got out of our chairs and went to the living room window to see what Mother was doing. She was walking at a fast clip down Brandt Avenue toward her house.

"Maybe you should follow her, John Carl," I said.

He gave me one of his "why me?" looks. "I think she needs some time alone. She just had an old wound opened up, and then we poured some salt into it," he said. That was a good way to put it.

Mother would let us know when she was ready to talk about it. I stepped outside for a better view and some minutes later saw her turn, and head down her driveway.

We gave her an hour then John Carl and I drove over to check on her. A living room lamp was the only light on in the house. Mother was sitting in a chair beside it with a box of letters she and Carl had exchanged when he was in the service.

Mother looked up with a concerned expression on her face. "All these years you've had a sister you didn't know about. How do you feel now that you know?"

John Carl stared straight ahead, and I shook my head because I didn't know the answer.

"Your father was such a good man. I've known that all my life, with our parents being close neighbors, and growing up together. I don't know what got into me our junior year in high school, but I questioned whether I really loved Carl after all. A couple of boys had crushes on me, and I think that went to my head. I broke up with Carl and went on some dates with them." So mother had started it.

She paused and had a faraway look in her eyes. "It didn't take me long to realize Carl really was the one for me. No one else even came close. He was hurt when I was seeing other boys, and Wendy took the opportunity to go after him. I can't blame her for that. When we made up, Carl told me about his one-night stand with her. I was pretty devastated, and he felt guilty because he didn't have deep feelings for her. But their relationship was over, as far as he was concerned. Now it turns out that wasn't quite true.

"I would never have guessed Wendy had it in her to keep a secret like that. And she actually protected Carl's reputation. Her own, too, I guess. She could have named Carl as the father and insist that he marry her or pay child support, but she didn't. This may sound strange, especially to the two of you, but knowing there's another part of Carl in the world actually makes me happy."

Grandma hadn't shown Mother Taylor's photo so I took it out of my pocket and handed it to her. She sucked in a quick breath, and she put her hand on her neck as she studied the image. "Dear Lord in heaven." After a moment she looked from John Carl to me. "I'd like to meet her, find out what she's like." That's when John Carl agreed to think about it. I'd already decided I needed to do that. And my mother's consent gave me permission to feel some excitement about it.

Sheriff Twardy settled in well at Parkwood, and in the following days, he slowly showed signs of improvement. As his brain healed, he remembered more and more, mostly from many years back. But the doctors, nurses, and therapists were hopeful, and the rest of us were encouraged. Whether he'd be back to where he was before suffering the stroke, and the fall, no one yet knew.

I stopped in to see the sheriff on Sunday. I'd visited him a few times before and mainly sat with him, telling him what was happening without going into too much detail. I kept my account of the Whitetail Lake case on the general side, not spelling out its ensuing drama and trauma. I'd been cleared to go back to work the next day, six days after the shooting. I shared that with him. "I've been off work for a few days, and I'm raring to get back."

The sheriff watched me as I talked on for a while. When I stood up to leave, he reached out his hand. I took it in my own, and shook it. When he spoke it was the first time he'd indicated he knew who I was. "Thanks for stopping by, Sergeant. Now get back to work and catch some bad guys."

His words were music to my ears and caught me completely off-guard. He was healing. I grinned and said, "Yes, sir."

26

Tuesday late afternoon was T-Day. Taylor Day. Two weeks had passed since the bodies of Wendy Everton and Sheldon Viets were recovered from Whitetail Lake. It was the day the Evertons had chosen to hold Wendy's memorial service. For the Aleckson family, it was the day we were to meet another one of Carl's children.

I was not normally one to primp and polish much, but I wanted to look my best when I met Taylor, to make a good impression. When I got home from work, I put on a navy waist dress with a fuller, knee-length skirt, and open-toed taupe shoes with two-inch heels. My hair had been pulled back in a ponytail for work, so I brushed it out, and styled it into a looser bun near the crown of my head. I applied a little more makeup than usual and tried to quiet the butterflies fluttering around in my stomach.

John Carl was driving Mother, Grandma, and Grandpa to the church. Gramps had difficulty with the news and decided he'd wait to meet Taylor another time. Smoke offered to pick me up, and I was ready when he pulled in my driveway.

"Have I told you lately that you clean up very well?"

"No, but thanks. You too." He looked darn near dashing in his dark navy suit, white shirt, and navy, gray, and burgundy patterned tie. "And we match."

Smoke smiled. "Big day, huh?"

"Yeah. I'm glad we decided to meet in the church basement before the service. That way, if things go south, we can leave. And if they go well, Taylor will know we're sitting in the back supporting her and Wendy's parents."

"I'm holding good thoughts," he said.

"When I talked to her the other day and introduced myself, she wanted to know some Aleckson family history. She's easy to talk to and is looking forward to meeting everyone."

Smoke shook his head. "Who'd have guessed the Alecksons and the Evertons would be brought together this way."

A tall, elegant-looking woman was waiting for us in the United Methodist Church basement with the Evertons. Her eyes were the color of cornflowers, and her straight brown hair was pulled back with clips and fell just below her shoulders. There was no need for a genetic test to confirm she was our father's daughter. Her resemblance to John Carl, and Carl, and Grandpa Aleckson was remarkable.

She took not only Mother's breath away, as Grandma had predicted—it happened to all of us. I grabbed John Carl's arm and we walked over to Taylor. We studied her, she studied us, and after we gave each other hugs, we stood like three points on a triangle. There were a million things I could have said, but what came out of my mouth was, "You're gorgeous."

She smiled and the room got brighter. At least that was my perception. "Thanks, so are you. Both of you. I've learned a little about you, but I'd love to know much, much more. I hope we can get to be good friends."

John Carl smiled then nodded.

"I hope so, too," I said with a big grin.

Grandma and Grandpa joined us, and each took a turn hugging Taylor and admiring her. It felt strange, knowing they had another grandchild besides John Carl and me. And one they could feel proud of, from the looks of it.

"We have a lot of years to catch up on," Grandma said. "Where are your children?"

"With my husband, at the hotel. They're four, six, and nine so I thought it was better if they weren't here for our first meeting. But if you'd like, we can all get together later."

"That'd be nice," Grandpa said.

Mother was waiting in the wings with Smoke. "Taylor, we'd like you to meet our mother, Kristen."

Taylor and Mother moved in to face each other. "Very happy to meet you, Kristen," Taylor said and shook Mother's hand.

"And this is our good friend, and Carl's best friend, Elton Dawes," Mother said.

They shook hands. "Oh yes, I've read about you and Corinne in the news, and saw you on the YouTube video."

Smoke beamed. "Good to meet you, Taylor."

Mr. Everton cleared his throat. "Well, the service will begin in a few minutes, so we should head upstairs." Taylor fell in with the Evertons, and it was obvious by the way they positioned her between the two of them, and each slipped an arm in hers, how important she was to them.

The rest of us followed. The time had arrived when people who knew and loved Wendy Everton could say a very belated, final goodbye to her.

I was lying in bed that night with the window open. The spring breeze ruffled the top of the open blind, making a soft bumping sound. There were many thoughts swirling around in my mind and a variety of emotions coursing through my body. The members of my family, and the sheriff's office, had been on some rough waters the past two weeks and were all due for a long stretch of smooth sailing.

It was impossible to predict what having Taylor in our lives would mean for our family going forward and how it would impact us. She and her family lived two hours away, so our visits would need to be planned. Taylor wouldn't be dropping by unannounced because she was in the neighborhood, and vice versa. The Evertons were enamored with her, and rightly so. They'd lost their daughter but gained a granddaughter and great-grandchildren.

I believed my own grandparents were more cautious about embracing Taylor unconditionally because of Mother, John Carl, and me. If not for us, they likely would be waiting in line behind the Evertons. Their only son had died young. Now they had another one of his children, and his grandchildren, to get to know, to love.

It felt like we'd all been dropped into the middle of a party where we knew who people were, but didn't know enough about them to start an intelligent conversation.

I thought of meeting Taylor's children after Wendy's service and smiled. The oldest, Katie, looked a lot like my grandma. Shorter in stature, on the sturdy side, with those same blue eyes. Charles, next in line, bore a strong resemblance to his mother, Taylor, and his grandfather, Carl. The youngest, Isabelle, looked the most like her father with hazel eyes and curly, dark hair. I wanted to get to know all of them better and spend time with them, doing fun things.

A couple of years before, a felon requested that I act as the guardian of her young granddaughter, Rebecca. She had the good fortune of finding a loving family who wanted to adopt her, as Taylor had, and I was delighted Rebecca was growing into a fine young woman. Unfortunately, I didn't see her as often as I liked, but would make a point of introducing her to my newly-found nieces and nephew when the time was right.

My mind drifted back to the day Whitetail Lake's secret was revealed because of side-scan sonar technology. Then DNA technology made it possible to identify Wendy and eliminate Toby as the victims in the Dodge Charger. We were still working to positively identify Sheldon Viets, and that would take some time.

David Fryor had called me and echoed what he'd told Chief Deputy Kenner. Toby needed to be stopped, and they knew, without reservation, I had no choice in doing what I did. His brother, Wade, was traveling from California, and the two of them would take turns staying with their father for as long as he needed them to.

Smoke, Vince Weber, and I had gone through a debriefing two days after the shooting. It helped me deal with the nagging question, "What could I have done differently?" because the answer was, "nothing." Toby Fryor had refused to be taken into custody and saw no other way out except to die. By my hand or his own. He'd chosen mine.

I thought of Wendy, and Sheldon, and Rudy Medlin. They were kids who had unwittingly gotten involved with the worst of the worst. I prayed they knew that Toby Fryor had been banished from the earth forever and were all now at peace.

I focused on the night sounds and was lulled to sleep.

Winnebago County Mysteries

<u>Murder in Winnebago County</u> follows an unlikely serial killer plaguing a rural Minnesota county. The clever murderer leaves a growing chain of apparent suicides among criminal justice professionals. As her intuition helps her draw the cases together, Winnebago County Sergeant Corinne Aleckson enlists help from Detective Elton Dawes. What Aleckson doesn't know is that the killer is keeping a close watch on her. Will she be the next target?

<u>Buried in Wolf Lake</u> When a family's golden retriever brings home the dismembered leg of a young woman, the Winnebago County Sheriff's Department launches an investigation unlike any other. Who does the leg belong to, and where is the rest of her body? Sergeant Corinne Aleckson and Detective Elton Dawes soon discover they are up against an unidentified psychopath who targets women with specific physical features. Are there other victims, and will they learn the killer's identity in time to prevent another brutal murder?

<u>An Altar by the River</u> A man phones the Winnebago County Sheriff's Department, frantically reporting his brother is armed with a large dagger and on his way to the county to sacrifice himself. Sergeant Corinne Aleckson takes the call, learning the alarming reasons behind the young man's death wish. When the department investigates, they plunge into the alleged criminal activities of a hidden cult and the disturbing cover-up of an old closed-case shooting death. The cult members have everything to lose and will do whatever it takes to prevent the truth coming to light. But will they find an altar by the river in time to save the young man's life?

The Noding Field Mystery When a man's naked body is found staked out in a farmer's soybean field, Sergeant Corinne Aleckson and Detective Elton Dawes are called to the scene. The cause of death is not apparent, and the significance of why he was placed there is a mystery. As Aleckson, Dawes, and the rest of their Winnebago Sheriff's Department team gather evidence, and look for suspects and motive, they hit one dead end after another. Then an old nemesis escapes from jail and plays in the shocking end.

A Death in Lionel's Woods When a woman's emaciated body is found in a hunter's woods Sergeant Corinne Aleckson is coaxed back into the field to assist Detective Smoke Dawes on the case. It seems the only hope for identifying the woman lies in a photo that was buried with bags of money under her body. Aleckson and Dawes plunge into the investigation that takes them into the world of human smugglers and traffickers, unexpectedly close to home. All the while, they are working to uncover the identity of someone who is leaving Corky anonymous messages and pulling pranks at her house. A Death in Lionel's Woods is a unpredictable roller coaster ride to the electrifying end.

Firesetter in Blackwood Township Barns are burning in Blackwood Township, and the Winnebago County Sheriff's Office realizes they have a firesetter to flush out. The investigation ramps up when a body is found in one of the barns. Meanwhile, deputies are getting disturbing deliveries. Why are they being targeted? It leaves Sergeant Corinne Aleckson and Detective Elton Dawes to wonder, what is the firesetter's message and motive?

www.ingramcontent.com/pod-product-compliance
Lightning Source LLC
LaVergne TN
LVHW091347150225
803821LV00028B/500